W9-CFA-421

SIX IMPOSSIBLE THINGS

Nicholas Wayne, like Alice in Wonderland, finds it hard to believe impossible things: to believe that he could forget Estelle Dryden who went to America ten years ago or that his sister Julia, who had always been a scraggy child, should come back from Rome tall and attractive with a supple figure and delicate auburn hair. But after a good deal of plain speaking from a pretty woman, Nicholas is obliged to change his mind.

This is the third of Elizabeth Cadell's trio of lovable and witty novels about the Waynes of Wood Mount, Greenhurst. The others are *The Lark Shall Sing* and *The Blue Sky of Spring*.

Books by Elizabeth Cadell in the
Ulverscroft Large Print Series:

BE MY GUEST
THE HAYMAKER
THE PAST TENSE OF LOVE
MONEY TO BURN
THE LARK SHALL SING
THE BLUE SKY OF SPRING
SIX IMPOSSIBLE THINGS

———————◆———————

This Large Print Edition
is published by kind permission of
HODDER & STOUGHTON LTD.
London

ELIZABETH CADELL

SIX IMPOSSIBLE THINGS

Complete and Unabridged

85 33352
1-18502

ULVERSCROFT
Leicester

12·95

CAD

First published in 1961 by
Hodder and Stoughton Ltd.
London

First Large Print Edition
published March 1976
SBN 85456 417 9

Copyright
© 1960, 1961 by Elizabeth Cadell

Published by
F. A. Thorpe (Publishing) Ltd.
Anstey, Leicestershire
Printed in England

The characters in this book are entirely imaginary and bear no relation to any living person

CHAPTER I

NICHOLAS WAYNE stepped off the ladder, walked backward for a few paces and stood surveying his newly-painted home.

"Looks all right, don't you think?" he asked his brother-in-law.

There was no reply: Jeff Milward was completely absorbed in putting the finishing touches to the board on which the name of the house — Wood Mount — was painted. His shirt and jeans, like Nicholas's, were paint-splashed; white paint streaks matted his hair and gave a Halloween look to his features.

He finished the last brush stroke, placed the board carefully against the wall and walked over to stand beside Nicholas. The dark green, wooded background and the sloping fields beyond the garden seemed to accentuate the pale, fresh look of the house.

"Looks all right," he said.

"That's what I just told you. Three weeks hard going, but in my unprofessional opinion a nice job. What do you reckon that saved us in decorator's fees?"

"Let's see," murmured Jeff. "Say three workmen doing — "

"They wouldn't have put in the hours we did."

"No, they wouldn't." Jeff removed his glasses to wipe the dust from them, put them on again and spoke with his habitual calm. "I reckon it saved you — not us — something like seventy pounds."

"That's right — saved me. I'm always forgetting you don't live here any more. Well . . . thanks for the help." Nicholas spread his arms above his head in a long, luxurious stretch. "It's finished. I'm about finished, too. In future, I shan't talk so much about the disadvantages of life in an office."

"In future," said Jeff, "I'll take my holiday in July instead of in May — and I'll take it in a car, with my family." He blinked through the spring sunshine at the lovely house before them, and something in the glance made Nicholas look at him curiously.

"Ever regret leaving?" he asked.

"No. I don't. Living here was all right when Roselle and I were first married, but when the babies began to put in an appearance — "

"I know. But while it worked, it worked," said Nicholas. "And while it was working it gave me time to get on my feet financially."

Jeff was still studying the house.

"Pity they don't build more of these, so to speak, Colonial type houses in England," he mused. "Why is it?"

"Probably because they're better suited to, so to speak, Colonial climates. Big rooms, wide corridors, gracious staircase — how many years is it since we slid on trays down that gracious staircase? — wide, sheltered verandahs; no, they're for places where the sun hits harder."

"It's a lovely house, all the same."

"Yes." Nicholas wiped a paint-brush thoughtfully. "And we kept it in the family. I've been lucky," he said slowly

His brother-in-law's reply was made to himself. Nicholas had been lucky yes, and lucky no, he reflected. Lucky in his job, perhaps; who could have foretold that a travel agent's office in a small town like Greenhurst would grow and prosper so swiftly? But was it luck? Or was it some-

thing about the tall, handsome, thirty-two-
year-old Nicholas and his easy, casual
charm? Or was it those eleven or so years
of hard work he had put in? At all events
the luck, if it was luck, hadn't operated as
far as love and marriage went; a sawn-off-
short romance ten years ago, a girl loved
and lost to another man, and since then —
Jeff reviewed them without pleasure — a
few half-hearted excursions in the direction
of some attractive and only-too-co-
operative women; affairs that got nowhere
and died of inaction on the part of Nicholas.
Ten years; a hell of a waste of life, mused
Jeff. Now take himself; only a little older
than his brother-in-law and with nothing
comparable in the way of looks or charm,
but he had in the same period acquired a
wife and four sturdy little sons. He might
point out that that was the kind of luck to
have — but the subject of marriage was not
one it was safe to bring up with Nicholas.

"What about lunch?" he asked.

"I'm ready. It's almost warm enough to
eat out here."

"We might have to eat out here. I don't
think there's much more room left in the
kitchen."

"Nonsense." Nicholas led the way into the house. "We can heap a few more of those plates on to the piles on the floor and . . ." He halted on the threshold of the kitchen and for some moments there was silence. Then he spoke in an incredulous tone. "Did we . . . did we really do all this?"

Jeff looked round the room, his expression midway between dismay and disbelief.

"We couldn't have," he stated at last. "Not in the time."

They had been alone in the house for three weeks. Pietro, the voluble Italian who for years had been attached to the household as cook and not-too-handyman, had at last been persuaded to pay a visit to his brother in New York. Miss Cornhill, the quiet, efficient housekeeper who kept the house so immaculate, had been sent on a three-weeks cruise. Nicholas's sister, Lucille, and her husband now used their quarters on the top floor only for infrequent visits. His younger brothers and his sister, Julia, were away. His sister, Roselle, with her husband, Jeff, had moved out of the middle flat on the death of old Mr. Mil-

5

ward, and now lived with Jeff's mother in Greenhurst, four miles away. Nobody but Nicholas and Jeff had been at Wood Mount, and when they began their self-imposed task of painting the house, Jeff remembered hazily, they had decided to leave the clearing up and the washing up of plates and dishes until the evenings.

But the evenings had found them stiff and exhausted after the unaccustomed work out of doors; they would, they said, wash up in the morning. In the morning, as there was a great deal of crockery available, it had seemed sensible to put off the washing of the dirty plates and take a supply of clean ones.

There must, Jeff figured, taking off his glasses to give them another clean, putting them on and staring through them at the chaos, there must be no fewer than . . . Well three weeks, seven days a week — that made twenty-one; three meals a day, that came to sixty-three. An average of three plates a meal . . .

"Anyway" — Nicholas's voice broke through his calculations — "we didn't use any dishes. Or any saucepans."

This was true. One frying pan had

6

sufficed for their needs, for they had cooked nothing but slice after slice of bacon, an incalculable number of fried eggs, squares of bread dipped in bacon fat, and some tomatoes to use up the last vestiges of the appetising grease. They had discussed other dishes; they had looked them up in recipe books and had made lists of the ingredients they would require — and then they had torn up the lists and telephoned for more bacon and bread and eggs and tomatoes.

"Hadn't we better do some clearing up?" asked Jeff soberly. "This is Saturday and Miss Cornhill gets back on Monday. If she sees — "

"By Monday, the place'll look as though she'd never left it. Stop worrying," directed Nicholas, "and see if the milkman left those extra eggs I ordered. And there's the post; you might fetch it at the same time."

Jeff brought in several letters; Nicholas, glancing casually at the envelopes, put them aside until the business of cooking and serving was completed.

"Any news from anybody?" Jeff asked sometime later, through a mouthful of food.

"Something from Dominic," said Nicholas, taking the topmost letter, opening it and scanning the contents. "Sounds as though he's enjoying himself. They climbed a peak yesterday . . . they're going on to do another climb somewhere near . . . can't read it; looks like Bergen. And one of them's dropped out. Looks like one of the Norwegians; can't read the name. Hellish hand-writing Dominic's got." He peered. "Somebody's injured his foot and is coming home."

"Wouldn't be Derek, would it?"

"Might be. Yes, it is." He put the letter down and looked at Jeff. "If Derek Arkwright had hurt his little toe ten years ago," he said thoughtfully, "his mother would have chartered a plane and flown over to nurse him. That's one thing he owes Dominic and Julia — they got him out of his mother's clutches."

"He got himself out. Incidentally, have you done anything about Miriam Arkwright's wedding present?"

"What's the hurry?"

"The wedding's exactly two weeks off, that's what's the hurry. I must say," Jeff added, "I'm looking forward to seeing the bridegroom."

"Julia saw them in Rome."

"Miriam and the Count?"

"Yes. She said he's about forty, tall and thin and motherless."

Jeff grinned.

"I know what she means by motherless. Funny, isn't it? Miriam Arkwright must have had a try, in the past, for every eligible Tom, Dick and Harry in the district — including you and me — and she ends up with an Italian Count called Leopold. Why Leopold? That's not Italian."

"Austrian mother, deceased," Nicholas explained. "I hope she'll be happy; she turned out a nice girl. She might have started off as a general nuisance, but that wasn't her fault; it was her mother's. Having Lady Templeby as a mother was too much of a handicap for any girl. It's a pity she didn't escape as early as her brother Derek did."

"She must be — how old?" calculated Jeff. "Two years off my age makes — "

"About thirty-one. She deserves a decent husband and I hope she's getting one."

"Do we get separate wedding presents," asked Jeff, "or one big thing from the whole family?"

"One small thing from the whole family."

Jeff looked at the other letters.

"No word from Julia ?" he asked.

"Nothing. And if she can't take the trouble to write and tell me when she's coming home, I can't be expected to meet her, can I ?"

"Two years," said Jeff slowly, "is a long time. I wonder if she's changed ?"

"She hasn't changed her mind."

Jeff looked across the table.

"You feel it's been a waste of time and money, don't you ?"

"Her time and my money; yes. But who am I to decide ? Paul Moulin said she ought to go — so she went. She didn't want to go, but he talked her into it. I didn't want her to go, but he talked me into it. And the two years are over, and she hasn't changed her mind, and the only one who's made anything out of it is that fellow Albano, who's made a whacking sum in fees."

"If she hadn't gone, how would you ever have known whether she could be a top-ranking pianist or not ?"

"We went through all that two years

ago," said Nicholas. "I thought at the time, and I still think that Julia could have put in these last two years more profitably with Lucille, shuttling between London and New York, meeting interesting . . . well, meeting well-known people, learning how to dress and how to do her hair and how to become a presentable member of society, instead of a scraggy girl with red stringy hair, clothes held together with safety pins, and with only one ambition in life: to lie on the nearest comfortable sofa and read and read and read — preferably poetry. That's all she's ever wanted — to live here at Wood Mount, reading poetry, until she dies. I'm grateful to Paul for discovering that she had musical talent, and for doing so much to develop it — but you know as well as I do that Julia never had the faintest wish to take it up professionally. So why did I waste the money?"

"To give her the chance to become one of the greats. You couldn't have let her — at nineteen — decide that she didn't want to go any further, and leave it at that. She — "

He stopped. The telephone had

rung, and Nicholas went to answer it.

"Who?" enquired Jeff, on his return.

"Telegram. Julia. Arriving on Monday afternoon."

A smile of pleasure lighted Jeff's face. Julia — home again.

"Will you go to the airport?" he asked.

"Yes. But I'll spend the morning in the office."

"And the weekend washing up all this lot — and cleaning the bathroom," said Jeff. He rose and looked round him. "Well, that's the end of the bachelor interlude."

"Thanks for the help. I couldn't have done it without you."

"Not in the time," agreed Jeff. "I enjoyed it. Nice change."

Nicholas looked at him curiously. You never knew, he thought, quite what old Jeff was thinking. During the three years he'd lived in this house, nobody had had any idea what he really thought of Roselle's inexpert efforts at housekeeping. He came home from his house-agent's office every evening to clear up the mess and wipe Roselle's tears, and gave no indication that he had expected anything else from marriage. Perhaps he hadn't. He'd known Roselle all her life, and he must have had a fairly good idea that her delicate, wild-rose look was about all there was to her. Funny how things turned out. Most marriages of that kind packed up — but this one was going as merrily as Christmas chimes. Old Mrs. Milward was happy running the house; Jeff was comfortable, the kids were well and happy, and Roselle — all Roselle did was push the pram and get prettier with each pregnancy. Four so far, and nothing to show she had any intention of slowing down.

"Will you be sleeping here until Monday?" he asked Jeff.

"No. I'll have to get home and get the place ready for my mother and Roselle."

"In that case, we'll start getting this place ready for Miss Cornhill," said Nicholas. "You wash, I'll dry. And after this interlude, life in the office'll seem like one long siesta. Now who," he demanded, as the front door bell rang, "can that be?"

"I'll go and see," said Jeff.

There was no need to go. Footsteps were heard outside the back door, and a moment later the head of a man with grey hair and a round, ruddy-complexioned face appeared at the kitchen window.

"Paul! Come on in," invited Nicholas.

But Monsieur Moulin, staring through the window with an awed expression, seemed unable to reply.

"It's all right; we're just wading in to clear it all up," Nicholas assured him. "Don't come in; I'll come out. Did you, incidentally, come to see me or to see Jeff?"

"I came," said Paul, in his correct but careful English, "to see you."

"Then we'll talk in the garden, and Jeff can carry on here."

"Make it short," ordered Jeff, his eyes on the disordered kitchen.

Nicholas went outside and joined the short, stout Frenchman, and together they walked round the house and sat on a bench on the lawn.

"If you'd like some coffee," offered Nicholas, "Jeff could make some."

"Nothing — no, nothing, thank you. I came because I had a letter I wanted to discuss with you."

"A letter from Albano, about Julia?"

"Yes." Paul paused, and seemed to be

choosing his words. "You will remember," he went on, "that when we discussed, two years ago, whether Julia should go to Rome and study under him or not, I said that I was sure he would agree with me about her . . . her capabilities. He did agree with me. But he knew — because, of course, I had to tell him — that she herself showed no desire to . . . to . . ."

"Go the whole way ?"

"Yes. Today, Albano writes to me. Like myself, he had hoped that he could persuade her to change her mind; to see the great future that might be for her. But — "

"But — ?"

Paul turned to face him.

"This is difficult for me," he said slowly. "I am, after all, responsible. It was I who first told you that Julia had talent — more than talent. It was I who persuaded you to let me direct that talent. It was I — was it not ? — I who from the first insisted that she should be taught the piano. You thought that it was too late for her to begin, because already she was eleven and a half — nearly twelve. But she began — " He stopped abruptly. He had been about to remind Nicholas of the circumstances in which Julia had begun the study of music; circumstances which had contributed much to her initial astounding, almost spectacularly swift progress. She had been unhappy; people, he thought, did not always assess accurately the pain, the agony that children could feel. At eleven, Julia had loved her English mistress — Paul's cousin, Estelle Dryden. Estelle had married and had left Greenhurst. She had been lost to Julia — but it was not possible to remind Nicholas of this, because Nicholas, too, had loved Estelle Dryden. Nicholas, too, had lost her. It was over — long ago — but one could not bring it up now.

"You're trying to say," said Nicholas, "that Albano couldn't make Julia change her mind?"

"Yes. That is what I came to tell you. I wanted to see you, to speak with you before Julia came home. He says that, in his opinion, she could become great; famous. But she does not wish to go on to do the study that would be necessary. She is not afraid of the work, but she does not wish to take up music professionally. And I am sorry; sorry, of course, that she has made this decision, but sorry also that you have had so much expense for . . . No, not for nothing. Nothing has been wasted — but perhaps at this moment you do not feel that?" He put a hand on Nicholas's arm. "Consider, Nicholas: how could one allow her, at nineteen, to take a decision that she might have regretted most bitterly later? How could I, her teacher, allow her at nineteen to refuse to place herself with the best teacher in Europe — perhaps the world? But . . . it was expensive for you."

"I'm not kicking," said Nicholas. "I'm grateful for all you did for her."

"But I am asking myself, now, whether it was right for me to persuade you to spend so much. You know that I am a rich man; you know that if I had not been certain you would never forgive me, I would have asked that I myself should bear the expense."

"This fellow Albano," asked Nicholas after a pause, "does he say that she could go to the top?"

"Without any doubt. But he is also convinced that nothing more can be done, or should be done. He does not wish that I should reproach her. And I . . . I do not wish that you should reproach her."

"Why should I reproach her? She said from the start that she didn't want to take up music. She didn't want to go and study in Rome, and she only went in the end because we made her see that if she didn't, she'd be breaking off something in the middle. She worked hard; I'll say that for her. She's always worked hard."

"But you feel that she worked for nothing?"

Nicholas stirred restlessly.

"I don't know," he said. "I've never been able to make up my mind about what's the right sort of education for girls. It seems to me that all this fighting to get them into a University, all this training for a career, parents pouring out money — where, half the time, does it lead to? Girls get good degrees, or they become pianists, or they cover large areas of canvas with daubs, and then what? In ninety-nine cases out of a hundred, they marry and go into the baby business, and the violin stands in some forgotten corner, and the canvases get stacked up in the attic and the degree comes in handy to work out formulas for baby-feeding, and the only time the piano's used is when the baby gets active enough to lever himself up and hammer on the key-board with a sticky fist. Waste? In my probably worthless opinion, yes. But then there's the hundredth case, where you find that the money was well spent after all. I know I'm giving off a lot of outdated and controversial opinions; the form nowadays is to give the girls the same chance as the boys. I'm all for it . . . in theory. But take it this way: the money I paid out for the boys is bringing in handsome dividends; Simon's going to be a first-class vet and he loves his job. Dominic's talking about the Diplomatic Service, and although I thought it was aiming a bit high at first, I've warmed up since Lady Templeby hinted that she'd back him. You see? In the boys' case, you sow and up comes the corn. With girls . . . As I said; you never know. Things might have turned out differently; Julia might have decided to push on until she was sitting on a piano stool on a concert platform, with her skirts spread out round her and the Philharmonic boys waiting for the first crash of chords. I've never been able to see her quite that way — but maybe you're right; maybe you have to give talent every chance."

"Yes. You have to," said Paul. "If you can."

"What do I know about it? My own musical talent began and ended with a few trumpet notes. Not the kind of music" — he grinned at Paul — "you teach your pupils. And I gave up trumpeting ten years ago."

"That was the trumpet that was auctioned by your brother-in-law at one of Lady Templeby's charity bazaars?"

"The same. Robert Debrett auctioned it in his best famous-actor manner, and it fetched no less than two hundred pounds. Not bad, when you remember it cost me ten and six in a junk shop somewhere in Chelsea."

Paul rose.

"You are not, I hope, going to auction Julia's piano?"

"No." Nicholas laughed. "No, I won't do that."

"When she returns — "

" — which will be on Monday afternoon."

" — will you ask her to come and see me? And do not, I beg you, try to make her reconsider her decision."

"If you're satisfied that she's gone as far as she's going, then so am I," said Nicholas. "What does she do now?"

"She is qualified to teach, of course — but I do not think that she will make a good teacher. Perhaps she herself will have something to suggest. Shall we wait until she comes home?"

"Seems a good idea. And thank you," said Nicholas, "for all you did for her. It wasn't only the lessons. It was a lot of other things. I don't know quite how to put this, but she was all over the shop at one time, and you gathered the pieces together and tidied them up."

"I put her to work at something she loved. That is all. And now I must go; I am very busy. But I had to come; I had to see whether you would be upset."

"At the thought that she'll never be world-famous? Curiously enough, I'm not. One international celebrity in the family's enough. Looking at Robert's life, I can't really help feeling that Julia's better out of the limelight. The money's nice, of course, but in my opinion most of these world-famous figures earn it. All I'm worried about at this moment is how Julia's going to earn a living."

"I think," said Paul, "that she will make her own plans. You have," he added thoughtfully, "done well for them all."

"Luck," said Nicholas lightly. "Sure you won't have that coffee — or a beer?"

"Nothing, thank you. I must return to my pupils."

Nicholas walked with him to his car.

"Do you ever regret settling down here?" he asked, as they went.

"Here? In Greenhurst? Never, never, never! To settle here, to use the house I inherited as a little Conservatoire . . . No. It was the best thing. How can I regret?"

Nicholas watched the car out of sight and walked thoughtfully back to the kitchen. Jeff turned from the sink.

"Julia?" he asked.

"Yes. The Italian — Albano — says she could go to the top if she wanted to. But she doesn't want to."

Jeff was silent for some time.

"Disappointed?" he asked at last.

"Yes and no. For ten years Julia has been wearing out her fingers to no — as you might say — specific end. Paul said it wasn't a waste, and who am I to contradict him? But the only future I can see for her at this moment is using her Italian to guide tourists round Roman ruins. Less lonely, when you come to think of it, than shutting herself up in a room for hours a day, polishing up her arpeggios." He picked up a cloth. "Oh well, let's get on with this job. From concert platform to crockery. From Debussy to detergents. Wonder how Miss B. Stocker's been getting on in the office for the last three weeks?"

Miss Stocker answered the question for herself when Nicholas entered the office on Monday morning.

"Good-morning, Mr. Wayne."

"Good-morning, Miss Stocker. Everything all right, I trust?"

That was what all executives said to their secretaries, and having Miss Stocker in the office made him feel very executive indeed. Even the wisest of men, he acknowledged, made mistakes — and his big mistake was knowing Miss Stocker for almost four years without taking her to his professional bosom. She had been an employee of the London firm that had once misguidedly given Roselle a job. A kind Fate had delivered Roselle into Jeff Milward's hands, and Miss Stocker had for four consecutive years come to Greenhurst to spend her annual holiday with them. During the fourth year, Nicholas's typist had left in a tantrum, and Miss Stocker had helped out — and he had almost let her go back to London; she had, in fact, been boarding the train when he had caught her and, panting, besought her to work for him permanently.

Without her, he wondered, would things have worked out so well? She had persuaded him, on the death of old Mr. Milward, to propose to Jeff that he should move his house-agent's office, rent with Nicholas the vacant building next door to the travel bureau, make the two buildings into one, instal his own office with Nicholas's on the ground floor, and let the upper stories to other firms. It had been a bold venture on the slender capital at their disposal, but Miss Stocker's calm and confidence had never once cracked. Now she occupied a vast desk in a small room overlooking the High Street, and carried the bulk of the travel bureau's work on her square, strong shoulders.

She looked the same as ever, thought Nicholas, with a detachment bred by three weeks' absence. A little over forty, short, stout in a tight, solid way, and as placid, as composed as Miss Cornhill. He marvelled once again at the complete unselfishness with which both women had given themselves up to the interests, the well-being of himself and his family. It was hard to remember that Miss Cornhill had ever lived anywhere else but at Wood Mount, or that Miss Stocker had any life of her own outside the office. His right hand and his left hand . . .

Miss Stocker, on her side, was admitting to herself that it was pleasant to have her employer back in the office. Looking for a word to describe the difference he made to the working atmosphere, she fixed upon stimulating, and then changed it to vital. That was it, she mused. That was really, when you came to think of it, the thing that made the Waynes different from all the other people she had ever met: they were vital. That is, with two exceptions: nobody could apply the term to Roselle, or to Simon; Roselle couldn't stand up without strong support, and Simon spent his time worrying about what their vitality would lead his brothers and sisters into. But the others: Lucille, Nicholas, Dominic, Julia — above all, Julia — they were really alive. What was more, they were interesting. Not many men of Nicholas Wayne's age could claim to have undertaken, at twenty-one, the care and expense and responsibility of two younger brothers and a sister.

"I did what you told me," said Nicholas. "I kept my nose out of the office for three weeks."

"Painting done?" She ripped open the morning mail and sorted it with the ease and dexterity of a bank cashier counting notes.

"The house looks very nice."

"Stiff in all your joints?" she enquired.

"Stiff in most of them."

"There." With the air of one putting aside the personal and coming down to business, she placed a file before him. "You'll find one or two things you ought to look at before you start on today's letters. Three hundred applications for that Mediterranean trip."

"Three hundred! And supposing we can't charter the boat?"

26

"The boat's fixed. There are some cheques for you to sign. Gas and electricity for Wood Mount. And a grocer's bill."

"Seems a lot," he commented, studying it, "for bacon. What's this memo?"

"You wanted to be reminded about Miss Arkwright's wedding present."

"Time enough for that."

"I don't think so, Mr. Wayne. It should go now. The wedding's less than two weeks off, and a bride likes to get her thank-you letters written before she goes off on her honeymoon."

"Well, what d'you suggest?"

"A travelling clock," said Miss Stocker without hesitation. "There's a nice one in Wilson's for ten pounds. It folds up, and it's got an alarm."

"Ten *pounds*!" repeated Nicholas, aghast. "Do you mean to sit there and tell me I've got to spend ten pounds on Miriam Arkwright, who's Lord Templeby's daughter, and probably has a *dot* of several hundred thousand pounds? Ten *pounds*?"

"You've all known her all your lives," pointed out Miss Stocker. "And after them, you're the leading family here."

"What — estate agents and travel agents?" asked Nicholas derisively.

"You're Mr. Wayne of Wood Mount, and you owe yourself something," said Miss Stocker in her flattest manner.

"That I believe," said Nicholas. "But I don't owe Miss Arkwright ten pounds. I could get her a nice little silver-plated toast-rack for — "

"Her mother," broke in Miss Stocker, "has just stopped at the door."

"What the hell," asked Nicholas irritably, "does *she* want?"

The office boy, new to his job and new also to the district, entered after the most perfunctory of knocks.

"Lidy outside," he announced.

"Try again," invited Nicholas coldly.

"Sorry. There's a lady outside wot wishes to see yer."

"What else?"

"Sir."

"Take your hands out of your pockets."

"Yessir."

"And swallow that gum you're chewing."

"Yessir."

"And remove that pencil from behind your ear."

"Yessir."

"And put that pocket comb out of sight."

"Yessir. Anythink else, sir?"

"Yes. Show Lady Templeby in."

"Yes, *sir.*"

Lady Templeby came in at her characteristic slow, stately pace, and before shaking hands with Nicholas, gave Miss Stocker a gracious nod, which Miss Stocker acknowledged by a respectful five-seconds' suspension of work. Making the usual enquiries as to the visitor's well-being, Nicholas looked at her large, commanding, tightly-corseted figure with its imposing bosom, and took in the well-preserved face, elaborately-dressed hair and feathered hat — another of the series of feathered hats he remembered from his boyhood. He thought there was more kindliness, or perhaps less aggressiveness, in her manner, and dated it from the time she had received the news of her daughter's engagement to Count Leopold Franzero. Not, Nicholas remembered, that she had given any sign of pleasure; before the engagement had been formally announced, there had been a considerable delay, which Lady Templeby, without saying anything, managed to make people feel was being used for the purpose of discovering whether a Franzero was worthy of an alliance with an Arkwright.

Nicholas, as he grew older, had begun to see the formidable old lady through eyes that took in more than her imperious and high-handed exterior. Since her marriage to Lord Templeby nearly forty years ago, she had shown a deep and unfaltering interest in Greenhurst and its inhabitants. The only flaw in this benevolent attitude had been the lengths to which it was carried, for though enough of feudal tradition remained in Greenhurst to enable those in it to accept gifts from the lady of the manor, enough of modernity had crept in to make the townspeople fiercely resentful of anything approaching patronage.

She had done much for the district, Nicholas reflected. For as long as he could remember, she had organised a series of charity concerts at Templeby, the majority given by foreign artists for the benefit of refugees from their countries. Few small market towns in England could have had so wide or so intimate a knowledge of European celebrities, for Lady Templeby, finding the few rooms at the George Inn inadequate to deal with each influx, had by degrees persuaded many of the housewives in the town to help her out by taking in, for a few days, one or more paying guests. Thus, conversational exchanges at street corners after the concerts ranged well beyond the usual small-town topics of weather or local gossip, and touched instead upon more exotic items, such as Zanini's habit of standing on his head for ten minutes before breakfast, Szorsky's remarkable feat of giving a flawless performance an hour after he had had to be assisted from the bar of the George and dipped in Mrs. Wilson's rain barrel, or Grunbaum's inexplicable rage at being offered by Mrs. Brett a nice bit of ham for his lunch.

Endless charities, and a whole-hearted interest in the welfare of the town; these were good marks, summed up Nicholas, and if one had to chalk up some bad ones on account of Lady Templeby's failure to understand her son and daughter . . . well, one had to strike a balance. And things had turned out happily: Miriam and Derek were free of her, although it was a

BIBLIOTHÈQUE INTERMUNICIPALE
PIERREFONDS / DOLLARD-DES-ORMEAUX

pity that Miriam, at twenty-five, had had to find freedom in escape, instead of learning, as her younger brother had learned, to manage and control his strong-minded mother.

"I have come," Lady Templeby announced, when the premininaries were over, "to ask you to confirm some travel arrangements for me."

"Won't you come into the other room?" Nicholas asked.

"No, thank you; I cannot stay more than a moment." Lady Templeby took the chair he brought forward, and loosened her beautiful furs. "I am, as I'm sure you must understand, extremely busy. Weddings" — she sighed — "take an enormous amount of organising."

Nicholas, whose sole contribution to the organisation of the weddings of his sisters, Lucille and Roselle, had been to give the brides away, nodded in agreement.

"They do indeed."

"I want you," went on Lady Templeby, "to complete the arrangements for Miriam's honeymoon. I wrote to her long ago; once, and then again, but I have not been able to get an answer out of her, so I told her that I would not wait any longer before confirming the arrangements I had made with you. It is going to be part of my present to the young couple, so I do feel that they might have let me know what they thought of my plan of a cruise to Greece and Istanbul."

Interfering to the last, mused Nicholas. He heard Miss Stocker bring down a paper-weight with some force upon her desk, and wondered whether this was a commentary on mothers who arranged their daughters' honeymoons, or whether she felt that a bride of thirty-one and a bridegroom of forty did not make a particularly young couple.

"The ship was the *Ulysses*, was it not?" said Lady Templeby.

Nicholas glanced interrogatively at his secretary.

"Sailing on the fifteenth," recited Miss Stocker, without troubling to consult her papers. "Double room and bath, three hundred pounds to Istanbul, picking the ship up at Venice, or four twenty-two the whole way. Use of ship as hotel at Istanbul, ten guineas each a day extra. Per person."

"That seems a lot," commented Lady

Templeby, "but" — she gave her wide, gracious, mirthless smile — "I shall be glad if you will confirm it."

"We'll do that. When will Miriam be home?" asked Nicholas.

"She is arriving this afternoon."

"Not by air from Rome, by any chance?"

"Yes." Lady Templeby paused. "You mean that Julia — "

"Well, not if Miriam's coming by B.E.A. Julia couldn't get on a B.E.A. plane; she's coming by Tiberia."

"Then Miriam and her fiancé will be on the same plane," said Lady Templeby. "Are you going to meet your sister?"

"Yes. My car," said Nicholas hesitantly, "will hold four, but — "

"I am going myself," said Lady Templeby, and bowed her thanks. "The Rolls will be more roomy, I feel."

Nicholas agreed that it would, and accompanied his client to the street, pausing only on his way through the hall to bestow upon the office boy a glance so deadly that it caused that gentleman to take his feet off the desk and hurry to open the door.

"I'm introducing," said Lady Templeby,

"something which I hope will be appreciated at the wedding."

"Oh, yes?"

"An orchestra. I have written to a friend of mine in London, and he has arranged it for me; the Borner Orchestra. You've heard of it, of course."

"I . . . well, I'm afraid . . . no."

"Well, well," Lady Templeby sounded indulgent. "They are very well-known. I thought it would be pleasant to have them playing rather light pieces; it will give the occasion a happy sort of garden-party touch. We shall of course be out of doors — at least, I very much hope so. There may be rain, but at this time of the year it shouldn't be heavy, and it will be nice for the guests — there are over four hundred, you know — to stroll about listening to the music. I've also arranged for three coloured films to be made of the wedding. A man who does these things very well is coming down to arrange it. He — "

"Not *Joey*?"

Nicholas's interruption was uttered with the first sign of genuine interest he had shown throughout the interview.

"I beg your pardon?"

"You once," explained Nicholas, "had a fellow called Joey Helyon down to take a movie of Templeby. He — "

"He is the man. I forgot that you must have met him when he came here years ago to — "

"He's been here twice since then. How is it that — "

He paused; he had been about to ask how it was that Joey Helyon, now a well-known and successful free-lance film camera-man, had accepted so negligible a commission as providing Lady Templeby with three colour films of her daughter's wedding. While he sought a tactful way of finding out, the visitor supplied the information.

"He has, I believe, other business in Greenhurst, so that I was fortunate in being able to get him to make the films for me at the same time."

"He hasn't been here for years; about four," said Nicholas. "It'll be interesting to find out what business he can have here."

He closed the door behind his client and turned to study the office boy standing behind him.

"Look, Charlie," he asked him, "how would *you* like to go into an office and see a fellow with his feet sticking up on a desk?"

"Well . . . I see wocher mean," Charlie acknowledged.

"If this were your office, would you allow your office boy to comb his hair in public — and chew gum?"

"Well, when you kind of put it that-away," admitted Charlie, "it sort of makes sense. Sir."

"I'm glad you see it that-a . . . like that," said Nicholas.

"But — " began Charlie, as his employer began to walk away.

"Well?" enquired Nicholas, turning.

"Well, this job's not wot I 'oped, and that's straight," said Charlie, coming into the open. "My mum said I'd enjoy it."

"And you're not enjoying it?"

"No, I'm not. Sir. You take it this way: how'd you like to be stuck in this dark little 'all all by yourself? I thought, when you said I'd 'ave to look after the clients, that I'd 'ave more to do with them than just trot 'em as far as your secre'ty's door, or Mr. Milward's door, and leave 'em there."

37

"What did you expect?"

"Well, I didn't expec' to interview 'em, but I thought I'd be inside the office, like. I thought I'd be able to 'ear somethink going on. I thought I'd be, if you follow me, part o' the set-up. I didn't expec' I'd be ready for wot you call responsi-bility just at first, but I didn't think I'd be shut in this 'all all day, waitin' for the main door to open and watching people 'oo don't want you or Mr. Milward goin' upstairs in the lift. It was orlright at first; I like watchin' people — but I didn't know they'd be mostly the same people over and over."

"We advertised for a boy to act as office boy for this office and for Mr. Milward's office, and you — "

"Yeah. But apart from postin' the letters and that, I don't get out enough," complained Charlie. "I mean, it'd be more interestin' if I was to be a sort of commissionaire, and then I'd be able to step out into the 'Igh Street and see wot's going on. See? Sir."

Nicholas looked at him. He was sixteen, and looked twelve; small, thin, undersized, shabby and not too clean. His mother had been a Greenhurst girl, and had married a

38

Covent Garden market porter; all she had got out of marriage, she explained, on her recent return to the home of her girlhood, had been two rooms in a district pervaded by the smell of decaying fruit, and a son who took after his late worthless father.

"I thought it best," Charlie said, when the silence began to lengthen, "to be frank wit choo."

Nicholas studied him for some moments in silence.

"If you could choose a job — a job you felt you'd really enjoy — what would it be?" he asked at last, and the friendliness, the simple curiosity of his tone, the man-to-man freedom it seemed to betoken, brought down the last of Charlie's reserves.

"I never got as far as thinkin' of jobs," he said despondently. "All I think about is girls. Girls, girls, girls. But the girls 'ere won't go out with me. Why? One: I've got a Cockney accent. I like the way I talk better than I like the way they talk, but that ain't neither 'ere nor there. Two: I got no dough. Three: this is the only suit I got."

Nicholas sat on the edge of the desk.

"Didn't you ever think about a trade?"

"Trade? Yeah. If my mum hadn't been so set on comin' back to this one-'orse town, I could've got m'self a barrow and—"

"If you belonged to me, d'you know what I'd do?"

The question, so often asked with a grim threat behind it, this time was uttered in an entirely friendly tone.

"No. Wot?"

"I'd take you up the High Street to Bretts, and—"

"The motor shop?"

"Yes. You know how Mr. Brett started? He had a small cycle shop where Capper the grocer is now. From cycles to scooters; from scooters to cars. Now, as you see, he's got the biggest and the most successful garage in Greenhurst. I'd take you to him and I'd say, 'Look, Mr. Brett, here's a bright young fellow who wants to get somewhere; how about taking him on and using him and teaching him all about cars, and—'"

"Apprenticeship? That takes money," pointed out Charlie scornfully. "My mum tried that—not at Brett's, but up in London. Oh yes, they'd all 'ave me; oh yes, they'd all love to 'ave me. But if it was a case of teaching . . . Nope. Pay — or get out."

"How about leaving that to me — and Mr. Brett?"

There was a long silence. Charlie's eyes, small and keen and suspicious, bored into Nicholas's. With all his sixteen years' accumulation of distrust in the motives of his fellow-men, he pondered the proposition. Little by little, suspicion seeped away and surprise took its place.

"What's in it for you?" he enquired frankly at last.

"What's in it for anybody who puts money on a horse? Nothing — unless the horse comes in."

"I'm the 'orse?"

"That's right."

"And you're the . . . the backer?"

"Subject to your mother's agreement — yes."

Charlie swallowed hard.

"When?"

Nicholas rose.

"How about now? We could do the Mr. Brett end of it and then you could go home and get your mother's reactions. If all goes well, you can come back here and write out your resignation and hand it to Miss Stocker."

Charlie took a deep breath.

"Come'n," he said, and with a deference he had never shown a client, flung the door wide for Nicholas to pass.

Mr. Brett, emerging from a little glass compartment in the depths of his garage, listened to Nicholas's brief proposition, and decoded correctly the message in Nicholas's glance.

"You say" — he looked down at Charlie appraisingly, his manner so reminiscent of a farmer buying a calf that Charlie backed apprehensively — "you say he's been working for you?"

"Yes. In my opinion, he's built for something more active — both physically and mentally. All I propose at this stage is that you should try him out. Give him a month, and at the end of it you'll know, and he'll know — and I'll know — how he's shaping. What do you say, Mr. Brett?"

Mr. Brett, after giving a good imitation of a man weighing the pros and cons, at last agreed to the month's trial. Three seconds later, Charlie was moving with a rapidity never before seen in him towards the cottage in which his mother and grand-parents lived.

"I hope you're justified, Mr. Wayne," said Mr. Brett, looking at the retreating form.

"What happens," asked Nicholas, "to poor little devils like that if somebody doesn't give them a chance?"

"You can read it in the papers," said Mr. Brett. "Did he want to do something mechanical?"

"Hardly. What drew me to him," said Nicholas, "was his frank admission that all he thought of was girls."

Mr. Brett's laugh echoed over the wide spaces of the garage.

"Well, that's healthy," he said, sobering. "Healthy to admit it, at any rate. But may-be some of my boys'll be able to give him a bit more meat to chew on. I'll start him as I start all the other youngsters — teach him to drive. Not out on the road — they're too young for that. I've got a field I use. It lets them get the feel of a car, and that eases a lot of the strain out of them. Well, leave him with me, Mr. Wayne. I'll see what I can do."

Nicholas thanked him and made his way

back to the office, pausing on the way at the open door of the George to exchange a few words with the landlord.

"Good-morning, Mr. Trent."

"Good-morning, Mr. Wayne. Everything all right with the family, I trust?"

"Yes, thanks. I just stopped to ask whether you can tell me when you're expecting Mr. Helyon. He's coming to Greenhurst for the wedding, and as he always stays here —"

"Well, to tell you the truth," said Mr. Trent, "I didn't see the booking myself, but I'll just pop inside and —"

"Don't bother; if you'll look it up and phone my secretary, I'll be grateful. I've got to hurry back."

"I hear your sister's coming home."

"She's arriving this afternoon," said Nicholas, and walked on reflecting that it was odd, and might perhaps be put down to the fact that only one of his sisters was unmarried, that whenever anybody in Greenhurst referred to his sister, they meant Julia. Always Julia.

He entered the office and stopped before Miss Stocker's desk with a brief pronouncement.

"We've lost our office boy. He was sitting out there getting rust all over him, so I took him along to Brett's. Perhaps he'll learn something and go somewhere."

"Perhaps," was all Miss Stocker said. And perhaps, she added to herself, office boys — like tramps in the old days before the Welfare State put tramps out of business — left secret marks on door or on gates, to show those that came after them that something good was to be had within. The last office boy had pinched the petty cash and had been placed with a family somewhere in Surrey, and the one before that had had a delicate chest and Mr. Wayne had found him a job down by the sea, and the one before that . . . and before that . . . Oh well. A few more Nicholas Waynes, and the world would be a better place — for office boys.

"The George phoned," she said aloud. "Mr. Helyon's expected tonight."

"*Tonight?*"

"With a party of five."

"A . . . Tonight, with five other people?"

"Yes. That's what they said."

There was no pleasure in her voice, and Nicholas had expected none; Miss Stocker was almost the only person in Greenhurst who had remained unaffected by Joey Helyon's cheerful, forthright, uncomplicated personality. She kept him at a distance and gave him no more response than bare courtesy demanded. If Joey had been a ladies' man, mused Nicholas, there might have been reason to suppose that she resented his advances — or the fact that he had made none. But Joey wasn't a ladies' man; he was a hearty, jovial, carefree bachelor who was more at home in men's than in women's company, and it was difficult to see what Miss Stocker had against him.

Miss Stocker could have explained, though she would have added, in fairness, that her first impression of Joey Helyon had been a mistaken one. He had been in Greenhurst about four years ago on a brief visit, and he had come into the office to see Nicholas. As he came towards her desk, large, loud, red-faced, breezy of manner, greeting her with the cheerful familiarity one old friend would use to another, something deep, something forgotten, some instinctive animosity stirred within her, for he recalled to her mind a type which of all others she feared and detested, and which she termed the Commercial. She had fought since her schooldays to overcome the disadvantages of her beginnings in the East End of London; the way had been hard, but nothing had made it harder than the witless, insensitive, often cruel jibes of the less desirable members of the commercial travellers' profession. At Joey's entrance, the old distaste had welled up, clouding her normally keen perceptions.

She had learned that her first impressions had been wrong; active dislike receded, but wariness and suspicion remained. And now he was coming back again, and everybody would be very pleased; but if they asked her, she'd tell them that she could do very well without Joey Helyon.

"You going home to lunch today?" she asked Nicholas.

"No. I forgot to tell you: Julia's arriving at London Airport at three, and I'm going to meet her. Perhaps you'd kindly see that my car's all right for petrol and oil. Oh — and send a taxi to the station to meet the three fifteen; Miss Cornhill's on it, thank

God. When I go to Heaven," he ended on his way to his room, "remind me to ask Them what it was I ever did to deserve dear old Cornhill." He closed the door of his room, opened it and put his head out for a last word. "And you, of course."

Miss Stocker, left alone, dwelt with pleasure on the thought of seeing Julia again. Her mind went back over the years she had seen her coming into the office; Julia in a school uniform, Julia in a skirt and blouse; long, thin legs, red, untidy hair, a thin eager face, a quick, eager way of talking. When she left for Italy two years ago, she hadn't looked very different; nineteen or not, she was the same Julia. Perhaps the time in Italy had changed her. People did change. It seemed to her that even Nicholas Wayne had changed a little in the past few months. There was a touch of something new in his manner. Arrogance? Well, that wasn't a nice word to apply to anybody as nice as he was, but truth was truth, and he'd been having things a bit too easy lately. And when things became too easy, people got into the way of thinking that perhaps there was something clever about them that made them manage their affairs better than their neighbours did.

Trouble . . . Nobody wanted trouble, but there was no doubt that a touch of it kept people from becoming too . . . arrogant. Dogs needed a flea or two, and people needed a few irritants to keep them on the go. It was a long time since real trouble had touched Nicholas Wayne. How long? Miss Stocker did some calculations; it must, she decided, be about ten years since that girl Estelle Dryden had turned him down and gone off and married someone else. That was bad trouble, and she didn't want anything of that kind to happen to him again — but ten years were a lot of years to get over it, and for the last few of them she couldn't really say, not honestly, that he'd had much to worry him. He was beginning to look as though he expected life to roll along without bumps.

Well, life didn't. It had ups and it had downs, and Nicholas Wayne had had the ups for so long that in her opinion, if anybody wanted to hear it, there was every chance of a down or two being on the way. Trouble was bound to come, and something told her that it was only just round the corner.

And in this, as in all other matters concerning the Waynes, Miss Stocker was quite right.

CHAPTER II

NICHOLAS reached the airport to find, to his annoyance, that the Tiberia flight from Rome was delayed. He swore softly under his breath and stood for a moment hesitating: it was too early for tea, too late for coffee; there was nothing for it but to buy an illustrated paper and pass, as well as he might, the hour before the plane was expected. The fact that the B.E.A. plane, scheduled to leave Rome almost at the same time as the Tiberia flight, arrived punctually, did nothing to lessen his sense of grievance. Nobody minded hanging about when there was fog or bad weather, but on a calm, still day of this kind there was no excuse for any plane to keep people waiting. These Tiberians ought to get themselves some new engines.

There was nothing in the paper to hold his attention. He folded it irritably, leaned back in his deep chair and, idly watching the crowds hurrying to and fro, found himself in the unusual situation of having time for reflection. The reflection presently took the form of a review, and he surveyed, not without satisfaction, his progress during the past few years. The house, Wood Mount, his own; his brother Simon entering a good profession; Dominic getting through Oxford, Julia trained for a musical career — only she didn't want a musical career. Himself with a job he liked and a secretary who could run the office unaided. He could not have visualised ten or eleven years ago, that he would find himself so well settled in so short a time.

Marriage? One day, perhaps. There was no hurry. One thing about having a knock when you were young — it gave you a kind of immunity in the future. Or perhaps it would be more accurate to say that it made you walk warily where women were concerned.

In other ways, things had worked out pretty well. You had to give yourself credit if you felt any credit was due, but it didn't do to let the back-patting go too far. He'd got on — and most of it was luck and he was grateful.

He opened the paper again and took out his pen to fill in some of the solutions to the crossword puzzle — and then the arrival of the Tiberia flight was announced, and he got to his feet with an unexpected sense of excitement. Julia; funny little Julia was back, and in a moment he'd see her; good. And better still if she'd taken a look at some of those glamorous Italian beauties and . . . well, Julia could never be a beauty, but perhaps she'd outgrown the ragbag look.

He found himself hurrying to a point at which he could scan the incoming passengers, and a moment later bumped with some force into a man of his own age who appeared, like himself, to be anxious to see the Tiberia arrivals. Nicholas began an apology, only to find the other man pushing roughly past him with a brief and uncomplimentary summary of his opinion of those who didn't trouble to look where they were going. Nicholas, watching the retreating figure, noted its unusual breadth of shoulder and look of strength, and walked on with a feeling of deliverance; if the fellow had waited to hear his opinion of him, he would have given it — but not, definitely not after having seen those muscles. An ox like that could do quite a lot of pushing without finding anybody with the nerve to push him back.

He forgot the incident as he sighted a group of people climbing out of the coach that had brought them from the aircraft. They were easy enough to identify, for every passenger carried a bright green plastic flight bag on which the word TIBERIA was painted in huge scarlet letters. Nicholas stationed himself beside a group of people waiting to greet the arrivals.

A rustle behind him, a faint, familiar, expensive scent prepared him for the presence beside him of Lady Templeby. They greeted one another absently, each intent on watching the incoming passengers. An old man, an old lady, three schoolgirls, some young men who looked like students; Nicholas glanced at them as they appeared. A girl — and a beauty; well worth studying, if one weren't looking for . . . There was Miriam. And behind her — yes, that must be her fiancé, the Count.

Nicholas looked him over, and liked what he saw. For the first time, Julia's adjective — motherless — assumed its full significance in his mind. It was perhaps sad to be motherless, but Miriam had enough mother for two. Studying the Count's tall, thin figure and rather plain, strong, serious face, Nicholas came to the conclusion that here was a man who would have no difficulty in coping with the mother-in-law situation. Lady Templeby could be kind, sensible and pleasant — but she could in certain circumstances become very unkind, far from sensible and very unpleasant indeed. This man looked perfectly able to manage her in all her moods.

"There," murmured Lady Templeby into his ear, "is the Count. He looks charming, don't you agree?"

Nicholas, agreeing, was thankful for Miriam's sake that he also looked like a man who would not tolerate too much interference in his affairs, and turned to scan the arrivals in an effort to locate Julia.

Still no sign. Could she, he wondered, have missed the plane, and why should he be surprised if she had? Hadn't she missed every bus and every train she'd ever been scheduled to travel on? There they all were, all off the coach, all waiting the signal from the stewardess — but . . . the stewardess seemed to be waiting . . . And there was Julia!

Julia coming out backwards, picking up

her belongings as she came; a brown paper parcel had burst and she was stuffing the contents as well as she could into her Tiberia bag. Now the students had gone forward to help her — and the stewardess, too. And the Count. Trust Julia to hold up the whole show. Now she was ready — she had turned, and . . . Nicholas studied her for a long moment. Yes, she'd changed in a way; hair or something — it was shorter, or Julia was longer. But why had he hoped that she would grow curves, grow soft and rounded and feminine? She was as slim, as straight as he remembered her; there was her thin, odd face between the curtains of red hair. There were the same long legs — longer now — and there was the same complete lack of self-consciousness, which he felt uneasily to be, in a girl of almost twenty-one, an ominous sign. If she wasn't yet aware of herself, how could she make anybody else — any young men — aware of her? There she came, in the middle of the bunch of students, chatting and laughing as impersonally as though they'd all been her brothers. Oh well, Julia was Julia and he'd better get along and wait until she got through the Customs.

It was some time before she saw him. A Customs official began to deal with her luggage and then two and then three officials grouped themselves round her. Had she brought in a sackful of contraband, Nicholas wondered uneasily. If somebody had asked her to bring in a parcel, she probably wouldn't have stopped to worry about what was in it. Should he make his presence known and . . . No. It was all right. She was through, and all the luggage, with the rows of green Tiberia bags, was being placed on the assembly line and sent below.

He saw Julia gazing eagerly at those waiting to greet the passengers. Then she saw him, and her arm came up in wild, delighted greeting. She came hurrying towards him, through the barrier, and threw her arms round his neck.

"*Nicholas!*" She released him and drew back. "Let me *look* at you! Nicholas, you haven't changed a *bit*! Not a tiny, tiny *bit*! You're just exactly the same!"

"You, too, Julia. Nice to see you."

"Oh, Nicholas, it's *Heaven* to be home! Are you alone? Is anybody with you? Have you heard from Pietro? Is Miss

Cornhill back from her holiday? Did you hear that Lucille and Robert are coming to Miriam's wedding after all? Miriam's over there with her fiancé — did you see them? Doesn't England smell gorgeous? Nicholas, does Simon really like that job? Did you know that Derek had done something or other to his foot? Oh, Nicholas, did you really paint the house yourself? Did you — "

"Quiet," said Nicholas. "Come downstairs and let's claim your luggage and get home. What were you doing with brown paper parcels?"

"It was this way." Julia, her hand loosely in his, allowed herself to be led down to the luggage. "I hadn't any time to pack properly, and I hadn't changed into my travelling things, and my landlady got hold of everything I couldn't fit in at the last moment, and you know how Italians pack parcels, and just as I got off the plane, it all went Whang. Nicholas, did — "

"Hold on. What were all those Customs men doing round you — did you bring in a lot of contraband?"

"No, I didn't. They were just being friendly. Nicholas — "

"One moment. Which is your stuff?"

She looked at the rows of assorted luggage and then pointed.

"There's one of my suitcases. I've got two."

Nicholas stared at the battered case she had indicated.

"*That?* You mean to tell me that that's the suitcase I bought you just before you left home? What the hell did you do with it? Take a sledge hammer?"

"Well, I sort of used it when I went away on weekends. You know how Italian porters bang luggage about? Nicholas, have you —"

"Well, go and find the other case. I'll hang on to this one. Anything else?"

"Yes — that green bag. The one marked Tiberia. They gave them to us for nothing. Will you wait here?"

"Yes."

While he waited, Nicholas allowed his eyes to rest on the girl he had noticed earlier. Tallish, he noted; slender, fair; interesting eyes — greyish, as far as one could tell at ten yards distance; yes, greyish, with long black curling lashes which, if not stuck on, were pretty arresting. Wonderful skin — but there again, girls could manufacture wonderful skins . . . only this girl had a look about her that didn't look manufactured. What was called the best English type — knew how to move, knew how to stand still. Nothing of that ghastly deb vivacity about her, thank God. Age? Twenty-four, at a guess. Clothes expensive. Most clothes would look expensive on that figure, of course. Wonderful lines. Clean lines. She —

"Excuse ME!"

The two words, uttered in a tone Nicholas could only term belligerent, came from the man who had collided with him earlier and walked on without apology. Turning to face him, Nicholas saw no reason to change his earlier unfavourable opinion; the man was a boor. An outsider. Powerfully built, not bad-looking as features went, but with a manner so offensive that Nicholas felt it the duty of every right-minded citizen to try to correct it. Every right-minded citizen with boxing experience.

"I beg your pardon?" His voice was cold.

"I'd be glad if you'd hand over that bag," requested the man tersely.

Nicholas glanced down. He was holding the green Tiberia bag that Julia had claimed as hers. Also grasping it, in an attempt to wrest it from him, was the stranger. With an access of anger that surprised himself, Nicholas gave a sharp pull and placed the bag on the counter before him.

"That bag," he said, "belongs to my sister."

"That bag, on the contrary, belongs to my fiancée," said the man in loud and menacing tones. "Hand it over."

Nicholas, not easily roused, found to his dismay that a pink film was rising before his eyes. It cleared, and he was able to register the fact that the girl he had been watching was the one the man had indicated as his fiancée. With the realisation came the knowledge that the man had no doubt noted his frankly admiring survey of the girl, which accounted for the belligerent attitude. But people couldn't talk to people like that. He addressed him calmly.

"I think you'd better wait until I can ask my sister about the bag," he said.

"Sorry; I'm in a hurry. Come on — hand it over."

"If you'll forgive me," said Nicholas frigidly, "I'll hand it over to you when — "

" — when I ask you." The man glanced at the girl, who had drawn near and stood watching the scene with what Nicholas considered quite unjustifiable detachment. "Shan't be a mo," he told her. "Spot of bother; this chap took a fancy to a bit of your luggage."

"My sister," Nicholas told the girl, "said that this bag was hers. Perhaps she was mistaken, but I should like to — "

"Come on, come on," broke in the man insolently. "I told you I was in a hurry."

Nicholas's gaze rested on him benignly.

"Yes? His tone was gentle. "But I'm not.

The man's face came close to his own.

"Look here; if you want to make trouble — "

"Kenneth," said the girl in a restraining tone.

Kenneth, unfortunately, was past the stage at which he could be pulled up. He stepped close to Nicholas, who resisted an impulse to step back.

"If you want to make something of it,"

he offered menacingly, his face thrust forward, "the name is Springer."

"How do you do?"

"Sir Kenneth Springer."

"My name is Wayne. Plain Mister," added Nicholas, to his own surprise and regret. He warned himself that this thing was going too far. There was no need to get embroiled in an indignified dispute with this aggressive stranger. This man . . . and that girl! She was a girl who could have taken her pick — and she had picked this! She ought to be certified.

He looked round. To his relief, Julia was approaching, a porter and a suitcase in tow.

"Julia, is this your bag?" he asked her.

"Yes. They gave them to us for nothing — I told you," said Julia. "Nicholas, did Miss Cornhill — "

"Just a moment," broke in Nicholas. He addressed the girl standing beside them, studiously ignoring her fiancée. "I'm sorry," he said. "The bag is, as you heard, my sister's."

"Oh — but wait a minute." Julia was peering into the green bag. "Oh Nicholas — it isn't!" Her eyes went to the girl.

63

"I'm terribly, terribly sorry! I sort of mixed it up — you know how it is, with all of them all exactly alike! I thought this was mine, and I told my brother to hang on to it. *This* is mine — this one here. It's all my stupid fault, but I do hope — "

"It's nothing." The girl smiled, and Nicholas was confirmed in his opinion that there was something appallingly unsuitable about her choice of a life partner. Somebody ought to talk to her. Somebody ought to make her think again. Somebody —

"How about an apology?" demanded Kenneth in a loud voice. "First you grab somebody else's luggage, and then you — "

"We're going, Kenneth," said the girl, and this time something in her voice brought her fiancé to a stop. "Good-bye." Her smile, this time, included Julia and Nicholas, and Nicholas found himself regretting her interference. If she hadn't stepped in, Kenneth would soon have got above himself; Kenneth would have overstepped the bounds of decency, and one would have been justified in taking him by his expensive but unsuitable shirt and dragging him to the door and — with the aid of a porter or two — throwing him outside. Women ought to keep out of rows and let men settle them.

"Ready?" he asked Julia.

"Nearly. All I can't find," said Julia, "is a brown paper parcel."

"But you had it," said Nicholas. "It broke in the — "

"No — that was another one. Oh — there it is!"

"Let's get it," said Nicholas.

He walked away, bowing to the girl and ignoring her fiancé. He saw the man walk in the opposite direction to collect the rest of the girl's luggage, and then he had given his mind, with an effort, to Julia's brown paper parcel. Having with difficulty located it, he picked it up and turned to walk back to the place in which the rest of Julia's luggage had been left, pausing on the way to say a word or two to Miriam Arkwright and to shake hands with her fiancé.

The grey-eyed girl was still standing where Nicholas had left her. For a moment their eyes met and he saw in hers a look which he could not identify. Leading Julia out to his car and thinking about the matter, he came to the surprising conclusion that she had been looking pleased about something. There didn't seem to him anything in her situation to merit satisfaction of any kind. How a girl like that could . . .

His browsing was brought to an abrupt halt. A hand hit his back, sending the breath from his body. A voice, as loud as Kenneth's, but ringing with joy and friendliness, rang in his ears. His hand was grasped and pumped up and down, and before him he saw the broad, heavy figure of Joey Helyon.

"Nicho-las," he roared. "If it isn't my old pal Nick. Nicholas, my old pal, what are you doing ? . . ." He came to an abrupt stop, his eyes, round and wondering, upon Julia. "*Not* Julia ?" he brought out slowly. "Not my funny little Julia. Julia my pat — "

"She's just the same," Nicholas said, smiling.

Joey's glance came round to him.

"What was that ?"

"I said Julia hadn't changed."

"Julia hasn't changed ?"

"Her hair's a bit shorter, of course."

A curious look came and went in Joey's eyes.

"Have it your own way," he said. "Julia,

66

when are you booked to do a concerto with the London Philharmonic? And are you going somewhere, or have you just come back?"

"I've been in Rome for two years — studying. I'm just back."

"Studying music or studying life?" Joey wanted to know.

"Mostly music. What are *you* doing here, Joey?" Julia asked.

"Me? I'm just in from Athens. And I'm on my way to Greenhurst."

"Greenhurst?" Julia's delight sounded clearly. "To stay with us?"

"Not with you, no; the way to keep your friends," said Joey, "is to stay at the local pub. I'm putting up at the George. I've got a bunch of technicians with me. Tell me: how's my old pal Simon, and his dog — what was that dog's name? Long John! That was it. They all right?"

"They're both up in Yorkshire," said Nicholas. "Simon's all set to be a vet. Dominic's with a party of undergraduates, climbing in Norway, but he'll be home for the wedding. I understand you're going to film it."

"That's not why I came," confessed

Joey. "I had other things in mind — but I didn't want to turn down Lady T's proposition and then be around Greenhurst watching some lesser photographer doing the job. I'm taking it, so to speak, in my stride."

"What other things have you in mind?" Nicholas asked.

"I'll pop into the office in the morning and tell you. And get all your news. But now I've got to get back to my boys."

"There's a girl with them," said Julia.

"Girl? No girl," corrected Joey. "That's Delphi, and she only looks a girl from where we're standing. Distance, and all that make-up, lend enhancement, if not enchantment." He looked despondent. "I got stuck with her."

"Why the regret?" Nicholas asked. "She's rather picturesque."

"Well, she's not beautiful, but she's photogenic — and if you asked girls nowadays to choose, they wouldn't hesitate," said Joey. "One of my boys decided he'd like to marry her, and one of the conditions she made was that I should sign her up. I pointed out that signing her up didn't mean a thing, but she got this fixed idea that I could start her off on the road to fame, so when I found I couldn't talk this fellow out of marrying her, I gave in. She's a Greek and she's been married before — her last name was nothing but x's and k's, but now she's plain Delphi Dunn. What I'm going to do with her I don't . . ." Once more he broke off abruptly, his glance fixed on something over Nicholas's shoulder. "Nicholas, my boy," he begged, "speaking of beauty, take a look at that girl over there."

Nicholas looked back.

"I've already taken a look," he said. "The muscular gentleman with her is her fiancé."

"Fiancé?" echoed Joey, shocked. "He doesn't look up to her standard."

"He isn't."

"You know them?"

"I had a slight argument with him."

"Then you hadn't ought," reproved Joey. "You don't argue with muscles like that; you just stand off and admire them. Well, I'll be seeing you. I'll drop into the office tomorrow."

"We could drive you down," offered Julia."

Joey took her hand and patted it.

"Julia, my pet," he told her, "you've got to remember who I am. I'm not just any old camera-man, you know. I'm Helyon. I'm even more famous in the world of films than your sister's husband, Robert Debrett. When I touch down at an airport — "

"I know," broke in Julia. "The way to keep your friends is to drive your own car, hm ?"

"Right," said Joey.

Julia looked at him.

"I wouldn't mind coming with you," she said. "There's a lot Nicholas is going to say to me on the way home that I don't want to hear."

"All I'm going to say to you," said Nicholas, taking her arm and leading her away, "is that I'm glad you're back. See you at Greenhurst, Joey."

He supervised the disposal of Julia's luggage into the car, and took his seat beside her.

"I could drive if you like," she offered. "I drive quite a lot in Rome."

"Oh ? Whose car ?"

"Various people's." She watched him

as he threaded his way out to the road, and edged closer to him. "Nicholas, can I say something?"

"It can wait. Why not enjoy the English scene?"

"Did you get a letter from Albano?"

"No. I didn't."

"Well, did Paul get one?"

"Yes."

"Did Paul . . . Was Paul . . . I mean, have you seen him?"

"He came to see me on Saturday. Why can't this wait? You've just got home, and — "

"All I wanted to know was whether you and Paul — "

" — were going to hold anything against you? No, we're not."

"Honestly?"

"What did you think?"

"I thought . . . Aren't you terribly disappointed in me?"

"Strange to say, no. All I'd like from you, now that you're home again, is a suggestion or two as to how you can earn a living."

"Nicholas" — her voice was low with an intensity of gratitude that recalled the child

Julia and brought a smile to his lips —
"I'll work and work and *work*."

"Good. What at?"

"I . . . I haven't had time to decide.
Shall I come and work in your office and
send people to — to where? Seaborn
Salamis? Or to Thebes, home of Epamin-
ondas?"

"I think most of them prefer to stick
closer to home. So shelve it for the moment
and tell me about Rome. Are you glad you
went?"

"Oh . . . Nicholas, living there was
Heaven! Were my letters awful?"

"They weren't particularly informative."

"There were so many people to write
to! You, and Lucille and Roselle and the
boys, and Pietro and Miss Cornhill . . .
Have you heard from Simon?"

"Yes. He's settling down and so is Long
John. Dominic won't be back until the day
before the wedding — neither will Lu and
Robert. Derek Arkwright's home; he hurt
his foot."

"So Miriam said. Badly?"

"I don't think so. He gets around: I
caught a glimpse of him in town this
morning."

"Is Miss Cornhill back?"

"She should be"

She was. When they reached Wood Mount and went up the long flight of steps to the front door, it opened before Nicholas could use his key, and Miss Cornhill stood before them, as neat, as cool, as quiet as ever.

"Well, Julia?" she said, disengaging herself from an enthusiastic hug and holding Julia at arm's length. "You look very well."

"Miss Cornhill, darling, it's Heaven to be home again!"

Miss Cornhill merely smiled — but she had on returning to the house that afternoon experienced the same sensation of thankfulness. Fate played strange tricks, and when she retired from a long and honourable career as Matron of a girls' school, she would not have dreamed that another career lay before her. Housekeeper, adviser, settler of disputes, keeper of order; all these were part of the position she held at Wood Mount. The Waynes had become her own, their affairs hers, their problems, their hopes and fears all hers. She had taken a holiday reluctantly, and had enjoyed it not at all; this was where she belonged and where she was happiest.

"I hope," Nicholas said to her a trifle nervously as he carried Julia's suitcases into the hall, "I hope you found the house looking all right."

"The kitchen and your bathroom," said Miss Cornhill, "needed some attention."

Julia had vanished. She was upstairs, going along the corridor to her bedroom. She reached it and threw open the door and went in slowly, her eyes searching the room for familiar things but her mind already aware, after the first instant, that something had gone. Nothing material; the furniture and its arrangement, the carpet and the curtains were the same. And yet, she realised, standing in the middle of the room and slowly circling to view it from every angle, nothing was the same.

She was really seeing the room, she knew, for the first time. She noticed things she had never noticed before: its unusual shape, its deep windows, the colourful pattern of books on the shelves that lined one wall. This had been Roselle and Jeff's bedroom when they lived at Wood Mount; when they went, Miss Cornhill had helped her to make it into a bed-sitting room. The piano had been a combined gift from all her relations and friends on her fifteenth birthday.

She walked to the window and stood looking out. The garden — almost all under grass, since grass was easier to keep tidy than the flower beds which had once bordered the lawn. Up there the Tree House in which she and Simon and Dominic — and Derek — had spent so many hours. A tree house no longer; for her small nieces and nephews, who had made it their own, it was a space ship round which satellites — empty tins on long strings — could be put into orbit.

She turned and leaned against the window frame and looked again at the room and saw other things: the curtains were faded and the carpet in places threadbare. The furniture, she realised for the first time, was old, good and probably valuable.

Home. She was here, as she had dreamt of being. She had been happy in Rome; she had worked hard, but between periods of work there had been periods of rest and sightseeing and amusement. She had not been particularly homesick — but she had looked forward always to the time when the two years would end and she would return to Wood Mount. And now she was here. The two years had passed; she had booked an air passage and Nicholas had met her and brought her home. Here she was. And home . . . was changed.

Everything the same — and everything quite different. She faced for the first time the fact that Simon was gone, and Long John — Long John of the shaggy coat, the long, waving tail, the swift legs and slow brain — Long John had gone with him. Yorkshire was not, geographically, far away — but Simon would live there always, work there, and come back to this house only for brief holidays. Dominic would go — where, he had not yet decided, but he would go away. Pietro had gone; temporarily, Nicholas had said in his letters to Rome — but it was not likely that Pietro would return. He was gone, English and incomparable cooking and deep devotion to herself; Pietro would not return. He would marry, perhaps; he would find an Italian girl in New York and he would settle there and be lost to Greenhurst for ever.

Derek would go — but only for a time; he was to study farming, and when he had learnt all he could, he would return and would in time inherit Templeby and live there. But the old days, the old ways, were gone. Gone, she realised with a sense of shock that shook her, gone for ever.

She walked across the room and stared at herself in the glass. Twenty-one — almost. Twenty-one wasn't old — but twenty-one was older than childhood. That was what had gone: childhood. That was what had gone before she left Wood Mount two years ago — but she had not been able to read the signs, or she had not cared to read them. Twenty-one — it sounded young, but it wasn't. Looking forward one could see a stretch of years — but it was true, she told herself, staring unseeingly at her reflection, it was true to say that the greater part of her youth had gone. Older people would laugh if she voiced the conviction aloud, but nobody could deny the fact that the greater part of real youth was dead. Twenty-two, twenty-five, still young. Twenty-seven, twenty-eight . . . thirty. They called you young then, but it was only by comparison with the forties and the fifties — and the sixties. Real youth, golden youth, carefree youth, utterly irresponsible youth ... gone, and for ever.

It was too short, she thought rebelliously, and something in her stirred in pain. Too much had to be fitted into youth: learning, growing, preparing, shaping. You went through it all, pushed, urged, encouraged or bullied by your elders; you went through it blindly and without any sense that the years were slipping away. And suddenly you came home and found that you were twenty-one — and grown up. Perhaps other girls reached this stage of awareness earlier; she couldn't tell. For herself, it was enough to understand that childhood was over, and that it had been a time of great happiness. The bad times went unremembered, the memory of the good times endured. Wood Mount and Greenhurst, and the family as it was — when she, Simon, and Dominic were the young ones. The family as it was now, when the young ones were the new generation growing up; Lucille's children, Roselle's children.

She drew a long breath and shook off her mood of depression. It was no use standing here staring at herself and waiting for the grey hairs to sprout. Life was still fun, and she wasn't old yet. Life would go on being fun — with luck. All the same, it was a pity that you lived most of the best part of your life without realising that it was the best part.

She walked to her wardrobe and opened the door and inspected the row of dresses she had left hanging up when she went away. A slow smile appeared on her face, and she found herself murmuring a line or two that sprang to her memory.

> ... hang
> Quite out of fashion, like a rusty mail
> In monumental mockery.

Maddening, the way Shakespeare thought of all the good bits first.

She closed the cupboard and went down-stairs and Nicholas, hearing her swift foot-steps, smiled at Miss Cornhill.

"She's going to find it quiet without the boys — and without Pietro," he remarked.

Miss Cornhill said nothing. She herself found Wood Mount far more pleasant without the excitable and unmanageable

Italian. It had been a mistake, in her opinion, to let him stay for so long. She had never voiced the opinion, but she had sometimes hinted to Pietro, in a delicate way, that the household had shrunk and that his superlative cooking was really wasted on an English family. Hints, she had found, had no more effect on Pietro than they would have had upon Long John, but at last Nicholas had persuaded him to go to visit his brother, and she hoped that his brother's family would enjoy food cooked in olive oil and redolent with garlic. Perhaps they would find Pietro a wife and induce him to stay in New York for ever. And perhaps she missed him more than she had anticipated — but she was not getting any younger, and peace and quiet were more than compensation for his loss — and she was perfectly well able to manage, with the aid of two daily women from the town, the cooking and the work of the house.

"Roselle telephoned," she said, as Julia came into the kitchen. "She and Jeff are coming to tea. It's laid in the drawing-room."

"Are they bringing the children ?"

"They're bringing Nicky," said Miss

Cornhill. "I think" — she paused at the sound of wheels on gravel — "yes, here they are."

The only miscalculation people had made when they likened his sister Roselle to a wild rose, reflected Nicholas, as he went to welcome her and Jeff and their youngest son Nicholas, was that wild roses bloomed briefly, while ten years of marriage and four children had left Roselle's bloom untouched. She still had all her fragile, shy, blue-eyed charm — and she'd keep it, he decided, so long as her husband and her mother-in-law went on taking the weight. It was a sort of magic circle: they shouldered the tough jobs because Roselle looked like sugar-icing, and Roselle continued to look like sugar-icing because they shouldered the tough jobs.

There were other surprising things about her, Nicholas remembered, as he followed her into the drawing-room. She gave birth to her children with an ease and a swiftness that was the envy of every other young matron in Greenhurst — and the children, far from being reproductions of her own delicate, feminine loveliness, all turned out to be thumping great boys.

Nicky, aged five, went impatiently through the polite forms of welcoming back his Aunt Julia, and then fixed unblinking eyes upon her.

"What did you bring for me?" he demanded.

"How did you know I brought anything?" enquired Julia.

"When you come home," said Nicky, with a conviction that was the result of pleasant experience, "you bring things. Presents."

"You think I've got a present for you?"

"Yes. What present?" was the only detail that interested Nicky.

"Not before you've eaten your sponge cake and drunk your milk," said his father.

Nicky, on the edge of rebellion, paused to reflect that the long way round was sometimes the shortest way home. He ate his cake and drank his milk, handed his empty mug to Julia, and spoke through a mouthful of crumbs.

"Present," he said.

"It's locked up in my luggage," said Julia, "You'll have to come into the hall while I unpack it."

"Presents for Nicky and Robin and Dom'nic and Jeff," said Nicky, revealing both an admirably unselfish nature and his mother's regrettable obstinacy in insisting on reproducing, to the confusion of all, the existing family names.

"If you unpack in the hall," pointed out Nicholas, as they went out, "you'll have to pack again; I'm not going to carry your things upstairs piece by piece."

"I'll shove it all in when I've unpacked their presents," promised Julia.

There appeared, presently, to be a hitch; the presents were in the big suitcase, but where was the key?

"You must have had it at the Customs," pointed out Nicholas, when appealed to by a worried Julia. "Didn't you have to open your suitcases?"

"No. I told you, they didn't make me open anything. You don't think I could have left it in Rome?"

"I'd almost lay odds on it," said Nicholas. "You always liked to have the case in one place and the key in another. It made unpacking so much more interesting."

"Don't joke," she begged. "I've got lots of presents in that case."

"Then you should have insisted on opening it for the Customs officials."

"I'll ask Miss Cornhill," said Julia, "if she has a key that fits."

"Why not see if your keys are in your bag?" asked Nicholas.

"I looked," said Julia. "I turned every single thing out."

"In the middle of the hall?"

"I'll pick it all up again. Where do you think — "

"How about turfing everything out of that green plastic monstrosity the airline issued to its passengers?" suggested Nicholas.

"Oh — *that's* where they'll be," said Julia, her face clearing. "Come on, Nicky."

She was not long in the hall. When she returned to the drawing-room, she was holding the green Tiberia bag, and on her face was an expression which brought a frown of apprehension to Nicholas's brow.

"What's wrong?" he asked.

"The . . . the bag." Julia's voice was dazed. "I mean it isn't . . . it isn't . . ."

"It isn't what?" asked Nicholas impatiently.

"Well, it isn't mine."

84

There was silence. Nicholas, rising slowly to his feet, walked across the room and took the bag from his sister's nerveless fingers.

"You mean — this isn't yours?"

"No."

"Good Lord! But I *asked* you, Julia. When we had that mix-up, I specifically *asked* you which — "

"But it *was*!" cried Julia. "Honestly, Nicholas, it *was*! The first time, I didn't look inside, and so we all got mixed up — but when you asked me the second time, I looked inside, and it *was* my bag. It was! I checked; there were all the things I'd stuffed in from the brown paper parcel that had burst. It *was* my bag."

"What happened?" asked Jeff in the silence that followed.

"I got hold of what I thought was Julia's bag — and it wasn't," explained Nicholas. "It was owned by a girl who owned a fiancé who owned well-developed muscles. He didn't like me."

"You mean," came in Roselle's gentle voice, "you mean he spoke to you about it?"

"He brought his face close to mine and told me to hand it over — but I didn't. I held him off until Julia confirmed that it wasn't hers."

"And this bag?" asked Jeff. "Is it the same as the one you — "

"Can't be," said Nicholas. "Why Julia can't decide once and for all which luggage she owns and which she — "

"But it *was* mine!" persisted Julia. "I looked *inside* it, Nicholas. I looked — you *saw* me look!"

"I saw you peer into the bag for a moment," said Nicholas, "but that doesn't mean that you — "

"It was mine." Julia's voice had the calmness of certainty. "I don't know how you managed to get it wrong twice, but the second bag I pointed out was mine, and nobody else's. And my keys must've been in it, and if I haven't got my keys, how can I give the children their presents?"

"What was in your bag?" enquired Jeff.

Julia coloured.

"Well — it had all the things that fell out when my parcel burst. I'd sort of pushed things into a parcel at the last minute, and it fell apart just as I was getting out of the — "

"Well, what was in it?" asked Nicholas.

"Well . . . it had the things I'd been wearing before I changed to go to the airport," said Julia. "It had a white slip, and a pair of white sort of panties, and a sort of suspender belt . . . and . . . and that sort of thing."

"A nice haul for whoever got hold of it," commented Nicholas dryly. "Well, what's in the bag you're accusing me of getting hold of?"

Julia opened it and peered inside.

"Nothing much," she reported. "Just a newspaper — an Italian newspaper — and books. Two English books."

"Show me," said Jeff.

"Nothing," said Nicholas, "to cause anybody to lament its loss. I wonder who got Julia's underwear?"

Jeff was looking at the fly-leaf of one of the books.

"*Elaine Morley*," he read out. "*Redwalls, Crayke, Wilts.* Scribbled in pencil," he ended, laying the book aside and opening the other. "In this," he reported, "no name and no address. Funny . . ."

"What's funny about it?" asked Nicholas.

Jeff's tone was thoughtful.

"Both the books are new," he pointed out. "One of them has a name and address, obviously written in haste; the other hasn't."

"So what?" asked Julia.

"Nothing much," said Jeff. "I was just thinking that people don't as a rule write their names and address in books. Names, perhaps; addresses . . . I would have said not."

"Well, it isn't important," said Nicholas. "What Miss — or Mrs. — Elaine Morley has lost in literature, she's gained in lingerie."

"And keys," said Julia. "Couldn't we ask Enquiries for her telephone number — if she's on the phone — and ring her up and say we're sorry but we took her bag by mistake?"

"She might have taken your bag by mistake," said Nicholas. "There were several old ladies in the offing, and any one of them might have been Miss Morley. Before we start the wires buzzing, how about asking Miss Cornhill to let you try the keys out of the key box?"

Miss Cornhill, appealed to, produced a

large wooden box filled with keys of every sort and size. Julia, choosing the likeliest, sat with the silent but deeply interested Nicky on the floor of the hall, and in due time announced that all was well: a key had been found to fit, and all that remained was to unpack the suitcases and distribute the presents.

"And Miss or Mrs. Morley," said Nicholas, "can go without her reading matter for a day or so. Julia, you can write her a letter of apology and demand your property in return for hers."

"I'll write tomorrow," said Julia absently, showing her nephew how to work his new Italian car. "Nicholas, did you tell Jeff and Roselle about Joey?"

"Joey Helyon?" asked Jeff in a voice of lively interest. "What about Joey?"

"He was at the airport. I forgot to tell you," said Nicholas. "He's coming down this evening."

"Here?"

"To the George. He's staying there with a team of what he calls technicians. Five of them."

"Four of them — and Delphi," corrected Julia.

"What's he coming to Greenhurst for?" asked Jeff. "And who's Delphi?"

"He's doing three movies of Miriam's wedding; commissioned by Lady Templeby."

"I would have thought that Joey would have turned down a small job like that," commented Jeff. "He's an important fellow nowadays, in his line."

"It's not the only thing that's brought him here. He's got something else in mind; he's coming to the office in the morning, so we'll hear what it is."

"And Delphi?" enquired Jeff. "She coming, too?"

"She's married and her other name's Dunn," said Julia. "Nicholas can't tell you much about her, because he had both eyes on the girl with the fiancé. We need more hot water; I'll get it."

She went out, and Jeff's eyes followed her. Then he turned to Nicholas.

"Do you remember," he asked, "what Pietro always used to say about Julia?"

"I remember," said Nicholas. "He prophesied, among other things, that she'd be a beauty. Well, he was wrong, and she isn't, but I like her as she is."

"You don't think" — Jeff's voice held an odd note — "you don't think she's changed?"

"I didn't say that. I said she wasn't a beauty."

Jeff's comment was an echo of Joey Helyon's.

"Have it your own way," he said.

CHAPTER III

JOEY HELYON arrived early at Nicholas's office on the following morning, and after hesitating in the now untenanted hall, pushed open a door and found himself in the presence of Miss Stocker, who was typing with the speed and rattle that always made so sharp a contrast with her calm bearing. She paused on Joey's entrance, her hands resting on the keys to indicate that as soon as the courtesies were completed, she would return to her task.

"Good-morning, Mr. Helyon."

"Hello, hello, hello; and how's Miss Stocker after all this time?" Joey wanted to know.

"I'm very well, thank you. Mr. Wayne isn't in, I'm afraid."

"Oh wait a minute, wait a minute! One old friend at a time," protested Joey. "Let me look at you. You're not," he announced after a benevolent survey, "looking any older than you did when I was last here. By that I mean," he added hastily, "that you're not — well, looking any older," he finished lamely.

"Mr. Wayne came in," said Miss Stocker coldly, "but he had to go round to — "

"I can wait, I can wait," said Joey. "Nice to have this opportunity to have a chat with you. Ever regret settling down in Greenhurst?"

"Never. If you'd go into Mr. Wayne's room, he'll — "

"I'll just perch m'self here," said Joey, lowering his bulk on to one of the small wooden chairs lining the wall. "You just go ahead with whatever it is you're doing; I'll watch you."

Miss Stocker, without further exchange, returned to her typing, and Joey watched her admiringly.

"Middle name Lightning," he observed when some minutes had elapsed, "I bet you've won competitions."

Miss Stocker, without pausing, gave a brief nod to acknowledge the compliment.

"You the only one here?" enquired Joey. "Working here, I mean.

Miss Stocker nodded, her fingers flying.

"You mean you and Nicko-boy do the whole lot between you?"

"Yes."

"Seems a lot of work to me," said Joey commiseratingly. "You ought to see about getting a junior. You ought to — "

"I shall be obliged," broke in Miss Stocker, her fingers stopping for a moment, "if you will go and sit in Mr. Wayne's room and let me get on with my letters."

"If you want to write letters" — Joey waved a huge hand—"who's hindering you?"

The noise of the typewriter answered him, and he sat watching for a minute or two in silence.

"The trouble with you, he said presently, "is that you don't allow yourself enough leeway. You ought to be more elastic. You ought to — "

"I am not here," said Miss Stocker, tearing out a completed sheet and neatly inserting another, "to entertain visitors. I take them to Mr. Wayne — or they wait for him. Excuse me."

Her fingers flew, and Joey, watching, tried to assess her speed.

"Good, solid training you must've had," he remarked. "I always say you can't get good results on a poor foundation. I can see you put your mind to it from the word 'Go,' and — "

"Perhaps *you'll* be good enough to go," requested Miss Stocker, pausing with an air of desperation. "Do you expect me to work with you sitting there and going on?"

"You said you were writing letters."

"So I am. Mr. Wayne's letters."

"Oh well now, you misled me! My mistake. I thought you were just catching up on your correspondence. All I was doing," said Joey, raising his voice above the renewed clatter, "was making a few pleasant observations to my friend's secretary while I'm waiting for him to put in an appearance. Anybody who can't stop a minute just to listen to a bit of conversation when it's addressed to them by somebody they haven't seen for years, is in my opinion in need of a nice — "

"Nice nothing!" Miss Stocker bounced round on her chair and glared at him, her face red and angry. "You go away and — and mind your own business."

At the sound of her own words, uttered in a tone and accent that for more than twenty years she had endeavoured to correct, the colour faded from her cheeks. Turning her back on Joey, she applied herself once more to her work, but the spring had gone out of her fingers, and there was a blur before her eyes. Bitterness filled her mind. She, B. Stocker, had said that! She had let herself down. She'd gone straight back to where she'd started from. Instead of ignoring that ape, that monkey, that . . . There she went again. What was the use of all that trying, all that care for years and years, when one moment of temper could blow all the effort away?

She became aware that the visitor had left his seat and was standing before her with her hands on her desk, leaning on them and looking at her with round, reproachful eyes.

"I'll tell you something," said Joey slowly. "You're overworking."

"Fat chance with you around," said Miss Stocker bitterly.

"You got cross, didn't you? And why? You thought you got cross with me. But no; you didn't. You're doing too much and you've got yourself into such a state that whenever somebody — some quite innocent bystander — does anything to disturb your routine, you go off at half cock. Tense, that's what you are, my girl, and — "

"All I said" — Miss Stocker, with an effort, spoke calmly — "all I said was would you please go away. Just because you haven't got anything to do, is no reason why I shouldn't get on with what I have to do. If I was rude, as Mr. Wayne's secretary, I apologise. You needn't bring tenseness into it."

"If I asked you" — Joey's tone and attitude were fatherly — "if I asked you to get up out of that chair and walk out of this office and take a nice drive in the country with me for your health, what would you do?"

"Leave my job? Walk out at this time of the morning? You're crazy! Walk out!"

"Drive out."

"Walk or drive — what's the difference?"

"Some women would soon tell you. What have you got to be afraid of? If Nicholas Wayne doesn't know what a treasure he's got in you, then you ought to leave him and offer yourself to some other boss. If he does know — and I bet he does — then you're in a position to down tools without wrecking the organisation. How long have you been working here?"

"Six years."

"Holidays?"

"I don't need holidays. I like my job."

"And so the only thing you do in the whole wide, interesting world, week after week, month after month, and year after year, is bang that machine? Granted," admitted Joey, "you had to bang it until you'd banged your way into a good job and proved you could hold it down. But if you go on banging it to the ex-clusion of every other interest, then soon you're not going to be much use to anybody, including yourself. Take this morning, for instance: I'm not such a bad chap — single, clean-living, well-behaved — and I come back after four years or so and address a few harmless remarks to you, and what do you do? You get the jim-jams. You get all steamed up. You bark right in my face. Is that friendly? Is that nice?"

"In Mr. Wayne's room," said Miss Stocker, "you'll find pen and paper. You can write all this down and hand it to me on the way out."

"You mean you won't relax?"

"I mean" — Miss Stocker's voice had regained its habitual flat calm — "that what you see me doing may seem like hard work to you, but to me it's second nature. I do it in my sleep. And it's what I'm paid for. If you want to find somebody to listen to all those theories of yours, you'll have to go somewhere else."

Joey seemed about to reply, when the door opened to admit Nicholas, and he addressed him instead.

"Nicholas boy, I'm just trying to get your secretary to walk out on you and drive out with me."

"She's too busy," said Nicholas, ushering Joey into his own room. "Have you," he asked, giving Joey a chair and putting cigarettes beside him, "been annoying Miss Stocker?"

"I never in my life annoyed any lady," said Joey. "I offered friendly chat, and she rejected it." He looked at Nicholas in bewilderment. "What is it about me that she dislikes so much?"

"The fact that you interrupted her work?"

"No." Joey shook his head. "No, it's more than that. She's never, if I can put it that way, felt the magic of my charm. When I came into the office this morning,

I said to myself, 'Now watch your step with Miss Beryl Stocker' — and before I'd said twenty words, I'd put my foot right into it. Funny, isn't it?"

"You can make your peace with her on the way out. Cigarette?"

"Thanks." Joey drew his chair up to the desk and leaned over it to hold a light for Nicholas's cigarette and his own. "There's something about her," he brooded, "that I can't seem to get round. Ever since I got into town last night, I've been greeted everywhere like an old friend. Warmed me nicely; I never thought I'd got myself a little niche here, but I found that that's just what's happened. Glad to see me back; everyone: old Trent, all the lads at the George, all the people in the shops I popped into this morning. And then I walk into your office and there's this same old fish-eye from your secretary. I read it the moment she looked up; here's that pest again, she said to herself. Like cold water, it was."

"Well, tell me about Delphi; that'll warm you up again."

"Delphi?" Joey leaned back. "Well, in a way, she's my fault; I mean, I found her.

She was working in a café in Athens — a respectable café; none of your dives. She was doling out something they said was tea, and she was dressed in something thick and unrevealing which the customers took to be the national costume. Well, I haven't been standing behind a camera for all these years without being able to spot lines. I told her I was a film man and I dressed her in wisps and paid for her posing against some of the historic ruins — and the results took your breath away, Nicholas boy. They were — don't laugh — sheer beauty. Classic woman against classic column; it lifted my artist's soul high. But it had a different sort of effect on my assistant, Jimmy Dunn; soul didn't come into it at all — not at all. He fell for her with a thud; you could hear it all over Athens. He tried a few side doors, but no go, and he fell back on the good old-fashioned proposal, and as I told you, she only said Yes when I said I'd sign her up."

"Sign her up for what?"

"Well, sometimes I talk too much," confessed Joey. "When I was persuading her to pose, I told her about a girl I'd used in a documentary I made in France; Anglo-

Gallic bought it and it made them a packet; made me a packet, too. But they also signed up the girl I'd used in the film — and Delphi's hoping for the same kind of luck. I lose either way; if she doesn't get a job she'll make trouble among my nice tight little bunch of boys — every one of them a specialist in his own line. If she does get a job, I'll lose Jimmy Dunn. Oh well . . . that's my trouble, not yours. Now I'll tell you why I came to Greenhurst. It wasn't, as I told you, to photograph the Templeby wedding."

"Then what?" asked Nicholas.

"It was to do the second of a series of documentaries I've started off on: the life of small towns in various countries. The first one was in France — the one I told you Anglo-Gallic bought. It was a try-out; I did it in a small town in the Midi; name of Tourvalles. The boys and I made a good job of it. Nothing spectacular; just simple, everyday life."

"Don't tell me you're going to film the simple, everyday life of Greenhurst!"

"That's just what. I've talked to a number of people this morning and I've met with nothing but co-operation."

"What are they going to co-operate in? What's Greenhurst *got*?"

"Just what I want. It's a plain, ordinary little market town, with plain, ordinary citizens — and that's what I'm after."

"But — "

"Look at it this way. You take a tourist: he comes to this country or to any other country, and what does he see? He sees the highlights; the sights. Then he goes home, and if he's a small-town fellow, he goes home without having found out anything about his counterpart in the country he's been travelling in. So the idea came to me to do a sort of — as you might say — distillation of small-town life: the baker, butcher, grocer, the kids going to school; who eats what, and where? How does the washing get done, and who does it — and by what means? Washing machines, or banging off the buttons in the local stream? How do the kids amuse themselves out of school? What do the teenagers do? Courting couples; how long do they wait, what kind of money do they need before they marry? I film the people going about their business; all they need is — "

"But you said you had a girl who — "

"Well, yes. You have to have a central figure."

"And is Delphi going to be the central figure in the Greenhurst film ?"

"Well" — Joey gave a rare, worried frown — "I've got to try her. She's over at the George now, asking Jimmy how long she's got to stay in this town; she's got her eye on London and useful interviews, and I only got her quiet by telling her that the famous Sir Robert Debrett was going to be here for the wedding, and when it was over I'd get her a couple of minutes with him."

"That's a fine way to use old friends, isn't it ? The one thing Robert has always had in Greenhurst is — "

"Yes, yes, I know; people leave him alone. Well, I won't let Delphi worry him; I swear it." Joey rose. "And now I've got to get out there on the High Street and get busy. I'd like to get some shots of this office and — "

"No, you don't," said Nicholas with decision.

Joey looked at him in astonishment.

"What's the objection ?" he asked. "If you don't want to appear, all you do is walk in — young local business-man coming into his own firm — and we get a back view of you opening up and interviewing customers. I'd insert some shots of foreign resorts at that point, to underline the travel-agent motif. Then — "

"Nothing doing," said Nicholas. "And if I know Greenhurst, you won't get much co-operation. We're not publicity seekers, I hope."

"There's no publicity, Nicholas boy. Everybody's strictly anonymous. *This is England*, I state. This is a small part of — "

"You can go ahead, and I wish you luck — but leave this office out of it. Did you say — did I hear you say that Delphi was going to appear ?"

"Not as she looks now, of course. She'll be toned down and down — and down. When I've got her into the right clothes, anyone could pass her in the street and think she's just out of commercial school. That is" — Joey grinned — "if they pass her."

"You're really going to do it ?"

"I'm really going to do it."

"Then I wish you joy. If you use a girl in the film, why don't you use a man ?"

"I've got one. He doubles as commentary writer. Chap named Luke Hayman. Nice looker; Canadian. He wants an introduction to Julia."

"To Julia? He's never set eyes on Julia."

Joey crushed out his cigarette, rose, leaned over and patted the other man gently on the arm.

"You'll learn," he said. "He saw her at the airport."

"You're sure he's not mixing her up with that other girl?"

"Which other? . . . Oh, I remember. No; Luke doesn't get mixed up."

"What did he find so devastating about Julia?"

"How would you understand? You're her brother," said Joey. "Well, so long. Be seeing you."

"Oh — Joey."

Joey turned.

"Well?"

"Come and dine with us tonight. Miss Cornhill would like to see you again."

"And I," said Joey, "would like to see dear old Miss Cornhill. How old would she be now?"

"She's nearly sixty."

"Active?"

"She runs the house. I said something, a year or two ago, about her not wearing herself out in our service. It didn't go down very well."

"Give her my love. Will I do in this suit?"

Nicholas looked at him, taking in Joey's figure, broad and burly but not gross; his face, ruddy but not coarse; his manner, expansive, exuberant but never overpowering. He remembered his cheerfulness and kindness, his warm, impulsive generosity.

"You'll do in any suit," he said.

He opened the door, and Joey went out, pausing for a moment at Miss Stocker's desk.

"I apologise," he said. "I don't know what I do to you, but I apologise for doing it."

"Don't do it again," warned Nicholas from the open doorway of his room. "If he does whatever it is, Miss Stocker, throw him out."

Miss Stocker raised her brown, rather prominent eyes to Joey's.

"I'm busy, that's all," she explained.

"I like my work, and I don't like people who stop me from doing it."

"Well, that's fair enough," said Joey. "One day, perhaps you'll let me talk to you when you're not doing it. So long, Nicholas. See you tonight."

He went out into the High Street and walked back to the George, to be met at the door by his assistant, Jimmy Dunn.

"Well, what's the local reaction?" Jimmy asked.

"It's even better than I hoped," Joey told him. "Co-operation all round. We've got a lot of work to do. Where are the rest of the boys?"

"In the bar — where else? Not Luke — he's out souvenir-hunting. I don't think he'll be long."

They went into the bar, where they were joined by Luke Hayman, a tall, rangy, good-looking young man of about twenty-three. For the next hour or so, seated at a sunny table by the window, they discussed Joey's plans for filming the people of Greenhurst, and then Joey pushed his notes aside and called for beer. As he did so, he caught sight of Julia going past, and opened the window to call to her.

"Hey — Julia! Do you always pass your old friends without a look?"

"I was told never to peer into bars," said Julia, coming back a few paces and stopping beside the window. "Is this the important business you had in Greenhurst?"

"It's the preliminary," said Joey. "We — " He broke off to turn and protest to Luke, who was prodding him violently in the back. "All right, all right, I'm coming to it," he told him. "If you'd just go outside on to the street, instead of trying to shove me out through the window, I could perform a formal introduction. Julia," he said, turning to face her once more, "have you a moment to meet somebody who's anxious to make your acquaintance?"

"I haven't much time. I'm going to lunch with Paul."

"Paul? Ah! Mon-sieur Moulang?"

"Yes."

"Well, before you go, there's somebody you've got to meet," said Joey. He waved a hand towards Luke, who had gone out into the High Street and who was now standing beside Julia. "This, Julia, is Luke

Hayman, who wishes to pay his addresses to you."

"Really?" Julia turned to smile at him.

"Really," said Luke, and grinned engagingly. "Saw you at the airport."

"He's Canadian, twenty-three, and rolling," said Joey, and closed the window, his part in the affair over.

"There's nobody like Joey," commented Luke, "for skipping the preliminaries. Were you going somewhere I could go with you?"

"I'm going to lunch with my old music teacher — he's a Frenchman and he lives at the Red House, not far from here."

"Mind if I walk with you?"

"Of course not."

"You live out of town some way, don't you?" said Luke, falling into step beside her.

"Four miles out. A friend of mine brought me in — Derek Arkwright, brother of the Miss Arkwright who's getting married next week."

"Is he the guy with a bandaged ankle?"

"Yes. He thought he couldn't drive his car, but he found he can. He drove me into town and then took his mother shopping.

You're going to be here for the wedding, aren't you?"

"I needn't be; Joey won't need me. But I think I'll stick around and look at the tents and the band and the foreign notabilities."

"Marquees and an orchestra and almost everybody in Greenhurst. But no bridesmaids and no pages, which I think is a pity."

"You play the piano, don't you?"

"Yes. And this is going to be a difficult lunch, because I've got to explain, fully and finally, that I've come to a grinding halt and I'm not going to take up music professionally."

"He wants you to?"

"Deep down, I think, yes. But he's been kind enough to pretend that he knew all the time I wouldn't. And this" — she stopped — "is the house, so I have to say good-bye."

"When," enquired Luke casually, "will you be out again?"

"Out? Oh — I suppose about three."

"I'll be here," said Luke, and sketched a salute.

"And who," enquired Paul Moulin, as

she entered the large, beautiful drawing-room, "was that?"

"You were spying on me?"

"I happened to be in the room that overlooks the drive. You arrive with a handsome young man wearing those American trousers and a check shirt and a suede jacket. He is one of those film-makers, no?"

"Yes." Julia ignored the chair he pushed forward for her, and went to a sunny patch on a window seat. "Paul—"

Her tone brought his hand up to halt her.

"Nothing serious before lunch," he warned. "Are you old enough to take an aperitif?"

"Of course—but I'm not awfully good yet at deciding which aperitif is which. Tell me!"

He told her, and some of the tension inside her relaxed. This had to be got through, but it was not going to be easy.

She had reckoned without Paul's gentleness and affection. He talked throughout lunch of Italy, of her Italian friends, of her loved friend and slave, Pietro; not until he was watching the coffee dripping through the glass percolator did he touch on the subject that had brought her to see him.

"And now," he said, taking the coffee tray from his housekeeper and carrying it to the drawing-room, "your future."

Julia stood in the middle of the room, her eyes on him, her expression frowning and absorbed.

"Paul — "

He held up a hand.

"That tone," he prophesied, "means that you are going to put forward a case. What is it called? The case for the defence." He brought her coffee to her, and smiled. "Julia, my dear, why do you think you are doing wrong?"

She took the cup, but put it down, unregarded, on a table. He sat in a comfortable chair, sipping his coffee, and she dropped in a heap at his feet.

"You can't say it wasn't waste, Paul," she said, looking up at him earnestly. "Waste of time, waste of money and a terrible waste of all those hopes you and Nicholas had for me."

"We had hopes? Not, I think," Paul corrected, "in the sense that you mean. Why did we insist, nearly two years ago, that you should go to study with Albano?

Because there was a chance that you might change your mind, that you might find your full powers and decide to use them."

"But — "

"Wait. You are well aware that Albano is one of the most sought-after teachers in Europe; in the world. I could not send you to him unless I told him the truth: that you were not sure that you wished to make music your whole life. This I told him; I did not tell you that I had told him, but when you went to him, it was on a special agreement between himself and me: that if he felt, after first hearing you play, that it would be a waste of his time, or of yours, for you to go on — then he would send you home again without further study."

"You mean . . . He *knew* that I — "

"He knew that you loved music, but that you might not care to lead the life of a professional musician. Yes, he knew. But he wrote to me that you had an exceptional gift, and that he would keep you there — in hope."

"Paul — I tried! I honestly tried! I worked — terribly hard. I did all I could — but all the time, inside, I knew it wasn't what I wanted. But how can I come home now and throw all that wasted time in your face, all that wasted money in Nicholas's face, without being able to say *why* I don't want to go on? I don't *know* why! And what's worse, I can't even say: 'This is what I want to do instead.' If I had some alternative talent I wanted to develop, some life work I wanted to be free to do . . . that would make things a bit better." She hesitated. "There's only one thing . . . I did get an offer of a job."

"Oh? Tell me about this job."

"Well, it was a recording job."

"Recording? Making gramophone records?"

"A rather new kind. Have you ever heard of Student-Discs?"

"Never."

"They're experimenting with a new form of accompanying: records for purely practice purposes. They're trying to provide soloists with accompaniments on records. Trying to give the student the chance of playing to a first-class accompaniment — on a record."

"The solo part is not recorded?"

"No."

"They are doing away with the accompanist?" asked Paul, who had once earned his living as one.

"They can't do that. All they want to do is — "

"They will record, for example, a concerto — without the soloist?"

"That's it. Then the pianist, or the violinist, or whoever's working on the piece, buys the background on record and — "

" — and pretends he is on the concert platform?"

"He practises with the recorded orchestra?"

"But you — you are a soloist; how shall you help them?"

"They want me to do the piano part of some violin-piano works, for a start. Then the two piano parts — separately — of two-piano works, because they feel that this, for the student, is the most difficult thing of all — having to find a place where he can — "

" — where he can find two pianos?"

"Yes. You're on their list, too."

"*I* am?"

"You. Didn't you accompany the great,

late Gonzalez? Don't you think the idea's good?"

"I shall have to think about it. Yes, I think that in some cases, it would be very good. Sometimes soloists become discouraged by the — "

" — the *thin* feeling. The lack of background. There's no stimulus, on your own, when you're tired of going over and over the work alone. I'd like to do it for them. If the company finds the records selling, they'll sign on people like myself — and yourself, if you wanted to be signed up."

"And you would enjoy this?"

"Yes. Albano recommended me to them. If they wanted me, I'd have to go up to London and talk about fees."

"And when would this begin?"

"Not until the beginning of September."

"You have spoken to Nicholas about it?"

"Not yet. I wanted to see what you thought about it first. It's a job, isn't it? And if the idea catches on, it'll be a good job."

Paul reached across for her coffee and handed it to her.

"Drink that," he said. "We shall wait and see how this Student-Disc develops.

And in the meantime, you must not talk of throwing away time or money. Has study, has learning ever been wasted?"

"Shouldn't one *use* it?"

"Commercially? It is not always possible. In other ways, you will use it all your life. Sometimes, you will not even know that you are using it — but inside you there is a store; a store of beautiful music, of knowledge of what makes music and musicians. Most important of all, you have got, for ever, something of incalculable value for yourself — that is, an outlet. Whether you live the life of an artist or not, Julia, you *are* one. *I* am one. And artists are not quite as other men — or women. They have a fire; small or large according to whether they are good artists or not good artists. There are many disadvantages in being an artist, but we, more than others, have got a means of using the energy that wells up inside us. And you do not, at your age, know quite what a blessing this is. Forget about this talk of waste. We took a risk, let us say — and it was well worth it. And now we can forget the past and talk about the future, and for the near future, I have a little proposition to make to you. More accurately, I am going to ask you for your help."

"How?"

"In this way: I have not had a holiday, a real holiday, for more than eight years. Next week, my little Conservatoire closes its doors and my housekeeper and I are free for the three weeks of the vacation — but I would like to go away for longer than three weeks. I would like to go for three or four months to France, to see all my friends, to see my father's people. I cannot do this unless I arrange that somebody of — may I say — of my own ability is here to take care of my pupils, and I have waited until you came home, saying to myself: Perhaps Julia will undertake this for me. Perhaps she — "

"*Perhaps?* Oh Paul, I'd love to do it — if you thought I could!"

"I told Nicholas that I did not think you would make a good teacher, but by this, I meant that you would not be content, would not be satisfied to teach all your life. That is a pity, because it can be a very rewarding profession. But there is not one of my pupils who will not benefit much from what you know. It will be a business arrangement; I shall be free for three, four months, and I shall have somebody to leave with my pupils. Will you agree to this?"

"Oh Paul — of course! I'd love to do it!"

"Good. That is settled. Later on we shall talk of the details. But today, there is something else I wish to ask you. It is about wedding guests."

"What wedding guests?"

"That is what I do not know. But my housekeeper, who hears everything, says that she thinks Lady Templeby is in a little difficulty about the accommodation of wedding guests. There are — so the rumour says — some extra people who are coming. And I have been thinking: why should I not offer this house for them?"

"This house?"

"Why not? It will not be easy, so late, to find a place for extra guests — and you know what Lady Templeby will do?"

"Of course I know. She'll go to Nicholas again and ask him to have them at Wood Mount."

"Yes. So why should I not offer this house instead? I have never been able to do this before, because it is not possible to have strangers in the house when it is being used for music lessons or music practice — but for the first time, Lady Templeby has chosen a date on which the Conservatoire will be closed. There will be no pupils to make a difficulty."

"But you've just said you're going away, too — you and your housekeeper."

"Yes. We are going away a few days before the wedding. But Lady Templeby will not need me, or my housekeeper; she will need only beds, cups for coffee, some little things to eat. Why should you not come and stay here and look after the guests ?"

"*Me ?*"

"Why not you ? Can you make beds ?"

"Yes. But — "

"Can you cook a little breakfast, make a little coffee ?"

"Of course. But — "

"The other meals they will take at the George. To help you, you could ask Mrs. Bush to come. She is the mother of the boy who worked for your brother — she is a Greenhurst woman who went away when she was married, and has now come back; I needed somebody to help my housekeeper, who is not as young as she was before, and Lady Templeby heard this and asked me to have Mrs. Bush, and I did and Mrs. Bush is a good worker. She and you together — could you not manage this?"

"Yes, I could manage it, but — "

"There is no need for you to decide now. It is not even sure that Lady Templeby will be in any difficulty. I shall not be here to know if she wants the rooms or not — but you will be here. You need not say anything — unless you hear that she needs rooms for guests, and unless you are willing to come and stay in the house to look after them. Keep the idea — how do you say?"

"In reserve?"

"Yes; in reserve. But I shall be happy to lend the house. I owe Lady Templeby something, do I not? I shall be glad to do this. The house will not be closed; Mrs. Bush will have the key, to get into the house to clean it."

"I'll wait and see if Lady Templeby needs any rooms," said Julia. "If she does, I'll tell her what you said. But . . . you won't be here for the wedding."

"No. For that, I am sorry — but perhaps they will not miss me."

Julia got to her feet, leaned over and dropped a kiss on his thinning hair.

"I'll miss you," she said. "Paul — "

"Yes?"

"I love you with all my heart."

He sighed.

"All the girls I teach, they all love me with all their heart," he said. "And then they trip out of the gate, as you are going to do, to forget me with a young man of their own age. Ah yes! they all love me, but not too seriously."

But when Julia left the house a few moments later, she had forgotten Luke Hayman, and as he stepped forward to meet her, her moment of non-recognition brought a smile to his lips.

"I sure made an impression," he said. "Let me recall to you: Luke Hayman, on Joey Helyon's payroll."

"Oh . . . I'm so sorry. I wasn't thinking."

"You sure were — but not about me. How about coming with me to that funny little café and having tea — or a Coke?"

"I'd much rather go home — wouldn't you?"

"Home with you, or home with myself?"

"With me, of course."

"The 'of course' has it. Transport? I don't own a car, but I could hire one."

"If we worked out the time schedule cleverly," said Julia, "we could take my brother's car, and you could drive it back here in time for him to drive home in it after office."

"He knows about this borrowing?"

"He will when we tell him. Come on. We'll go to his office."

"How about the small matter of a licence?" Nicholas asked, when they got there. And when Luke produced one: "And how do I know how you drive?"

"If the car isn't back on schedule, you can begin to doubt," said Luke.

He led Julia away, and Nicholas went back to his work, only raising his head when Miss Stocker came in with his tea. He left the office in good time, drove back to Wood Mount, had a bath, changed and went downstairs to prepare for Joey's arrival. At the door of the drawing-room, he paused; Julia was playing. He went in quietly and stood for a moment behind her, watching her fingers flying over the keys and wishing he had a keener appreciation of some of the music she played. He had grown out of touch; he had left his trumpet and popular music behind him and had never graduated to the kind of thing Julia was playing at this moment. Weird harmonies . . . But it was only a question of getting his ear accustomed to the discordances; once he'd swallowed the idea that music needn't necessarily be musical, he'd catch on. It was no good having a sister who could play stuff of this kind, and stand here wishing she'd play something out of the Mikado.

"Like it?" asked Julia, lifting her hands from the final chord and twisting round to face him.

"I was just getting used to it."

"But you didn't like it?"

"Well, it was a bit above my head," he confessed. "I haven't really been with you since you played 'Early in the morning we're off to London' — with one finger."

Julia, smiling, turned to the keyboard once more and with one finger picked out the old familiar air.

"Oh Nicholas" — she spoke over her shoulder — "Derek's coming to dinner. You don't mind?"

"Did you ask Miss Cornhill?"

"Yes."

"Then I don't mind. All I mind is your bringing in people for meals without seeing that there's enough food for them. I've sat too often in the past, watching my own food go down their throats."

"Miss Cornhill said it was all right."

She was adding harmonies to the melody, at first with one hand, then with two. Nicholas, coming to sit on the piano stool beside her, played the air on the top octave of the piano, and Julia supplied full, rich chords below. He began to sing, and Julia joined in, and they came to the end and sat laughing.

"That's it?" she asked.

"That's it."

"That's it," corroborated another voice from the doorway, and Joey advanced into the room. "That was magnificent. For ten minutes of that, I'd give all your concert-platform stuff, and I bet Nicholas would, too, and we're both ashamed of ourselves."

"Don't you like modern music either?" asked Julia.

"Well, I will," said Joey, "when I get round to it."

"Explain," requested Julia, swinging her legs over the piano stool and facing him.

"Well, I'm a bit behind," said Joey. "I'd only just finished educating myself in what I took to be the arts — you know: Madonnas, Mozart — when an entirely new set of johnnies started this slap-on-the-paint school and weird-sounding music. So I'm trying to make up my mind whether to start learning all over again, or whether to shut my eyes and my ears and hope the whole thing'll be over soon. And in the meantime, can you play 'Now thank we all our God'?"

"Hymns?" asked Julia in surprise.

"Nothing like them," asserted Joey, "for good, strong simple even though out-of-date harmony. Play it as you did that piece you were playing when I came in just now; you know: put in plenty of meat and gravy. Good fat chords, but stick to the melody."

Julia played the hymn, and Joey's rasping voice took up the air and the words, breaking off now and then to encourage Nicholas to join in.

"Splendid, splendid, splendid!" he roared at the conclusion. "You wouldn't think, to listen to me, that I was forty before I discovered that Rigoletto wasn't spelt with a W at the beginning. Now we'll have it again. Nicholas, my boy, you sing the tune and I'll sing the discount. One, two, three . . ."

"Steady on," said Nicholas. "Visitors."

"It'll be Derek, I think," said Julia.

But with Derek came his sister Miriam and her fiancé.

"We're only here for a minute," she explaimed. "We're on our way to dine at the George, and we dropped in because Leopold hadn't met you all properly, and we wanted to talk to you."

Nicholas handed round drinks and came to sit beside her on the sofa.

"Well?" She smiled at him and then looked across the room at Leopold, who was in deep conversation with Joey. "You like him?"

"We all like him. How does he get on with your mother?"

"Beautifully. He listens to everything she says, agrees politely — and then does exactly what he was going to do."

"Good." He glanced at Derek, talking to Julia beside the piano. "Julia's glad to have Derek around; I think she finds the house empty without Simon and Dominic."

"Derek's glad to have her around, too," said Miriam. "He'll miss all the fun they had in the old days. He's got a lot to be thankful for. And so," she added, "have I. For you making me get away from Greenhurst."

"All I did was find you a family in Italy who'd put you up and give you a job."

"That's not quite all. Don't you remember my mother's behaviour at the time?"

Nicholas grinned.

"Well, she didn't exactly like it."

"She created hell, and you know it," said Miriam. "And left to myself, I'd have given in and stayed here. It was you who backed me up. It was you who took no notice of my backslidings and went on calmly booking my air passage and writing off to the family in Italy and telling them when I'd arrive. You even packed for me."

"And sneaked down the back staircase with your suitcases and brought them over here so's you could walk out without impedimenta. Yes, that was quite a morning," mused Nicholas. "Your mother never forgave me — until the news of your engagement."

"That brings me to what I wanted to

say to you," said Miriam. "About the honeymoon plans."

"The Greek trip?"

"Yes. Wash it all out, will you? Leopold and I decided long ago that we were going to spend our honeymoon motoring in Scotland. I've told my mother I'm asking you to cancel the bookings. I'm sorry" — she smiled — "I'm sorry you've been troubled."

"Think nothing of it. What do you think of Joey's plan to film Greenhurst?"

"Is that what he's talking to Leopold about?"

It was not; Joey was giving the Count some advice.

" — and your future mother-in-law is a wonderful woman in many ways, but you've got to know how to manage her. I can say this out in the open, with both her children present — can't I, Nicholas?"

"I dare say," said Nicholas.

"What's it like," Joey asked Derek, who on Julia's departure to help Miss Cornhill in the kitchen had come over to join the others, "what's it like to be the future Lord Templeby and to inherit one of these landed properties or whatever you call them? Will you be the next owner collecting half-crowns from visitors and turning the lawn into a fairground?"

"Not me," said Derek. "If I couldn't have it except on those terms, I'd rather not have it at all."

"It is a beautiful home," said Leopold. "It is very much more beautiful than the one Miriam will live in in Rome." He turned to Joey. "Why," he asked, "if you have done so much work with film and stage people, do you not work permanently at one of the major studios?"

"Well, I get restive," explained Joey, "when anybody says the word permanent. It gives me a bad go of claustrophobia. I never fancied a job like Nicholas here, that kept a fellow in one place all the time. I like to be on the move. What's more, I like to be free to work out my ideas, instead of tagging along with other people's. What's even more, I wouldn't have lasted long in any studio, because nobody ever taught me to keep my opinion to myself."

Miriam had risen reluctantly.

"We've got to go," she said."

"Why dine at the George?" Nicholas asked. "Don't you like home cooking?"

"If you mean Templeby cooking, no; we wanted to be out of the house for a while. There are too many wedding preparations going on at home."

"I meant Miss Cornhill's home cooking. Why don't you stay and dine here?"

Miriam hesitated, but it was clear that both she and Leopold welcomed the suggestion.

"Two extra — " she began.

"Please stay." Nicholas turned to Julia, who had just re-entered the room. "Julia, will you tell Miss Cornhill there'll be two more of us?"

"Not me," said Julia. "Miriam, only just before you came, he was telling me how often in the past he'd *agonised*, watching his own food go down other people's throats."

"This time," promised Nicholas, "it'll be Julia's food."

When the general laughter had subsided, Miriam agreed to stay, but she and Leopold left soon after dinner. Nicholas and Joey sat on in the dining-room, talking, and Julia, after helping Miss Cornhill in the kitchen, took Derek into the drawing-room.

"I'm sorry about your foot," she told him. "Does it hurt?"

He shook his head.

"No." He limped across the room as though to prove it, and then came over to take his coffee cup from her. "What about your musical future?" he asked. "Are you going on with it?"

"No," she said. "Not in the way Paul and Nicholas hoped."

He looked at her. She was curled up in a deep chair beside the coffee table, her expression distant and dreamy.

"What d'you want to do?" he asked.

"That's just it. I don't know. I wish I did. All I'm sure about is that I can't go on any more shut up in a room, hour after hour after hour, just playing and playing and playing. Anyway . . . not playing the things I have to play, as opposed to the things I want to play. I was happy for the first few years. I loved Paul, and I thought he was wonderful to have taken so much trouble with me, and I wanted to please him, and to please Nicholas, and to . . . well, I suppose everybody thinks about being a success."

"Do you still recite poetry out loud to yourself?"

"Sometimes."

"Do you remember how you used to sit up in the attic, or in the garden, reciting? Do you remember the day Dominic and I went up to the attic to look for tennis balls, and found you standing up there shouting at the top of your voice?"

"I remember. I remember what it was, too:

'Bring hither the pink and purple
    Columbine
With Gillyflowers;
Bring Coronation, and Sops in wine,
Worn of paramours.' "

"That was it. And then we all sat down to figure out exactly what paramours were."

"Yes." Her smile flashed out suddenly, and the years fell away. "Fancy your remembering that." She twisted herself round in the chair and, leaning her elbows on the arm, cupped her chin in her hands and gazed thoughtfully across at him. "Funny thing, remembering," she said slowly. "I was thinking about it tonight, looking at Miriam and Leopold. I watched them, and I thought: They haven't anything to remember. They've only known one another a few months, and each of them had more than thirty years — thirty whole years of life before they even set eyes on each other. How can people ever catch up on thirty years of unshared things?"

"They don't have to catch up. They start off on something new — together."

"Yes — but she can't ever say to him, at least not for years and years:

'When to the sessions of sweet silent
    thought
I summon up remembrance of things
    past,'

because she and Leopold will be summoning up two entirely different sets of remembrances, won't they?"

"Perhaps it's just as well. You're one of the lucky ones, Julia; you can dig a lot of prizes out of the past. Some of us can't. The times I'll always remember are the times I've spent in this house — not the time I put in at home, or at school. And when I marry, I'm not sure that I want to spend much time reminiscing; marriage is a new life, and I'd like to start living it. Isn't that just growing up?"

"But your past is *you*. All Leopold can see is Miriam as she *is*. Even I know miles more about her than he does — and that seems odd to me."

"There's nothing odd about it. If he'd seen Miriam at most of the times you remember her, he wouldn't have fallen in love with her. Your past isn't you; it's just what piles up to make the present-day you. It doesn't matter to Leopold what she was or what she did — until the day he fell in love with her."

She gazed at him with a frown.

"You've changed," she said slowly.

"Well, you haven't."

She looked surprised.

"I've got better-looking."

"That's not what I was thinking of."

"Well — " She studied him long and frankly as he sat slumped in a deep chair, his long legs stretched out, his lean, brown, rather sober face expressionless, but his eyes amused. "*You've* changed. I don't know quite how, but . . . you *sound* different."

"You mean I've lost my boyish squeak?"

"No. I mean . . . well, you sound as if you're more sure of yourself."

"Perhaps I am."

"Well, *something's* different. Derek, what am I going to do here all alone without Simon and Dominic and you?"

"We come back from time to time, don't we?"

"Yes — but if I'm going to be at home for a long time, and none of you can be around, it's going to be pretty dull, isn't it?"

"Haven't you got to do some kind of work?"

"Yes. But at the moment, I can't see anything that's going to take me away from this house for long — and it's a bit empty without you all. There's Nicholas, of course, but he's not the same as you and Simon and Dominic. Will you write to me?

"Not if the ratio's the same as it was when you were in Rome. I sent off four to your one."

"If you'd practised for all those hours, you wouldn't have felt like writing. I'll make it two to one. Nicholas," she said, as the two men came in, "the coffee's cold."

"Don't bother to make any more for me," said Joey. "I've got to be off. Young man, are you staying, or can I run you back?"

"He's going," said Nicholas. "In his own car."

"You can't bundle him home any more," protested Julia. "He's grown up."

"If he doesn't need his sleep, I need mine," said Nicholas. "Say good-night and see the visitors off the premises."

She stood beside him at the top of the steps as Derek and Joey got into their cars and drove away.

"Nicholas — about my undies," she said, as they re-entered the house.

"What brought that up?" asked Nicholas in surprise.

"How do I get them back — my Tiberia bag, I mean?"

"Well, you get hold of the address in the book that was in the wrong bag — and you write to Miss or Mrs. Elaine Whoever-she-is telling her you've inadvertently taken her books and asking her if she inadvertently took your underwear."

"But I didn't," pointed out Julia. "You did. It was your mistake."

"Then tell her so — when you write," said Nicholas, and watched her going sleepily up the stairs to her room. Miss Cornhill came out of her sitting-room, and he looked at her with a smile.

"Nice to have her back," he commented.

"Julia? Yes," said Miss Cornhill. "I missed her."

"She's just the same, isn't she? Same old Julia."

Miss Cornhill's eyes rested on him for a moment.

"You see no change?"

"Not much. Not a great deal. She looks older, in some way. Next thing, I'll be buzzing round like a demented Mamma trying to find a husband for her."

"You don't think she'll find one for herself?"

"She might. But I always thought it involved a certain amount of co-operation on a woman's part — and can you see Julia putting out a finger?"

"There's plenty of time," said Miss Cornhill. "Oh — you will remind her, won't you, to see about getting her bag back and returning the one we have here?"

"She's going to write," said Nicholas.

"And once we find out whether the owner of the books has got Julia's underwear, we'll ring the changes and that'll be the end of that."

So believing, he went upstairs to bed.

CHAPTER IV

JOEY HELYON was not a man who wasted time. On the following Tuesday — eight days after his arrival in Greenhurst — the narrow High Street presented a scene that would have made a stranger entering the town feel that he had wandered by mistake on to a film set, and that the shops were mere fronts painted to give the appearance of a picturesque market town. Cameras were placed at strategic points, traffic halted at Joey's command, and groups of townspeople, actors for a day, assembled in docile groups round him, listened to his brief summary of what he expected them to do, and then rehearsed their scene. The baker closed his shop for the sole purpose of opening it again under the eyes of the camera. The fishmonger cleared his slab and then rearranged his wares in close-ups. Two dozen passers-by agreed to do their passing by to order; one was to enter the butchers, one was to stand and gaze at the array of goods in the confectioner's window, three women were to stand and appear to gossip. Nicholas, who had assumed that everybody was as busy as himself, and who had been certain that Joey would find many objectors to this bustling intrusion on their affairs, discovered that nobody was in the least averse to appearing in due course upon their own television screens.

"I told you so." Joey, waving a bunch of papers, dropped into Nicholas's office and spoke through the open door of Nicholas's room. "I told you they'd do it. They're doing fine; fine. What I dropped in for, Nicholas boy, was to ask if I could use Miss Stocker here to type me a few notices."

"Ask her," said Nicholas, and closed his door firmly.

Miss Stocker was staring at Joey in surprise.

"I thought you told me I was overworking," she said.

"This isn't work I'm asking you to do; it's recreation," explained Joey. "A change. And a change, as you know, is as good as a rest. I — "

"You can go and find one of those typists I saw walking down the High

Street for you, pretending they were young intellectuals going to the library. You'd better watch out, putting glasses on to people who don't need them. One of those girls nearly fell down the library steps on the way out. I hope you're well covered for insurance? Go and ask those girls; they'll type for you. I haven't time to help people with play-acting."

Joey, checked, looked at her with a puzzled frown.

"What've you got against this project?" he asked.

"Nothing. But this is our busy season."

"Who travels so early in the year? This is only the end of May."

"People make their arrangements at this time of the year. We have to make bookings at this time of the year. We have to write to coach companies, shipping companies, airlines, at this time of the year; we have to allocate seats and cabins and we have to work out single and double rooms, and baths, and meals en route and meals at hotels. We've got eight hundred applications to date, and more coming in. Buy yourself a typewriter and do your own typing."

She stopped, annoyed at having shown so much feeling. There was something about this Joey Helyon, she told herself angrily, that was making twenty years of slow, patient effort on her part go for nothing. She had taught herself to be efficient and detached; she had laboured to turn herself, during working hours, into a machine that churned out whatever was required of it with the minimum wear and tear. Her interest in the Waynes was deep and affectionate, but she had maintained, since her entry into Nicholas's office, unfailing formal relations with him and a steadfast aloofness from any matter bordering on the personal. She had taught herself patience and control; others about her might panic if they chose; she herself remained detached, untouched.

Until now. Nothing in her experience had prepared her for Joey Helyon's unique blend of sense and nonsense; she wanted to label him loud and uncouth, but there was something in his manner, something of authority, of underlying strength about him that made her hesitate. He used people, but in a way that gave no offence; his interest in them might be fleeting, fugitive, but while it lasted it was genuine and disarming. He had turned Greenhurst into a film location and the people into puppets, but his enthusiasm had infected them, and they were enjoying themselves.

"You don't understand what I'm doing." Joey pushed aside some of Miss Stocker's most important papers, and seated himself on a corner of her desk. "You've missed the point of all this."

"Why did you have to choose Greenhurst?" she asked irritably. "Why didn't you pick on some other place?"

"Because I *know* this town," said Joey, looking down at her with missionary zeal shining in his eyes. "I *know* this place. I knew that I'd find, right here in Greenhurst, what I wanted. And what I wanted was an atmosphere of plain, decent, ordinary living. You might say that out there in the High Street, they're pretending to be this and that — but when I've had time to get away and chop up this film and put it together again, what'll emerge will be something that people won't be able to put their finger on until they've left the cinema or switched off their sets: something human, something decent; a change from all this business of the burglar bashing the old lady on the head or the crooks beating up the cops. You get so much of it that people are beginning to forget the millions and millions of plain, decent, ordinary people living nice clean lives and getting on with their jobs."

"And you're going to show them?"

"I am. I've got myself into the position, professionally, where I can afford to do something I *want* to do. And I believe that if I do something I like, a lot of other people will like it too. What I like is serving up miles and miles of film showing the family getting up in the morning, dressing the kids, putting the baby out, doing the washing, fetching the groceries, cooking the dinner, shoving the pram over the common, fetching the kids from school, getting the tea going and giving father a welcome when he gets home from work, and — "

"Here." Miss Stocker held out a hand for the papers. "Give me whatever it is I've got to do, and let me do it. It'll be quicker than letting you talk."

"Beryl, my girl, you're a sport. Can I call you Beryl?"

"No, you can't. You can call me Miss

Stocker, same's everybody else. Give me that paper."

"Here's what it is." Joey came round the desk. "I expected co-operation from this bunch, but not quite such whole-hearted co-operation, and what I want to make clear — look, I've drafted it — is that all I'm doing at this stage is using a lot of film — but it doesn't mean I can use it all. There's a little process called editing, and I want the local parents to understand that although little Johnny came out looking cute running around the common, there's no guarantee that he'll show up in the finished film. Let's get that clear at the start. If you could type it out and run a couple of hundred copies through on that stencilling machine, I'd be your humble servant forever."

"Leave it with me," said Miss Stocker. "And now go away."

"All you ever say," complained Joey, "is go away. I want some sympathy; I've got trouble."

"Take it away with you," requested Miss Stocker, and Joey departed.

The trouble was Delphi who, spectacular in stills, was proving disappointing in action. Her hair neatly dressed, her beautiful figure in tweeds, her feet in low-heeled shoes, she looked the very embodiment of well-behaved English womanhood — but as soon as she took two steps, Joey's bellow stopped the cameras.

"No, no, *no*, Delphi. Not like that!" he implored, crossing the road to join her. "Keep your . . . I mean don't waggle your . . . Look; do it like this." He marched a few paces. "Make it *natural*. No, don't; don't make it natural. Just use your legs and don't worry about the rest of you. You're not in a dance hall; you're simply walking along the road to commercial school, where you're going to learn to type. Now try it again."

Delphi, watched by the waiting cast, tried it, sulkily and without success, and Joey, wiping the sweat from his forehead, called a halt for the day. Jimmy Dunn detached himself from the group of technicians and stood by Joey, watching his wife walking angrily towards the George, and then turned a wide grin on Joey.

"She'll get over it," he said.

"She's bored."

"Of course. She thinks she's wasting her

time in a place like this. You should hear what I get at night."

"Well, it won't be long," said Joey. "If she'd only put her mind to it and — "

"She won't," said Jimmy. "Why don't you leave her out of it and find somebody else? You've got any number of girls here you could use. Leave Delphi out of it, and I'll keep her quiet until the wedding's over."

"You think that's the best thing?" asked Joey.

"Best thing all round. Leave it to me; I'll tell her. She'll be glad."

He followed his wife up the High Street, and Joey saw Miriam Arkwright and her fiancé crossing the road to join him.

"Could you spare a moment, Joey?" she asked. "We'd like to talk to you."

"Then let's talk over a drink," said Joey. "I need one. Come on; come along, Leopold. We'll give you some English beer at the George and you can tell the landlord what you think of it."

He settled his guests at a small table in the bar and ordered drinks.

"Now," he asked Miriam, his huge hands holding his glass, his expectant gaze on her face, "what can I do for you?"

Miriam hesitated.

"It won't take long, but it won't sound very polite," she said. "We're here on my mother's behalf."

"Don't tell me she's interested in my small-town film?"

"She's only interested, at this moment, in the wedding plans — and there's a hitch."

"She's changed her mind about having the colour films made?"

"No. It's this: eight people — cousins of Leopold — who hadn't been able to come, wired last week to say that they could, after all. They live in Southern Italy, and my mother thought that as it was so far away, they — "

" — they'd send a nice present and stay away? That's the bride's mother's eternal hope," said Joey. "Proceed."

"Well, ever since then, my mother's been trying desperately to find somewhere to put them. She hasn't succeeded, and so this morning she came to the George to ask Mr. Trent if he could do anything, but — "

" — but Mr. Trent couldn't, because why?" asked Joey. "Because this guy

Helyon is cluttering up the place with his team."

"Yes. Leopold and I met her just as she was leaving home to come and ask you . . . to come and talk to you. And . . ."

She paused, and Leopold finished the story.

"Lady Templeby was a little tired from so much going here and there, looking for accommodation," he said, "and Miriam felt that perhaps she would not be so polite to you as we would hope. She intended, as I think you have guessed, to ask that you and your friends — "

" — give up our rooms ?"

"Yes," said Miriam. "There isn't the slightest justification for asking you, and I'm sorry to have to do it — but I promised my mother I'd put it to you. When she really wants a thing very badly, she can be very difficult to deal with, and Leopold and I — "

" — thought you'd spare me ? I'm grateful. But where," asked Joey with interest, "did she think we could move to — if we moved out ? All the available accommodation in this town is took; you've just said so."

"Her idea . . ." Miriam hesitated. "Well, you know that she allows the Guides to camp on one of our fields in summer, and — "

"She wants us to move in with the Guides ?"

Miriam smiled.

"You're making it difficult," she said. "She was going to suggest your moving under canvas — she would have provided the tents."

"Well, that's handsome of her," said Joey, "but it wouldn't do my rheumatism any good. And in strict confidence, I'll tell you that it won't be my team that'll be in those tents — it'll be Leopold's cousins from Southern Italy."

"Perhaps," said Leopold, "they will even enjoy it. So long as they are not wearing their wedding clothes."

"Well, we put it to you," said Miriam. "But don't think for a moment that we liked doing it."

"You saved me from saying a lot of indiscreet things to your mother, and I'm grateful to you," said Joey. "But I won't march my team down and put 'em in tents. They wouldn't like it — especially as the Guides aren't going to be there."

"It would hardly have been suitable for Delphi," said Leopold.

"I'd forgotten Delphi," said Joey. "No, she wouldn't have taken kindly to the idea. What other girl could I use for my film?" he asked. "Delphi's out."

"What about Julia?" suggested Miriam.

"I thought of that," said Joey. "Nicholas wouldn't let her."

"Have you asked him?"

"No. But I know what he'd say."

"Julia is old enough to choose for herself," pointed out Leopold.

"Well, I'll point that out to him," said Joey. "He's dropping in here for a drink with me on his way to dine with Jeff and Roselle."

Nicholas, sounded on the subject, was unco-operative.

"But you can ask her," he told Joey, when he had exhausted his list of objections. "If she wants to, I can't stop her. But you'll find she's too busy. For the past week she's been fully engaged with other things."

"Luke and Derek?"

"Yes. If you can get a word with her —

I can't, these days — you can ask what she thinks about it," said Nicholas.

He thought about the matter, without reaching any conclusion, as he drove himself home that night from Jeff and Roselle's. When he entered the house, he found a note from Julia on the hall table: Luke Hayman and Derek had dined and Derek had driven Luke home; Nicholas could lock the front door.

Under the door of Miss Cornhill's sitting-room was a light, but Nicholas did not disturb her. He stood in the hall for a moment, undecided whether to go up to bed and read, to go into the drawing-room and get himself a drink or into the kitchen and make himself a nice cup of cocoa topped up with the breakfast cream.

Bed and a book. He walked towards the stairs, and as he passed the window overlooking the drive, glanced out casually. Then he halted, a frown of amazement and anger on his brow. Julia! Julia — walking up the drive, alone. Having told him to lock the hall door, she had gone out again. And having gone out again, she was walking home by herself. If young Arkwright hadn't the common courtesy to drive her up to the house, it was time she learned the technique of making him. It wasn't late — not much more than ten — and it wasn't quite dark, but a young man didn't drop a girl at the gate and leave her to walk up a long drive alone. Not if the girl happened to be Julia.

He walked to the front door, unlocked it and opened it, prepared to confront Julia with an angry demand for an explanation.

And then he saw that the girl was not Julia.

It was not Julia. Coming towards the house, coming alone, coming on foot at ten o'clock at night, was the girl at whom he had stared so hard and so long at London Airport, eight days ago.

CHAPTER V

NICHOLAS spent the next few moments in a maze of bewilderment. Then with an effort, he pulled himself together and went out of the house and down the steps.

"A nice surprise," he said quietly, as he came up to the girl. "I've often dreamt that a beautiful girl would appear, unannounced, on my doorstep one evening — but this is the first time it's happened."

He waited, but no answer came from her. She seemed to be struggling to find something to say. Puzzled, Nicholas added a light sentence.

"You're going to tell me," he said, "that your car's broken down outside the gate and you want to telephone for — "

He stopped abruptly. The eyes looking into his had vanished behind a mist. As he watched, helpless between astonishment and horror, two tears appeared and rolled swiftly down her cheeks.

"I . . . I . . ." she began uncertainly.

Without a word, Nicholas took her arm

gently and led her up the steps and into the house. In silence he crossed the hall, ushered her into the drawing-room, switched on the lights, closed the door and settled her on the sofa. Still silent, he poured out and brought her a drink and stood watching her as she drank it. Looking down at her, he saw several things that had escaped him on her arrival: her pallor, her obvious distress, and an agitation that showed itself in the uncontrollable shaking of her hands.

He took the empty glass from her and stood waiting for her to recover her composure, but the tears continued to pour down her face. She held her hands in her lap, gripped tightly together.

"You're in some kind of trouble," he began gently. "I . . ."

"No, I'm not." Her eyes, tear-drowned, came up to meet his. "*I'm* not in trouble. *You* are."

Nicholas, after an astounded pause, sat down on a chair and took from his pocket a folded handkerchief. This he handed to the visitor; she had one of her own, but he felt that his action would bring home to her the fact that he wished her to dry her tears and give him a more creditable explanation of her presence. Shaking out the folds, she mopped her cheeks, and, as he had hoped, the action restored to her a measure of self-control.

"I'm s-sorry," she said shakily. "It's just that I . . ."

Question and answer; that was the thing, he decided, as she came to a halt.

"Are you staying in Greenhurst ?"

"N-no."

"Did you come here by car ?"

"N-no. By train. And bus."

"Were you trying to get to Greenhurst ?"

"No. I was coming here."

"To this house ?"

"Yes."

"To see . . . ?"

"You."

There was a pause.

"If you thought I was in trouble, you were mistaken," said Nicholas after a time. "I imagine this is a case of mistaken identity. I . . ."

"It isn't a c-case of mistaken identity at all." She was making strong efforts to prevent herself from crying. "You're Nicholas Wayne."

"Yes. But I assure you I'm not in any trouble. At least, not any trouble that I'm aware of."

"That's just it. That's why I came." She wiped her tears angrily and stared up at him. "I'm sorry I'm being so incoherent — but when I left home this morning, I didn't think it was . . . that the journey was going to take so long."

"Where did you come from?"

"Wiltshire. A village called Crayke. I didn't stop to look up trains and things; I just . . . I just came in a hurry, and I missed the bus into the station and I missed the early London train and then I had to cross London, and I had to wait for a train that would stop at Greenhurst. Then I got into it and I was thinking and . . . and thinking, and then the train stopped and I looked out and saw Greenhurst written on the station sign, so I got out of the train, but it . . ."

"It wasn't Greenhurst station; it was Greenhurst Halt, and you were stranded?"

"Yes. There wasn't another train stopping there until midnight, and there was an idiotic old porter, and there was nowhere I could phone — I mean there was no public telephone, and the room with a telephone in it was locked, and — "

"And you had to walk to the main road and get a bus ?"

"Yes. I didn't realise you lived outside Greenhurst. The bus came and I took a ticket to Greenhurst and after a time I thought I'd ask the woman sitting next to me if she knew where Wood Mount was, and she said we'd passed it, and I ought to stop the bus and get off and walk and . . . and I did, but . . ."

"But it would have been more sensible to go right into Greenhurst and take a taxi out here," said Nicholas. "But by the time you realised that, the tail light of the bus had vanished into the distance."

"Yes."

"That's what comes of talking to strangers. Misdirection. Or the stranger happened to be a countrywoman, who thinks nothing of plodding five miles on country roads in army-type boots." He glanced at her high heels. "You didn't come prepared for walking ?"

"I didn't come prepared for anything. I . . ."

Tears once again threatened to overwhelm her, and Nicholas spoke quietly.

"What kind of trouble did you imagine I was in?"

She met his glance squarely; tears appeared and trickled down her cheeks, but she took no notice of them.

"With the p-police," she said.

He stared at her in bewilderment, and then smiled.

"That settles it," he said. "You've got me mixed up with somebody else."

"I told you before — I haven't mixed you up with anybody. And I'm not imagining anything. Your name is Nicholas Wayne and you live here. My fiancé found it all out."

"Your fiancé? What in the world . . . I really don't see why your fiancé should — "

"He said he'd give you a week." She stared at him in a kind of despair. "Why did you keep it? *Why* didn't you send it back, or get in touch, or do anything — *anything*? Two days, three days — I didn't worry much. Then four days, and then five, and . . . He said he'd wait till a week had passed, and then he'd go to the police. I tried to stop him, but he — "

"But what," broke in Nicholas in bewilderment, "did he want to go to the police *about* ?"

"About the money," she said.

There was a long silence.

"About the . . . the *money*," he echoed at last, in a slow, flat voice. "The *money*."

"The money that was in the bag. The green bag. The Tiberia bag. You must have seen it! You must have found it! What I couldn't understand was why you *did* nothing. You could have telephoned, or wired, or gone to the Tiberia office, or — or anything. But you didn't do anything at all, and — "

"One moment," said Nicholas, and his tone brought her to a halt. For a moment they sat in silence, staring at one another, and then he walked across the room and poured out another drink for her. This time, he also poured one out for himself. He did not speak until the glasses were empty, and then he drew a deep breath.

"Now," he said, "we'll talk sense. My sister Julia had a green bag like yours. The wrong one got here by mistake. I brought it out of my car and left it in the hall. Later, looking for her keys, she found that the bag wasn't hers. We looked inside; there were newspapers and two books, and in one of the books was a name and address."

"Mine. I — "

"Later, I reminded my sister Julia to get in touch with you; I didn't think there'd be any tearing hurry on anybody's part to get their books back, but I didn't feel they'd want to be landed with Julia's underwear for longer than was necessary. She said she'd write — and from that moment to this, I haven't given a thought to the bag or the books — or her underclothing. But I can assure you that there was no money in the bag."

"But there was! Kenneth — my fiancé — put it in. Forty pounds."

"Forty pounds!" Nicholas brought the words out slowly. "Your fiancé put forty pounds into the Tiberia bag?"

"Yes. I sent him a cheque from Italy and asked him to cash it and bring the money when he met me at the airport; I was going to do some shopping on my way through London. When I saw him, I asked him if he'd brought the money, and he took it out of his wallet — six five pound notes and the rest in single pound notes — and as I was busy with luggage and things, I told him for the moment to put it into the green bag. So he did. That's why he was so angry and so upset when he saw that you'd taken the bag by mistake. And the second time, he said you must have seen the money in it, and he insisted that the first time might have been a mistake, but the second time, you . . . you must have seen the money in the bag the first time, and . . . and . . . Oh, *why* didn't you *do* something? You must have known, even seeing him for so short a time, that he wouldn't just let it go. You must have seen that he's a . . . a trouble maker? All you had to do was — "

Nicholas had risen.

"Come with me," he directed.

He led her upstairs. At the top of the first flight was a door; he opened it and she saw that it was a boxroom. Nicholas switched on the light; neatly arrayed by Miss Cornhill on shelves and along the walls were a variety of trunks, suitcases and miscellaneous travel containers. Close by the door was the green Tiberia bag. Nicholas took it off the shelf, put his hand inside, groped, and the next moment had extracted from the inside pocket a sheaf of notes.

"There!" said the girl.

He sat down slowly on the nearest trunk. Seating herself on one opposite, the girl watched him as he thought over the situation.

"Money," he said slowly at last. "Who thought about money? All I thought of, when the bag turned out to be somebody else's, was how in the world I could twice have got hold of somebody else's bag instead of Julia's; how in the world the bags could have got changed."

"I changed them," she said.

Nicholas scarcely heard the words — he was thinking deeply, and it was some moments before their import reached him. Then he sat staring at her, unable to speak.

"I changed the bags," she said again.

"You . . . you changed . . ."

"Yes. I didn't have much time. You had moved away and Kenneth had moved away. I wrote my name and address in one of the books. I picked up your sister Julia's bag and put mine down in its place. And that was all."

"All. That," repeated Nicholas in a stunned voice, "was all."

"Yes."

"And so I took the money and your fiancé is taking steps to have me jailed?"

"Yes."

"And that's all? You're sure that's all? You're sure — "

He stopped. What could a man do, he asked himself desperately, when girls cried? They put you in a hellish position, for some obscure reason they hadn't bothered to explain, and when you showed some small sign of disliking the position you'd been put into, they cried. Their fiancés pushed their unloveable countenances into your face and snarled at you, they —

"Perhaps," he said, "you'd better do some explaining."

She tried to stem the tears, and he sat watching her moodily. Life couldn't be called dull, on the whole; here he was sitting on one of Dominic's old school trunks in a boxroom, waiting for a girl he didn't know to explain why he was to be hounded by the police for something he hadn't done. Well . . . that was the devil of it. To all intents and purposes, he'd come into possession and remained in possession. Here it came; she was going to say something. She had one thing at least in common with Roselle: she could cry a lot and still look pretty.

"It's a long s-story," she began. "I don't know where to begin."

"At the beginning?" suggested Nicholas. He tried to keep the coolness out of his voice, and immediately wished that he had tried harder; at this rate, he thought despairingly, watching a fresh torrent of tears being dealt with, they'd both be washed downstairs and into the hall. Then he saw that the unfriendliness of his tone had, after all, acted as a tonic; she was sitting up, still clutching the handkerchief, but with a look on her face of something approaching calm.

"You can think what you like about what I'm going to tell you," she said. "If things had turned out differently, you'd never have known — and now I don't care any more. I wrote my name and address in that book because I hoped you'd see it and get in touch with me. I wrote it in desperation because I thought I saw a way of getting myself out of a situation I couldn't bear any more. That isn't the beginning of the story; it's the end. The beginning is that my name is Elaine Morley. My mother died when I was a baby, and when I was twelve, my father remarried. He married a widow with a son of eighteen. She was a Baronet's widow, and so Kenneth had inherited the title. And things were all right while my father was alive, because he kept up the fiction — it *was* a fiction — that we were all a happy, united little family. And last year, when I was twenty-three, I got engaged to Kenneth, because my father was old and ill and certain that it was the best thing for me, and I'd seen so little of Kenneth — his job was in Japan — that I thought things would work out and that I'd fall in love with him when I . . . when I got to know him better. And then my father died and left the house to my stepmother, and Kenneth gave up his job and came home for good, and I discovered that without my father in the house, and with Kenneth in it, my stepmother was only just one degree less repulsive than Kenneth himself. And if I'd had any moral courage, I would have broken my engagement and left the house — but I was born in it, and all the things I loved were in it, and I'd spent most of my life in it, and I didn't seem able to walk out and . . . and lose it for ever. So I went to stay with friends in Italy, to think things over. And the moment I got back and saw Kenneth at the airport, I knew I wouldn't marry him under any consideration whatsoever. And . . ."

She paused, and after some time Nicholas prompted her.

"And . . . ?"

"And then he had that row with you at the airport, and I suddenly saw, or thought I saw a way of breaking off the engagement without having to tell Kenneth — and his mother — what I really thought about them both. I thought that if I wrote my name in a book and changed the Tiberia bags, you'd read the name and address and get in touch. You'd do it in common politeness, but I'd represent it to Kenneth as the the result of the mad infatuation you'd formed for me on one single glance. You got in touch, to return the bag. I wrote to you from Wiltshire saying I'd meet you in London — and Kenneth would know that you were the man who'd stared at me, and he'd make the kind of scene he made at the airport — but this time, he'd make it in front of his mother, and I'd give him back his ring and explain that I couldn't marry him because he was too jealous and too possessive. Jealous and possessive are things you can call a man in front of his mother; loathsome and repulsive are not. After the row, I thought that relations between us wouldn't become so strained that I couldn't spend at least a few months a year at home. It all looked simple. Kenneth would go back to Japan and I'd be able to keep some small foothold in the house I loved so much. It may seem fantastic to you that I should want to keep a foothold in a house which didn't belong to me and in which Kenneth and his mother lived, but perhaps you don't know what being born and brought up in a house that you love means."

"Yes, I know," said Nicholas.

"Then you ought to understand — a little. When I changed those Tiberia bags, I saw the whole thing working out: I got rid of Kenneth; I sent somebody else to meet you in London; I sent a message thanking you for your kindness. You got back your sister's things and you returned my bag. It was so simple. I thought it could not miss. All I forgot was that the money was in the bag. I didn't give it a thought."

"I didn't give it a thought either," said Nicholas, and tried to keep his mounting sense of injury out of his voice. It was all right for her to sit there and tell a fairy story about a foothold in the home, without one single mention of having landed him in the probable position of having a foothold in the jail. It was all very well to cook up a fantastic scheme to rid herself of a man she should never have got herself tied up to in the first place, but it was going too far to mess about with other people's lives. All she had to do was take off a ring and hand it back, and instead, she had mangled the situation to the point of landing total strangers in prison. And before he was led away to prison, he could indulge in the pleasant mental exercise of working out what Kenneth would do when he realised that she had left home to pay a late-night call on him at his house. Jealous and possessive . . . and as strong as a bull, for a start. And as aggressive as a bull-terrier, to go on with. And mad as all hell, to top it up.

She was crying again. What had *she* got to cry about? he wondered morosely. *She* wasn't going to land in a prison hospital.

"So you see?" she asked shakily. "I didn't know who you were or where you lived. I could only hope you'd show some sign before Kenneth went to the police. I didn't really think he'd go. Right up to the last, I thought he was just uttering stupid threats. But he wasn't. He got your name and address through your car number — we'd seen you drive away — and this morning he told me he was going to the police. And I was so frightened that I forgot everything else, and I had the most appalling row with him and his mother, and then I just walked out of the house and . . . and came down here. But I hadn't stopped to wonder how far it was or how long it would take, or whether I'd be able to get here and back in one day. I just . . ."

Tears drowned her speech. Nicholas, watching her moodily, could think of nothing to say, but he found himself putting out his hands and taking hers in a firm and, he hoped, comforting grasp.

And then he heard a voice — Miss Cornhill's — speaking quietly enough, but the unexpected sound broke like thunder through his absorption.

"Whatever in the world . . . ?"

He got to his feet, and at the sight of the calm, grey-haired figure, relief rushed through him, and he cursed himself for not having remembered that here in the house was the person who of all beings in the world could most efficiently deal with weeping womanhood. Hadn't Miss Cornhill, for twenty years, held a post as Matron of a girls' school? Who but she could deal with, could manage a girl in the state that this one was in?

"Miss Cornhill," he said, "this is Miss Morley. There was some money in that bag that got mixed up with Julia's, and Miss Morley's fiancé — "

"Ex-fiancé," sobbed Miss Morley.

"Miss Morley's ex-fiancé is going to the police to ask them to recover it — from me. She came here — "

He had been about to explain the position in which Miss Morley's arrival had placed him, to enlist Miss Cornhill's sympathy and co-operation. But Miss Cornhill, he saw, was no longer listening. She had taken a step forward and was looking with distress and sympathy at the sobbing Elaine.

"When," she asked her gently, "did you last have a meal?"

Elaine Morley looked up, abandoning the attempt to stem her tears.

"I h-had b-breakfast," she sobbed.

"And nothing since then?"

"N-no. The t-trains didn't have any r-restaurant c-cars."

"Did Mr. Wayne offer you anything to eat?"

"I gave her a drink," said Nicholas, and was amazed to hear the note of defensiveness in his voice.

"T-two drinks," hiccoughed Miss Morley.

Miss Cornhill's gaze rested for a moment upon Nicholas; only a moment — but he read, shrinking, her utter contempt of his conduct. He had concealed a starving girl in the boxroom. He had seen her arrive, famished, and he had plied her with drink. He had made her cry. He had reduced her to this state.

Kenneth himself, he thought gloomily, watching Miss Cornhill lead Elaine downstairs to a full and satisfying meal, Kenneth himself couldn't have looked a bigger cad.

CHAPTER VI

"AND then?" asked Jeff, who ought to have been attending to his work but who was sitting at his desk listening, absorbed, to Nicholas's account of the events of the night before. "Miss Cornhill fed her, and —"

"Well, I was left up in the boxroom, and the general feeling was obviously that the whole thing was my fault. I chewed my thumb for a time, and then I went downstairs and opened the kitchen door. This Morley girl was sitting at the table, making short work of all the stuff I'd hoped to have for lunch today, and Miss Cornhill was standing over her with outstretched wings. As soon as I showed my face, she wove her way to the door, said 'Miss Morley is *very* tired' — and shut the door in my face. *My* door, mark you. *My* house. *My* food."

"Tough," said Jeff absently, being obviously more interested in facts than in feelings. "And then?"

"Well, I chewed the other thumb, and

then I heard Julia coming down. We met in the hall and went into the drawing-room and I poured myself out a stiff drink and put her into the picture and told her she'd better keep away until Miss Cornhill gave the word — but Julia said Miss Cornhill would let *her* in, and Miss Cornhill did. I waited an hour — a whole hour — hanging about wondering what was going to happen, and then I got fed up and went to bed."

"And this morning?"

"No sign. I'd heard them all come upstairs, and I knew there'd been bed-making and general emergency measures, but nobody bothered to come in and tell me anything. This morning I heard trays going up and down, but when I went downstairs for breakfast, all I found was a miserable bit of ham resting on a cold plate, and two boiled eggs sitting beside it. That was my breakfast — and Miss Cornhill knows very well I always have a nice, well-done bit of bacon, with some — "

" — with two fried eggs and some fried bread and four slices of toast and marmalade; yes, yes," said Jeff. "But what's to happen to the girl? She can't just walk out of her own home and come to rest in a strange — ”

“You’d say she couldn’t — but she has,” pointed out Nicholas. “When I’d finished what passed for breakfast, Julia came down in a dressing-gown and made me some coffee — did I tell you there wasn’t even any coffee made for me ?”

“You forgot. What did Julia say ?”

“She said Miss Cornhill had put a call through the night before to say that Miss Morley had arrived and was staying with us for a day or two. To give her, Miss Cornhill told Julia, a chance to get over the shock and inconvenience I’d put her to. I! Me! A girl appears out of the blue and — ”

“If you hadn’t feasted your eyes at the airport, she’d never have cooked up that silly scheme. And if you’d kept your hand on that green bag of Julia’s, instead of putting it down and leaving it for anybody to— But surely,” he broke off to observe, “her fiancé won’t leave matters as they are ?”

“Of course he won’t leave matters as they are. Would you, in his place ? And you didn’t see him; he looks like a champion heavyweight boxer. If Miss Cornhill spent less time thinking about Elaine Morley and more time thinking about what Elaine Morley's landed me into — "

"What's she like?" Jeff broke in to ask.

"Well, she's got a face and a figure, or why would I have gone into that bemused state at the airport? But she can't be a girl who has any feelings worth speaking of, or why would she mess up my life just to get her own straightened out? All she had to do, long, long ago, was throw this fellow's ring in his face and tell him to find some other girl. What was so hard about that?"

Jeff was silent. Fellows did forget, after all, he thought. Nicholas had obviously forgotten that ten years or so ago, a girl had not found it so easy to tell him that she was not going to marry him. A girl named Estelle...

His musing was interrupted by the appearance of Julia.

"Hello, Jeff." She bent to drop a light kiss on her brother-in-law's head. "Has Nicholas been telling you about last night?"

"How did you get here?" Nicholas asked.

"Derek brought me. Miss Cornhill wanted some things from town, so I rang Derek up and asked him to drive me in."

As she spoke, she was rearranging the family photographs on Jeff's desk and placing them in a different order: Roselle and the children in the centre, lesser relations on the fringe. "Miss Cornhill and I have been talking to Elaine; we think she ought to stay with us for at least a week, just to get things straightened out."

"Staying with us won't straighten anything out," said Nicholas. "It'll merely give her fiancé all the excuse he wants for being unpleasant."

"Ex-fiancé," corrected Julia. "That's all over and done with."

"That's what you think." Nicholas's voice was morose. "In my view, things are only just beginning."

"Where's Miss Morley now?" enquired Jeff.

"She was just getting up when I left," said Julia. "She slept well and she's feeling fine and she looks as good as new."

"Is she as pretty as Nicholas makes out?"

"Pretty? She's more than pretty; she's beautiful," said Julia. "What's more, she's nice. But she won't stay, she says."

"Where will she go?" Jeff asked.

"She didn't say; all she told us — Miss Cornhill and myself — was that it was quite impossible for her to stay in the house. And that's what I came to see Nicholas about. I've got an idea."

"We're waiting," said Jeff.

"Well, Paul told me when I went to lunch with him last week, that if Lady Templeby was stuck for somewhere to put wedding guests, she could have his house. And she *is* stuck; badly stuck. Derek told me just now. His mother's coming in later on to see Nicholas and make the usual appeal for us to have them at Wood Mount. So why can't they go to the Red House?"

"But Paul's going away," said Nicholas.

"Yes; tomorrow. So's his housekeeper, but Mrs. Bush — Charlie Bush's mother — keeps a key, because she goes in to clean the house. Paul said she'd help me to look after the guests."

"*You?*" asked Nicholas in amazement.

"Me. All that's needed, Paul says, is a bed per person, with breakfast, and I'm good at breakfasts. I wasn't keen on the idea when it meant just me alone, and so I didn't say anything about it, but if Elaine would do it with me, it'd be fun. Like playing houses."

"When do these guests arrive?" asked Jeff.

"Tomorrow morning,"

"Thursday," mused Jeff. "And the wedding's on Saturday. It doesn't solve Elaine Morley's housing problem for very long."

"For five days," pointed out Julia. "They arrive tomorrow — Thursday — and they leave on Monday. That's long enough. It would give her somewhere to stay over the wedding; it would keep her in Greenhurst and give her a breathing space and it would get over her objection to staying at Wood Mount. I talked to Derek about it just now, and he's gone back to put it to his mother. If I know her, she'll be here, sighing with relief, in about an hour." She looked at Nicholas. "It *is* a good idea, isn't it?"

"Yes, it's a good idea," said Nicholas. "Especially if it gets her out of Wood Mount before her fiancé turns up. That would put me in a slightly safer position."

"Well, I could talk to Paul and suggest

our staying there tonight," said Julia, "but I think it'd be better to let Paul have his last night in peace, and move in in the morning. There's another thing — "

"What other thing?" enquired Nicholas.

"Well, Miss Cornhill said I could have Derek to dinner tonight, and so I asked him."

"Good. Then Roselle and I will come to dinner, too," said Jeff, "and get a look at the beautiful Miss Morley. I'll ring up Miss Cornhill and fix it. And tomorrow you can move with Miss Morley into the Red House."

"If Elaine will agree," said Julia, and opened the door. "I'm going to do the shopping, and then I'll go and see Paul. 'Bye for now."

"Well?" asked Jeff, when the door had closed behind her. "What do you think of the idea?"

"It might work."

"That girl's right about not staying at Wood Mount. If her ex-fiancé is half a man — and from your description, he sounds a man and a half — he'll be showing up soon, with or without the police."

Nicholas was staring out of the window

at the once-quiet High Street, his expression morose.

"Things," said Jeff, following his glance, "ain't what they used to be."

"In any other town," observed Nicholas, "there'd be someone — at least one inhabitant — who'd raise strong objections when a fellow with three or four assistants and a brace of cameras cluttered up the main thoroughfare. All we're doing is edging round the cameras, stepping carefully over the chalk marks and getting on with our business as best we can. Joey's held up traffic for over a week, organised the tradespeople and disorganised the citizens — and nobody cares. Nobody's got any business that can't wait a week — or two weeks. Nobody down here is doing anything so important or so urgent that it can't be put aside until Joey's got his pictures." He turned to his brother-in-law. "Makes you think, doesn't it? I was getting into the way of thinking we were quite a bustling little community."

"So we are — but we're sane enough to keep the pace even," said Jeff. "There aren't many places left in this country where people of all ages can knock off work when a circus comes to town. We've all got time, God be thanked, to enjoy watching Joey and his boys."

"And Delphi."

"No, not Delphi; she appears to be out of it. So Joey said when he looked in just now. Incidentally, he was on his way to see you."

"To see me? Then why didn't you say so before?"

"There was no hurry; he brought some work in for Miss Stocker."

Nicholas went through to his own office and found Joey checking the finished sheets.

"Hello, Nicholas boy," he greeted him. "Shan't be a minute. Been asking Miss Stocker here to do me a few copies of Delphi's contract. She's talking of suing me. She came to my room last night with Jimmy Dunn and I told her I wasn't leaving Greenhurst until after the wedding. Jimmy got her quietened down, but it's a pity I ever set eyes on her. She wanted me to —" he broke off, staring with open mouth out of the window.

"What's the matter?" asked Nicholas.

"Nothing. Optical illusion. Could have

sworn I saw that girl who was at the air-port. As I was saying — "

"That was no illusion," said Nicholas. "She's here. But I didn't know she'd come into town."

"*Here*? Here in Greenhurst?" Hope and pleasure were equally evident in Joey's voice. "What brought her?"

Nicholas told them both, briefly and without details, what he had communicated to Jeff. Joey and Miss Stocker listened in silence, and at the end of the recital, dismay made Joey's eyes rounder than ever.

"No sign of the muscular chap yet?" he asked.

"None."

"He'll turn up," prophesied Joey. "He'll turn up, Nicholas boy. He'll come to argue with her, and if she won't listen to argument, he'll take it out on you."

"How about the police?" asked Miss Stocker.

"That'll fall down," said Joey. "We don't have to worry about policemen; all we've got to do is keep a watch out for this Springer. Well, well, well," he ended, "and I was the fellow who said that nothing out of the way ever happened in

Greenhurst. Mind if I wait here till Miss Stocker's done this little job?"

Nicholas shook his head and closed the door of his room, and Joey waited until Miss Stocker had checked the last pages. Standing at her desk with the sheets in his hand, he spoke soberly.

"If that fellow does turn up — and he will," he said slowly, "there'll be trouble. I mean real trouble. You didn't see him and I did. He's mean. He's the kind of fellow who runs out of ideas and then starts arguing with his fists. I know the type and I don't like the type. And I shouldn't like anything to happen to Nicholas."

"You're not the only one."

"No, that's right." Joey looked at her. "You like the Waynes, don't you?"

"Who wouldn't?"

"Ever have a family of your own?"

Miss Stocker, fully intending to brush the question aside, to her surprise found herself answering it.

"No brothers or sisters," she said, "and a father who disappeared and wasn't missed. My mother was a good sort."

"Why didn't you get yourself a husband?"

The fatherly tone in his voice was disarming.

"I had to push for myself when I was
young," she told him. "I wanted to do a bit
better than my mother'd done, and to do a
bit better, I had to push. I daresay I
pushed too hard and pushed aside a couple
of things that might have come to something. I don't know. I don't regret anything."

He looked at her: square, brown-skinned,
brown-haired, brown-eyed, with a manner
blunt and uncompromising. She bore his
scrutiny for a time and then put a question.

"Know me again?" she asked.

"Oh. Sorry. I was just thinking that I
always liked the look of you, right from the
first," said Joey simply. "You're like the
kind of tune one of my sisters used to play
— the only kind of tune she could manage;
she wasn't as you might say gifted. She
played slow, steady tunes; nice to listen to
but with no tra-la-las or twiddly bits. You
didn't get tired of hearing them. Did I tell
you I was one of twelve kids?"

Miss Stocker stared at him.

"*Twelve!*"

"That's right. I was number eleven. My

dad was a wonderful old boy. Bit of a — "

"*Twelve!*"

"Round dozen, yes. He was a bit of a philosopher — "

"*Twelve!* What time did he get for his philosophy?" demanded Miss Stocker, an angry spot of colour showing on her cheeks. "Philosophy, don't tell *me*! His poor wife with *twelve* kids. Philosophy! Why she stood for it, I can't think, unless she was one of those spineless, cringing — "

"She happens to be dead."

"And I don't wonder. So'd anybody be dead, with twelve kids to bring up. Somebody should've stopped him — the Salvation Army or someone. Going round with his philosophy and leaving a wife with twelve kids to— *Twelve!* You ought to be ashamed of yourself!"

"*Me?*"

"Yes, you. You take after him, standing there boasting about being one of twelve. That's one thing my mum didn't let herself in for, and if she'd met your father and his philosophy, she'd have given him something to philosophise about. If you'd thought more about your poor mother, instead of going round holding up your father to people as a paragon, when he was — "

"My dad's dead."

"And serve him right. And the sooner you stop going round holding him up to yewmane people as a — "

"I did not hold my — "

" — as a paragon, the better. And let me tell you — "

"If you'll kindly let me get a word — "

" — that you can keep the history of your father to yourself in future. What happened to the other eleven ?"

"They emigrated."

"Then you can go and join them. Go and see if you can find some bush-woman or other who'll have your twelve children while you follow in your dad's footsteps and — "

"I said nothing whatsoever about — "

" — and polish up your philosophy. What are you waiting for ? You'll wait a long time before you'll find any woman today with your mother's co-operative nature. And now you can go and spread your farmyard philosophy somewhere else, and shut the door after you."

"Will you please — "

"I said shut the door after you. You can't help what your father did, but you can help giving him away to people. A term in prison would've been more to the point than his philosophy. And now go away."

Joey went. Miss Stocker, breathing with difficulty, realised that the telephone was ringing, and picked up the receiver. When she felt sufficiently recovered to speak calmly, she went to Nicholas's room with the message.

"Lady Templeby," she told him. "She's calling here at twelve-fifteen. Says her business is important."

"And for once, she's right. She's got some extra wedding guests arriving to-morrow and nowhere to put them — except the Guides' field."

Lady Templeby arrived punctually, but immediately preceding her came Julia, who, laden with packages, narrowly missed colliding with Lady Templeby in the hall.

"Oh — I'm so sorry." Julia, her chin wedged firmly on the topmost package to keep the load firm, peered over the top and spoke contritely. "I was just going in to leave these things in the office." She freed a hand, opened the door and stood aside for Lady Templeby.

"It's very nice to have you home, Julia," said Lady Templeby, having bowed towards Miss Stocker. "I must talk to you soon about your plans for the future. You must remember that I have some very useful contacts in the musical world. But it must wait until after the wedding. Ah! the wedding!" She raised her hands to her head and stood for a moment, the imposing figure of a woman upon whose shoulders too much rested. "That is why I have come. Derek said that you may be able to extricate me from this dreadful difficulty of where to put these extra guests. I . . . Oh, good-morning, Nicholas."

Nicholas had opened his door and Lady Templeby went into his room, shepherding Julia before her. He allocated chairs in order of seniority: Lady Templeby in the large leather one, Julia on the small cane one.

"Did Paul Moulin ring you up?" Julia asked the older woman, as soon as they were seated.

"He did. He said that you had just been in to see him. I cannot tell you, Julia, how

grateful I would be if you would do this —
but I could not accept without coming in to
see whether Nicholas would have any
objections to your staying at the Red House
for a few days."

"I've no objection," said Nicholas. "Julia
thinks she may be able to get another girl to
stay there with her."

"I haven't asked her yet, but I'm sure
she'll agree," added Julia.

"Derek said that you had somebody
staying with you," said Lady Templeby.
"Is that the girl you mean?"

"Yes. She's a Miss Morley," said Julia.

"Do I know her?"

"No. I mean, she's rather a new friend,"
said Julia.

She paused, but the thing wouldn't rest
there, Nicholas told himself. Wedding or
no wedding, Lady Templeby wouldn't lose
her hold on everything that happened in
Greenhurst — or anybody it happened to.

"Morley? I know several Morleys," she
said, and waited expectantly.

"Well, this one was on my plane — the
plane Miriam and I came over on."

"Lady Templeby's eyes, half-closed,
were scanning the passengers.

"An extraordinarily pretty girl?"

"Yes."

"Not" — Lady Templeby's eyes opened, revealing disapproval — "*not* the girl who was with that dreadful young man called Springer?"

"You know him?" Nicholas asked in surprise.

"I had, once, some slight acquaintance with him." Lady Templeby's voice was cool. "I am surprised that Miss Morley—"

"She was engaged to him," said Julia. "She broke it off."

"Ah." Lady Templeby's face cleared. "I am very glad. Very glad indeed." She lowered her voice. "A horrid young man," she confided. "He came to see my husband when we were staying in London last year. Lord Templeby happened to be on the board of directors of a company in which Sir Kenneth Springer hoped to get a job. When he heard we were in London, he had the impertinence to call on my husband at our flat and ask him to use his influence on his behalf. My husband made rather short work of him. I cannot understand how a charming-looking girl like Miss Morley can have allowed herself to . . . But I am straying from the business that brought me here."

"Leave it all to me," said Julia. "I'll talk to Elaine and take her round to see Paul."

She had left her chair and was sitting on the corner of Nicholas's desk. Lady Templeby looked at the slight, calm figure for some moments, and there was a look of bewilderment on her face. Nicholas knew that she was trying to locate a small, thin, plain little girl who had on more than one occasion thrown mud at her little boy.

"Well, it's very good of you, Julia; I would be grateful if you could arrange it. And it's most kind of Paul Moulin, too."

"He said he'd like to do it," said Julia. "Because if you hadn't given that concert years ago, and if Paul hadn't come here to play at it, he wouldn't have been living at the Red House now, would he?"

"That is true." Lady Templeby smiled with genuine pleasure. "I may say that on that occasion, I played the part of Fate."

"Mrs. Bush is going to help us," said Julia.

"Mrs. Bush?" Lady Templeby flicked a mental file. "Mother of Charlie Bush, the boy who worked here for a time?"

"The same," said Nicholas.

"She was very wise to come back to her home after she lost her husband," said Lady Templeby. "I have — I say this in confidence — somebody in mind who will make her, in time, a far better husband than the good-for-nothing one she chose for herself." She rose. "Well, I will go and see Paul Moulin and tell him how grateful I am."

"I'm not sure how many bedrooms there are," said Julia, "but — "

"There are eight," said Lady Templeby. "I knew the house well in old Miss Dryden-Smith's time."

Even Lady Templeby, Nicholas noted, used the old name. Miss Dryden-Smith had, to the bewilderment of Greenhurst, been found, upon her death, to be not Miss Dryden-Smith, but Madame Moulin. Her son, Paul, had inherited the house and had for ten years lived in it — but nobody in Greenhurst ever thought of, or ever referred to his mother as anything but Miss Dryden-Smith.

"You have no idea," said Lady Templeby, as Nicholas opened the door for her, "what a weight this is off my mind.

These people are all cousins of Leopold, or I would have thought seriously of wiring to them to tell them that they must make their own arrangements and stay in London. The only available accommodation was at that dreadful little inn over at Stenby, and I wouldn't dream of putting anybody there. I had almost decided to ask you once again to have some of them at Wood Mount — but you have been so kind about it in the past that I didn't want to ask you again, especially as Miss Cornhill is doing the cooking herself now. But the Red House . . ." Her eyes narrowed, and she stared absently past Nicholas, calculating. "I shall rearrange the guests," she said. "I shall put Leopold and his brother Rudi there — Rudi is arriving tomorrow morning and he was to have stayed at Templeby for a night or two, but now I shall put him and Leopold at the Red House, and — as chaperones — Leopold's godmother and her French companion. And — well, I shall decide later. And now I must go. Nicholas, you're sure that everything is arranged about the guests coming from London?"

"Everything. The train will arrive at two

twenty; the coaches will meet it and go straight to the church and wait there to take people across the park to Templeby."

"What a mercy Leopold wasn't a Catholic!" Lady Templeby exclaimed. "We could never have got the guests into the tiny little Catholic Church. Thank goodness St. Mark's is so large— Oh, Nicholas, you're *sure* people will be able to get dinner in the train on the way back?"

"Quite sure. You did say, didn't you, that the orchestra was making its own arrangements?"

"Yes. They come in their own bus, and all I have to arrange is their lunch when they arrive and their supper before they go. I am putting them in the little temple on the other side of the lake; the music will float across the water and sound very nice — and if there is any rain, they will be sheltered."

And if they want any tea, added Nicholas to himself, somebody will have to walk a mile and a quarter to take it to them, and if the temple is as cold as I remember it from Templeby party days, the musicians will all suffer from frostbite.

Julia walked with Lady Templeby to her

car, and coming back to Nicholas's room, curled herself into the chair the visitor had vacated.

"Do you think Elaine'll do it?" she asked.

"She might," said Nicholas. "But what does she do about luggage? She didn't bring any."

"Pooh! Nylon undies she can wash out every night, and a couple of my blouses to ring the changes with the skirt she's got. I gave her a toothbrush, and she can buy anything else she needs. It isn't for long."

"She's got her own affairs to straighten out before she tackles Lady Templeby's," pointed out Nicholas.

"Well, Miss Cornhill's sure she oughtn't to go back yet — or if she does, and when she does, she says she oughtn't to go back alone. She's going to talk to you about it. She thinks she ought to go back with Miss Cornhill as a sort of escort. She — "

She stopped. Miss Stocker had opened the door and ushered in Elaine Morley.

"We were just talking about you— Come in," said Julia. "Sit down and listen to a proposition. Some of the wedding guests are homeless, and I suggested putting them into a friend's house while he's away

— my old music teacher, Paul Moulin. Bed and breakfast. I said I'd look after them, and I more or less offered you as co-worker. Will you do it?"

Elaine hesitated, and Nicholas looked at her. The night's sleep, he agreed, had had a renewing effect. Or perhaps tears acted like rain and left a fresh-as-spring look. Whatever the cause, the effect was good to see.

"How did you get into town?" he asked, before she could reply to Julia's rapid speech.

"Miss Cornhill telephoned for a taxi."

"And why?" he asked. "I could have fetched you, or my brother-in-law Jeff could have — "

"I met him."

"Met Jeff? When? Where?"

"Outside the George just half an hour ago. He stopped me and asked if I was Elaine Morley."

"And he's got the reputation of being a shy, retiring sort of fellow," commented Nicholas. "Then what?"

"He asked me what I was doing, and I said I'd just been into the George to ask if they could give me a room for a few days."

"You don't like staying with us?" Julia asked.

"There are some things," said Elaine, that one can't do. Staying with strangers when you've already put them to a lot of trouble is one of the things. Miss Cornhill didn't think the George had any rooms — "

" — because of the wedding," said Julia. "Nobody has any rooms."

"So Jeff took me to meet your sister Roselle, and his mother. They said I could stay there."

"Well, don't," said Julia. "It'll be fun to play at houses — you and I can move to Paul's house until after the wedding, and you'll be doing a job of work, and you'll be in a much stronger position if your ex-fiancé shows up, which everybody seems to think he will. You can — "

"Let Miss Morley think it over," broke in Nicholas.

"Well, I'll count ten," offered Julia, and for the first time they heard Elaine laugh, and it occurred to Nicholas that in happier circumstances she would be a girl who would have a light-hearted outlook on life.

"I think . . . yes," she said. "It sounds a crazy scheme, but if it can be made to sound like a home and a job for me for a few days, it'll give me something I want badly: a breathing space."

"Good." Julia rose. "I'm going to find Derek; he and I and Luke are going to lunch at the George — with Joey. Nicholas, will you take Elaine home?"

Nicholas glanced at his watch.

"In twenty minutes," he said.

"Then I'll leave her here. Elaine, don't forget the parcels; there's food in them. Nicholas, will you tell Miss Cornhill that it'll be Luke as well as Derek to dinner tonight? I bought enough to eat."

She went out, and Nicholas frowned at the closed door.

"Derek and Luke. Always Derek and Luke. How," he asked Elaine, "do you make a girl understand that three's a crowd?"

"If Luke's the Canadian I met this morning, he'll do the explaining," she answered calmly. "I saw it in his face. Am I disturbing you?"

"No, you're not disturbing me. But if you want to read anything, there's the morning paper beside you."

She picked it up and vanished behind it,

and Nicholas, after wondering whether she would emerge again and show a desire to talk, forgot her, and was only roused from his absorption by the sight of Miss Stocker in the doorway.

"Do you want anything before I go, Mr. Wayne?"

"Eh? Oh, no, no; thank you. I'm just off myself." He rose. "This is Miss Morley, who's staying with us."

Miss Stocker did no more than nod, and Nicholas looked at her anxiously.

"Not tired?" he asked.

"Not tired of work," she said. "Just a bit tired of Mr. Joey Helyon coming in and disturbing me."

"Joey?"

"I told him what I thought, and he went away," said Miss Stocker with some satisfaction. "Here, let me help you."

She took some of the packages out to Nicholas's car, and then turned and went with her firm, heavy tread to her boarding house farther up the High Street. Nicholas backed the car and turned it in the direction of home.

"Feeling better this morning?" he asked Elaine presently.

"Yes, thank you. And once and for all, I'm sorry. I'm sorry I changed those two bags, and I'm sorry I made a scene last night. I'm sorry to have made a complete fool of myself. But I'm not sorry I left Kenneth and his mother, because it was something I should have done long ago. All that was wrong was the — the manner of going."

"Your fiancé knows where you are, of course."

"Yes. Miss Cornhill telephoned last night and said that I was staying with you for some days. It was his mother who answered."

"Lady Templeby had heard of him."

"Of Kenneth?"

"Yes. He called on Lord Templeby last year in connection with some job or other. He didn't appear to have made a good impression. I suppose there's no doubt that we'll be seeing him in the near future?"

"None at all, I'm afraid — that's why Julia's suggestion of staying at the Red House is going to be such a godsend. When Kenneth comes, I can deal with him, and this time, you won't be involved. You've had about enough of me and my affairs."

Her tone was quiet, almost business-like; it was difficult to picture her seated on a trunk in a boxroom, weeping. A night's sleep was a good sedative, but Miss Cornhill was an even better one, Nicholas thought. He gave a glance at Elaine, and saw that she was sitting, relaxed and comfortable, her hands folded quietly on her lap. There was a quality about her that he liked; searching for a word to describe it, he hit upon restful, and discarded it in favour of sensible. She had behaved foolishly, had acknowledged it, had made a straightforward apology and was now turning her mind to the future.

"There's only one point," he said, "on which I'd like enlightenment — if you wouldn't think the question an impertinent one."

"Well?"

"This Kenneth. For a girl like you — you know, I take it, that you're exceptionally easy to look at? — the field of choice must have been a fairly wide one. How is it that girls like you consider, even for a week, teaming up with a Kenneth?"

"It's impossible to explain," she said slowly, "without filling in years of family history, family relationships. I shall never be able to understand why my father, who was so wise in some things, was so unwise about Kenneth. Perhaps he saw something in him that I didn't. Perhaps he hoped that marrying me would change him. Perhaps he thought that . . . What does it matter what he thought? All I know is that between him and my stepmother and Kenneth, I got manoeuvred into a corner — and I got engaged. And I'm glad I did, because it made my father very happy. I don't know what would have happened if he'd lived; all I'm certain of is that I couldn't have married Kenneth. But when my father died, it was frightening to see how quickly everything collapsed. I saw my stepmother and Kenneth for the first time without the softening effects my father had always been so careful to fill in. I must have known then that — thinking of them as I did — I couldn't have gone on living in the same house. But twenty-four years is a long time in one home; I suppose I'd been too blind or too lazy to think about getting out and starting a life of my own. And breaking off an engagement isn't ever easy, I imagine, but it's very hard indeed when the man is Kenneth and sees himself as a splendid specimen of manhood — "

"Which he is."

" — and who couldn't understand any girl failing to be impressed. I could have written to him from Italy, but I knew he'd come out there and remind me of the promises I made to my father. I came home still engaged to him — and the rest of it is this mess you know about already, and in which you're unfortunately involved."

"Are you going back? To live there, I mean."

"No. Never. My stepmother and I said a lot of things yesterday morning that . . . that cleared the air."

"Haven't you other relations? Uncles, aunts?"

"Nobody close. Nobody I'd like to go to. Money isn't a difficulty, thank goodness; I've got the money my mother left me, which isn't much by Kenneth's standards, but which makes all the difference between feeling desperate and feeling secure. All I've got to do is start again. Some people's past merges nicely and neatly into their future, but mine got cut off short; it ended in an ugly, jagged, horrible sort of way — yesterday morning."

"I don't have to tell you that you can stay with us as long as you want to. You know enough about Miss Cornhill to understand that she's a fortress of respectability."

"I'm very grateful to you. But — "

"But you don't want to. If you took this job of looking after some of the wedding guests, it would do one thing: it would fill in time for you until the George emptied. Once the wedding's over, the place will be yours. The only thing is that I'd rather you stayed here at Wood Mount, or — if you preferred it — with Roselle. Or — if you like — with anybody you care to pick out in Greenhurst."

She turned to look at him.

"Greenhurst or Waynehurst?" she asked, and he laughed.

"All six of us were born here. Four of us are still around. It's a narrow circle, but a friendly one."

He was at the gate of Wood Mount; soon he had brought the car to a stop at the foot of the steps.

The telephone was ringing as he entered the house. Nicholas, picking up the receiver, heard Paul's voice.

"Do you trust those two girls to keep your house in order, Paul?" he asked him.

"Why not? I ask only that you will ask Miss Cornhill to spare one of the women who work at your house, if Mrs. Bush should need any help. If this can be arranged, I have told Lady Templeby that the house is at her disposal."

"She was very grateful. She was in what you might call a state this morning."

"She need not be grateful. If I had not come, all those years ago, to play at her house in that concert, where would I be now?" asked Paul. "One thing more: this girl you have, Miss Morley — will you please bring her this afternoon? I would like the two girls to be here, to talk with my housekeeper about everything. Remember that I am going away tomorrow."

"I'll bring her after lunch," said Nicholas, and rang off to relay the request to Elaine.

He left her with Julia at the Red House after lunch, and Julia, dismissing Derek and Luke for an hour or two, took her to Paul, and the three went round the house, Paul's housekeeper leading them and issuing instructions regarding beds and bedrooms. Then Paul went to his room to pack, and Julia led Elaine to a sunny corner of the drawing-room.

"Luke and Derek'll be here soon," she said. "Sit down and relax."

Elaine, ignoring the proffered chair, was walking slowly round the room, stopping to look out of the windows at the smooth, secluded lawn. She sat on a window seat and looked at Julia, who was lying full length on the sofa, her legs dangling over the side.

"I'm a bit mixed up about your family," she said. "There are six of you?"

"Yes."

"Yourself, your brother Nicholas — "

"Starting at the top and working down — that's neater, isn't it? — you get Lucille."

"She's married to a film star?"

"Yes. He doesn't like to be called a film star. He's gone into management; he's got shares in a theatre in London and he's going to produce plays. He was knighted in the New Year Honours. Three children.

That takes care of Lucille. Next, Nicholas. Next, Roselle."

"Married to Jeff; four children?"

"That's right. Then a gap; a gap of about seven years, nobody ever explained why. Then Simon. He's up in Yorkshire; he's going to be a vet, and he'll make a good one. Then there's myself. Shall I here insert a brief history?"

"You needn't bother. Go on."

"There isn't far to go. Dominic's the youngest, the handsomest, the calmest, the deepest — because you can never really tell what he's thinking — and in some ways the steadiest, because he's always known exactly what he wanted. And how to get it. Now on the other hand, Simon — "

"All I'm trying to get is an overall picture."

"Well, outlines don't make a picture. I like talking about my family."

"Talk about Lady Templeby. Why is Monsieur Moulin so keen on doing something for her? What did she do for him?"

"She was the — what's it you call people who start something off without meaning to?"

"I don't know. What did she start off?"

"Well" — Julia loosened the jacket of her suit and stretched out her legs in the warmth — "as far back as I can remember, Lady Templeby has got up these charity concerts and brought foreign musicians and artists to her house, and when they overflowed, she's farmed them out all over Greenhurst and sometimes at Wood Mount and — "

"So she started off what?"

"I'm coming to it, I'm *coming* to it. You're just like Nicholas — he never lets you work up to anything. You just get into your stride with a few preliminary arpeggios when he — "

"So she started off — ?"

"Oh well." Julia sighed. "She gave a concert. Foreign artists. Paul accompanist to one of them. Miss Dryden-Smith dies suddenly and leaves this house to her son. Big scandal. What son? Son turns out to be Paul. Big surprise. Is that the way you like it?"

"That's the way."

"But that way," objected Julia, "you leave poor Miss Dryden-Smith with a smirched reputation, and you make poor

Paul out a bastard — and so you only get a distorted story. Miss Dryden-Smith was legally Madame Moulin, and if Lady Templeby hadn't had that concert, Madame Moulin wouldn't have found her son again after all those years, and Paul wouldn't have got the house."

"Who would have got it?"

"Miss Dryden-Smith's niece — Estelle Dryden. She didn't need it; she married someone with quite a lot of money. But that's the reason Nicholas doesn't often come here."

"Come where?"

"To this house. He loved Miss Dryden. He lost Miss Dryden. His sister Julia also loved and lost Miss Dryden, who happened to be an English teacher at Julia's school. Big tragedy." Julia, full length on the sofa, kicked her legs in slow march time, admiring the display of long shapely legs. "More accurately, two big tragedies," she ended.

"When?"

"About ten years ago." Julia twisted round on to her stomach and frowned across at Elaine. "You know something? It really *was* a tragedy — when it happened. For months after she went off with this man whose name — can you believe it? — I have to try hard to remember, for *months* I felt *ill*. Sort of sick inside."

"And then?"

"And then — nothing. That's the awful part. In that room across the hall, which I can see from where I'm lying now, I suffered — honestly — agonies because she told me she was going away. And now — nothing. It's gone. That's why I, more than anybody else, can understand how Nicholas feels."

"And how does Nicholas feel?"

"Well, I think he's got this feeling that I've got: this awful realisation that you can be shaken to your very depths by somebody, that your life can — for a time — be completely blasted, and that you can live through it and come, in time, to forget the whole thing."

"What's odd about that?"

"Odd? It's frightening. It's terrifying! It shows you that your emotions can't be relied on. It was different for me — all I had was a schoolgirl passion for a schoolmistress. But Nicholas . . . Nicholas was old enough to — "

"How old?"

"Twenty-two. She was about three years older than he was, but he had it terribly badly."

"And he's still got it?"

"No, I don't think so. If he had, there'd be some sense in it, wouldn't there?"

"Clinging for ten years to a lost love?"

"Well, your emotions are *you*," pointed out Julia. "You're attracted by somebody, and you go deeper and deeper until there seems to be nobody else who's quite real in life. Your thoughts, your hopes, your very inside is tangled up with this somebody. Then you suffer — and then what? Nothing. A sort of memory, and pretty dim at that. So next time you find yourself swooning off, what do you say to yourself? You say: Here it is again, and in five or ten years, this thing, which feels so real, could turn into a thread of smoke. That's all Estelle Dryden is now — a thread of smoke. She's got three children, but for Nicholas and myself, what is she but a thread of smoke? And once she was a sort of star in our lives, and that's what's so hard to understand. Do you ever read poetry? Do you know that Byron says that:

'In her first passion woman loves her
  lover,
In all the others all she loves is love.'

Isn't that a terrible thing to have said?
The more you think of it, the more
terrible you think it."

" 'And I was desolate and sick of an old
passion'," murmured Elaine.

"Who said that?" demanded Julia. "It
sounds like Swinburne."

"Well, it wasn't Swinburne. It was somebody called Dowson."

"Of the I-have-been-faithful-to-thee-
Cynara-after-my-fashion Dowson?"

"The same."

"You like poetry?"

"Who doesn't? Don't answer that. Kenneth doesn't, for one. Is your brother still
nursing this passion?"

"No. I told you: dead, I think. But we
don't talk about it."

"Why not?"

"Haven't you ever heard of a little thing
called delicacy?"

"So delicate that it's lived for ten years?"

"Well, perhaps other people talk to him
about it, I must say it's never cropped up

215

between him and us three younger ones:
Simon and Dominic and myself. We've
either taken it for granted, or forgotten it,
or — "

" — skated round it ?"

Julia hesitated, studying the other girl.

"Perhaps. Why not ?" she said at last.

"I don't know. Perhaps I believe in
dragging some things out into the daylight.
If my father had dragged out a few things
and aired them, I would be in a happier
position today."

"But you wouldn't have come to Greenhurst — and we like having you."

"Thank you. But I feel that ten years is a
long time to leave something that's been
folded up and put away. Taking it out and
shaking it might uncover quite a colony of
moths. I could be wrong."

"You could be right, but I don't think
I'll appoint myself as shaker-out, if you
don't mind. You've got to remember that
I've got more than a little-sister angle on
Nicholas; when Lucille married, about
eleven years ago, he took on Simon and
Dominic and myself and completed the
process of our upbringing. We were on the
point of losing our home — and he saved it

by making a three-cornered agreement with Lucille's husband and with Jeff to buy it. The Bank put up the money for Nicholas. Since then he's done everything for us — housing, food, clothing, and education. I only bring this up to show you that as well as being an elder brother, he's been a sort of parent, with a parent's authority, and you don't talk to your parents about their old love affairs, do you?"

"I suppose you don't."

"But it did give Nicholas, as I told you, a sort of immunisation. A number of quite passable girls have — "

" — made sizeable passes at him since?"

"Yes."

"Without success?"

"It depends what you call success. They were all," said Julia cautiously, "after different things."

Elaine had picked up a photograph from the bureau.

"Estelle?" she asked.

"Yes. And he loved her. And now . . . Can't you see it from his point of view? How does a man get down on one knee and chant at some girl: 'I love thee, almost as deeply, almost as passionately as I loved a girl ten years ago. I want to marry thee — almost as much as I wanted to marry Estelle Dryden, but since that's all over and forgotten, how about thou testing this new passion of mine and thee seeing whether it lasts as long as ten years.' You do see how complicated it makes life ?"

"I don't see. But that's only the opinion of a passing stranger, so you needn't take it seriously."

Julia was sitting up, her expression thoughtful.

"You mean he ought to — to wash it out ?"

"You don't have to wash things out. Time does it for you. Haven't you ever been in love — since you loved the school mistress ?"

"No."

"But it passed, didn't it ? It has to pass, if you're going to go on living a healthy, normal life. You have to accept loss — don't you ? You have to go on. When you get wounded in battles, you don't give up fighting; you take time off for convalescing and you go back and fight again. If you don't go on, what's the point of anything ? If Estelle Dryden came back, you probably wouldn't even like her much because you've changed; you've developed; you've become, in some ways, somebody else. So has your brother, unless he's been too busy nursing his disappointment."

"Nicholas didn't — "

"If he'd married her, they would have gone on together; they would have lived together, developed together, grown together. But she went one way and he's had to go another — and the point is to go. It frightens me when you say he won't come to this house."

"I didn't say he didn't; I said, or meant to say that at first, it was difficult."

"And does everybody in your family avoid mentioning her to him?"

"To Nicholas? No. My sister Lucille was Estelle's friend, and she talks about her when she's home. But Nicholas doesn't say much. He makes polite enquiries, and that's all."

"It's probably an effort to remember to make polite enquiries. After ten years, it ought to be. You keep faith with your own, not with somebody else's. And here come your swains."

"Derek and Luke?"

"Both. Your brother Nicholas is looking for somebody who'll point out that three's a crowd."

"Not this three," said Julia. "Luke's here for exactly one more week, and Derek was here when I was born and will probably be here when I die. And in any case, I don't think I'm quite the type that disturbs men too much. I hope I'm not; it must be a terrible responsibility. Will you come home with us and play records?"

"I told your sister Roselle I'd go in and see her." Elaine rose and walked to the door with Julia, and then paused. "You don't, by any chance, take your own family's assessment of your face and figure as the right one, do you?"

"When you say family's, you mean Nicholas's, I suppose," said Julia, steering the other girl through the doorway. "If I saw myself through Nicholas's eyes, I'd see a skinny eleven-or-twelve-year-old with red string for hair and ten thousand freckles for decoration. That's what you mean, isn't it?"

"That's what I mean."

"But isn't that what's so nice about him?" Julia walked towards the front door.

"When I came back from Rome, he gave a couple of tactful glances at me, and I could see he gave up hope. He thinks I'm still the old gruesome Julia — and he loves me. Wouldn't that make you feel good?"

The arrival of the two young men saved Elaine from the necessity of replying. Refusing offers of a lift to Roselle's, she walked slowly out on to the quiet road, pondering the answer she might have made. To be loved in spite of, or because of? Had her father known that her step-mother was a shallow and an ignorant woman, and had he loved her in spite of it? Or had he come to realise it slowly, and decided to keep up a pretence of love in order to keep peace in the home? Had he seen things as they were, or had he seen them as he would have liked them to be? She would never know. Would Nicholas Wayne have been the man he was if he had forgotten Estelle Dryden as soon as she left Greenhurst? Wasn't one of the reassuring things about love its dateless-ness? Was he clinging too long to the past and was his inability to see his sister Julia as she really was another sign of his disinclination to move on, move forward, leave the past behind? Like her father, did he go on loving when the reason for love was gone, or . . .

She arrived at the gate of the Milwards' house, and she had found an answer to none of the questions.

Jeff drove her back to Wood Mount for dinner, but Roselle was not with them, and Jeff was not, after all, staying for a meal. He parted from Elaine at the front door.

"You go and tell Julia and Miss Cornhill," he said, "and I'll break the news to Nicholas."

"What news?" asked Nicholas, coming down the stairs as Elaine disappeared in the direction of the kitchen.

"Oh" — Jeff's tone was airy — "just a message. Roselle didn't feel like coming along tonight, so I'm not staying."

"You'll stay for a drink, won't you?"

"Not tonight, thanks."

"What's up with Roselle?"

"She didn't feel like dinner. She hasn't been eating well for the last couple of days."

Nicholas eyed him.

"What's Elaine telling Miss Cornhill?"

he asked. "Two fewer places at table tonight and one more — "

"That's right," said Jeff. "One more place at the nursery table in another six months or so."

Nicholas accompanied him to his car.

"Aren't you rather overdoing it?" he enquired. "The world's over-populated; don't you ever listen to the news?"

"I swear to you," said Jeff solemnly, "I never go near her unless I've got my fingers crossed."

"You'd better uncross them and start counting your money. Four boys to educate as it is."

"State education," said Jeff. "I'm determined to be go-ahead. One of them's going to be a plumber and one a carpenter and one an electrician — and so on. Then they'll do-it-yourself for one another, and no labour charges."

"How does Roselle feel about having another?"

"Well" — Jeff climbed into his car — "while my mother's alive and in good health, the idea seems to be the more the merrier. But we'll have to move into a bigger house; I'll take a look at my files tomorrow and see what's going. Well, so long."

"Give my love to Roselle and tell her I'm . . . well, you'd better say I'm delighted."

He watched the car out of sight and went thoughtfully back to the house.

"Isn't it wonderful?" said Julia, emerging with Elaine from the kitchen.

"I'm glad you think so."

"Aren't you pleased?"

"I'm puzzled; how are they going to pay for their education?"

"Jeff's going to leave it to the State — didn't he tell you?" asked Elaine. "I think it's wonderful to see somebody going ahead and having a large family."

"Come and drink to it," said Julia, leading the way into the drawing-room. "Oh wait — here's Derek, with Luke."

Nicholas, in the drawing-room, took some records out of a cabinet. When Julia brought her guests in, he looked at Derek.

"You and Julia can do some sorting after dinner," he told him. "About half these records are yours. I got Simon and Dominic to clear theirs out and I actually got them to throw some away. See if you can persuade Julia to get rid of most of these."

He left the three younger members of the party on their knees on the carpet, surrounded by records, and carrying a drink to Elaine, settled himself beside her on the sofa.

"You watch them," he said. "They'll go through all those records and then Julia'll decide that they're all old treasures and can't be thrown away. She must be the keepingest girl who ever lived. She hates to part with anything but money — and money goes through her fingers like water."

"You sound like her father."

"No, I don't; I sound like her guardian, which is what I am."

"There's going to be a family reunion for the wedding, isn't there?"

"All except Simon. And Lucille's not bringing her children down until later; she and her husband are coming for the wedding, but they've got to go back to London after the weekend."

"I've seen pictures of her with him — she's lovely, isn't she?"

"Lu? Yes. She's a nice girl; you'll like her. She's not as easy to get on with as

Roselle is, but she's got more back-bone."

"You all lived in this house once, didn't you?"

"Yes. Lucille and Robert on the top floor, Jeff and Roselle in the middle and the rest of us on the ground floor. It was all right until the babies arrived."

She looked at him with frank interest.

"Did you ever feel you wanted to go away from Greenhurst?" she asked.

"No, I don't think so. When you launch out into a firm of your own, it sometimes helps to have some local backing. I was known here — at least, the family was known here — and it helped a lot. And I was lucky to start this travel business at a time when an entirely new class of people were beginning to go abroad. People whose idea of a yearly holiday had once been a trip to Blackpool or Margate or Southend suddenly began to buy tickets for the South of France, or for Mediterranean cruises. I took a little time to realise what was happening, but when I did, I began to work on the older people — the people who wished they'd been young enough to have the pluck to get out of England and take a look at them there furriners. That's where my local knowledge helped. I . . . Am I boring you?"

"No."

"Well, I tackled the older people personally. If they didn't want to go alone, I found companions for them. Sometimes I put them in charge of couriers; sometimes I even took them myself. If you were ever in a Spanish *plaza* or an Italian *piazza* or a French *place* and saw a fellow standing in the centre of a bunch of home-grown exhibits, pointing out the beauties of the local scene — well, that was me. I. And I discovered another . . . Look, this can't be very interesting to you."

"Go on."

"Well, I discovered another untapped stream. Are you a Holy Roman?"

"No."

"Neither am I — but if you're not, you won't understand what a tremendous pull all those Continental shrines exert."

"Pilgrimages?"

"That's it; pilgrimages. Would you believe that I organise no less than forty-two pilgrimages every summer? Whole coach-loads, some taking in the shrines and nothing else, others taking in the shrines on the way to somewhere else. Lately, I've got hold of three priests — nice fellows — on my regular list of guides. I enjoy sending them off. We all meet outside the George, and we take our hats off while the priest blesses the coach and the driver and the passengers and any stray passers-by who've happened to stop and watch what's going on. Then we say some Hail Marys, me leading the responses, and then away they go, as happy as happy. Lourdes, Santiago de Compostela, Fatima — I could list them for you. But I won't." He took her empty glass. "Same again?"

"No, thank you." She rose. "I'm going to help Miss Cornhill."

"That's Julia's job."

"Then I'll go with her."

He was left with Luke and Derek, but throughout dinner, he found himself looking forward to sitting beside her once more, talking to her, listening to her. He did not analyse his impatience to get the meal over; a conversation had been interrupted and he wanted to resume it; that was all, he told himself.

Luck, he felt, was with him this evening;

first, no Roselle and Jeff to take her attention, and, after dinner, Derek choosing and putting on records, Julia and Luke dancing to them, leaving him free to talk to Elaine. But this time, the talk was of her affairs.

"This idea of helping Julia at the Red House is a godsend," she said, "but it'll come to an end in a few days. After that" — she turned to face him — "can you get me a job?"

"Here in Greenhurst?"

"Yes."

"A temporary job?"

"Not necessarily. I like it here. I'd like to stay here. But I'd want a job. You said something before dinner about looking for a job in a place in which you've got local backing. Well, I haven't got local backing anywhere but here."

He was silent for some time, and then he looked at her with a frown.

"Are you being wise?" he asked. "Don't think I'm holding back on a job; I can get you one with half a dozen firms here — if you want one. But . . . you had a home, and you must have had friends and relations."

"The only home I ever had was at Crayke. I've got school friends, but they're either married or living in small flats in London — or elsewhere — and working. My father was nearly fifty when he married, and his two brothers were much older than he was and he didn't know them particularly well. I worked for some time in a solicitor's office in Crayke — he was a friend of my father's and I left when my father got ill. I've always lived at home; I liked living at home. I liked going back to my own rooms every evening after work. I could have done what most girls seem to do — leave home and share a flat with other girls in London — but I always thought it was a scrambling sort of way to live. The flats were mostly too small, generally not too well kept, and there seemed to be a strong undercurrent of man-hunting going on. But now . . . I've quarrelled quite finally with my step-mother and I shall never live at home again. Even if I wanted to — which I don't — she wouldn't have me."

"But you've got to tidy up ends. Nobody can just walk out of a house the way you did. You've got possessions, haven't you?

You've got clothes and pictures and records like Julia over there, and books — Julia's got over a thousand, most of them, thank God, up in the attic. You can get a job here, but first you've got to go back, even if it's only to claim your things."

"I won't go back alone."

"Then I shall ask Miss Cornhill to go with you. If you don't know by this time that she's the all-time expert on girls' problems, then I can't explain it to you. She fell in with us — fell is the correct word — after a long and honourable career as Matron in a girls' school, and besides knowing all about girls, she knows all about their parents and guardians. All you have to do is fix yourself a job here — if you want to — and write to tell your step-mother that you're coming back to fetch your things. The only thing you've got to decide is where you'll bring them."

"What about that boarding house where Miss Stocker lives?"

"No; you don't want a boarding-house life; you want to find a flat, or a couple of rooms — somewhere you could settle down and have your things round you and ask a few friends into now and then. When the wedding's over and the guests have gone, we'll put it to Miss Cornhill and she'll take over. She might or might not have taken me off her black list for having made you cry in the boxroom. Next time a girl appears on my front doorstep at night, I'll take her straight to the kitchen and hack large slices off the cold joint."

They talked until the dancers tired, and Derek drove Luke back to Greenhurst. Julia, yawning, went up to bed, looking so sleepy that Nicholas forebore to point out that the records lay round the record-player where she had left them, and none had been scheduled to be thrown away. He stood with Elaine looking down at the disarray, and stooped to restore some kind of order.

"Records and books," he said moodily. "You try to get her to sort them and throw them out, and what happens? She decides there isn't a single one of them that can go. When she marries, is her husband going to house all her accumulation of stuff?"

Elaine had picked up a record and was smiling at the label.

"Know it?" she asked, holding it out.

"That's an old one," he said, taking it

from her. "Has it got special memories for you?"

"No. I just remember it because it was the first tune I ever danced to — with a strange man. He was an Italian, and they were playing this tune and dancing on the terrace of the hotel, and he came up and took me outside, and we danced in the moonlight."

"Heady stuff," grinned Nicholas, putting on the record. "I can't offer a moonlit terrace, but this room's got a decent floor and so's the hall; we could open the front door and recreate the scene for you."

She was in his arms, and they danced into the hall, and he kept one hand round her waist while with the other he switched off the hall light and swung open the heavy front door. They danced silently, and the breeze from the open doorway stirred her hair and blew it gently about his face. He steered her into the long shaft of moonlight that lay across the hall, and followed it out of doors and on to the narrow terrace at the top of the flight of steps. They danced without speaking, and he felt at peace, happy and, after many, many years, happy without the persistent, nagging voice that for so long had made itself heard when he had held a woman in his arms. Tonight, there were no questions. Tonight, his arms held a woman and his only thought was one of gratitude for her slender loveliness, for the soft hair caressing his cheeks, for the smile that met his when now and then her face looked up to his. He had lived for a long, long time with a ghost; a gentle ghost, but one which had flitted across his consciousness at moments in which he felt a ghost had no place. Tonight he was at last alone with the present. Tonight, for the first time for longer than he could remember, he felt free. He had no regrets, scarcely any memories, and a feeling that he was at last on a road which led forward to happiness.

The music came to an end, and their footsteps halted, but he did not release Elaine. The moon went behind a cloud and they stood together in the darkness and her faint, delicate scent came to his nostrils and made him a little light-headed. He felt her stir in his arms and draw away, and he tightened his hold. It was dark, and they were alone, and she was beautiful, and in his mind, cleared at last of doubts and hesitations, was one clear thought: he wanted her.

He held her fast, and his lips sought and at last found hers. Darkness, and Elaine . . .

Darkness, stabbed suddenly by two blinding parallel lights.

Nicholas, still holding her, lifted his head and heard the roar of a car engine, and it needed only a glance to tell him that it was not a car he knew.

It was, he reflected long afterwards, a hell of a time for Kenneth to choose.

CHAPTER VII

THE next few moments were so confused that Nicholas, looking back on them later, was never able to recall them with any degree of clarity. He remembered only his reluctance to release Elaine; even when Kenneth's car had drawn up at the foot of the steps, his arms were round her, and he released her slowly and regretfully. He also remembered switching on the outside light, and recalled his momentary feeling of envy at the sight of the car out of which Kenneth was stepping; a car of greyhound proportions, silvery in colour, and of a beauty and power that Nicholas had in boyish dreams dreamed of possessing. The dream had materialised in the form of a utility waggon, chosen for its seating and luggage capacity and its low petrol consumption.

He had, he remembered, invited Kenneth to come in, and Kenneth, advancing into the hall, had instantly embarked upon loud and violent demands for an explanation, interspersed with some opinions of his own regarding the behaviour of Nicholas. His attitude was openly threatening, and Nicholas was ashamed to remember with what relief he had looked up to see Miss Cornhill, still fully dressed and quite unhurried, descending the stairs.

Her voice, calm, quiet, edged with contempt, had acted upon Kenneth like a jet of very cold water.

"Will you," she asked him, "kindly remember that Miss Wayne is trying to sleep? Will you please go with Mr. Wayne and Miss Morley into the drawing-room and continue your discussion there? I presume," she continued when they were all assembled beside the scattered records, "that you are — that you were — Miss Morley's fiancé?"

"She walked out." Kenneth's voice was furious, but under Miss Cornhill's cold eye, the fury was held in check. "She walked right out of my mother's house" — he snapped his fingers — "just like that. All I had said to her was that if people stole anything, it was the duty of decent-minded citizens to put the police on to them. 'It must be a mistake,' she said —

and, I told her, a pretty lucky one. Some nice, clean pound notes. Anybody'd be glad to make a mistake like that."

"You accuse Mr. Wayne," enquired Miss Cornhill politely, "of stealing your money?"

"I'm merely sticking to the facts. I said the money was in the bag, which it was. I said that the bag had disappeared — which it had. He'd tried once to get his hands on it, and I'd seen through it; I never should've let the thing out of my hand after that. I said he'd be bound to look inside the bag; when he looked, he'd find the money. If he notified the airline, well and good; that's what an honest man would've done. But did he? He did not. So if he wasn't going to give up the money, he was going to keep it — right?"

"I telephoned last night to your mother," said Miss Cornhill, "telling her that Miss Morley was with us and would be staying with us until — "

"I know all that; she told me," interrupted Kenneth. "What would you say if a total stranger rang you up in the middle of the night and told you that your son's fiancée was — "

"Ex-fiancée," said Elaine coldly, and regretted the words, since they immediately drew Kenneth's fire.

"I thought I knew something about women," he said, regarding her bitterly, "but I was wrong. I would have said you were the last girl in the world to act the way you did and walk out of a house you'd lived in all your life, and for no reason at all. Did you ever think of all my mother did for you? You were a daughter to her. She treated you as though — "

"We've been through all that," said Elaine. "I'm sorry you had to come such a long way to go over it all again. I'm not going back to your mother's house, and I'm not going to consider becoming engaged to you again, and I'd be grateful if you'd leave me alone."

"Leave you alone where? Here?" demanded Kenneth. "Here? With people you don't know the first thing about? Here with — "

"If you have anything more to say, Sir Kenneth, perhaps you would very kindly call and say it in the morning," broke in Miss Cornhill.

"Judging by what I saw in the glare of

my headlights as I drove in," said Kenneth, "the morning'll be too late."

"I wouldn't say that again if I were you," came from Nicholas in an even tone.

Kenneth swung round to face him.

"You wouldn't? Do you deny that you were holding Elaine in your arms?"

"I do not."

"Do you deny that you were kissing her? Do you deny that the moment she touched down at the airport, you got your eyes on her, and have kept them there ever since? Fellows like me know how to deal with fellows like you, only fellows like you take damn good care that there are always a covey of women surrounding them and protecting them. Like as now. You stand there making out that all this trouble with Elaine hadn't anything at all to do with you, and you try to make me out a big, nasty fellow who chases a girl and makes a big, nasty nuisance of himself. Have I got a grievance, or haven't I? You took that bag and you hung on to the money; those are facts, and I like to deal with facts. If you didn't take it to get the money, then you took it hoping to use it as an excuse to see Elaine again."

"It would have been a good idea," said Nicholas. "Unfortunately, it didn't occur to me."

"So you say. And when I decide, as any good citizen would decide, to ask the police to look you up and ask you a few questions, what happens? My fiancée walks out. She leaves me, leaves my mother, leaves the house, and when next seen, she's standing out in the moonlight being embraced by a total stranger. Quick work, that's all I can say. I get home and find my mother terribly upset; I drive off to find my fiancée and ask her to come home and discuss the whole thing reasonably, and I find her with — "

"I told you that if you insisted on going to the police, I'd leave," said Elaine. "For the last year, I've been trying to tell you things and you've been too busy listening to your own opinions to understand that anybody else had any. I've left home, Kenneth. I'm sorry, because I think my father would have been sorry — but I'm not going back. Not to live there."

Kenneth, without answering, strode to the door and opened it. He turned back to glare at Elaine.

241

"I'll be back in the morning to see you — alone," he said. "Perhaps I'll be able to make you see reason."

"Where are you going to stay?" she asked.

"What the hell do you care?" he snarled.

The door slammed behind him.

"Well, that's that," said Nicholas. "You don't mind," he asked Elaine. "if I say that I see no reason to revise my first impressions of Sir Kenneth?"

"Was *that* who he was?" Julia, tying the cord of her dressing-gown, came into the room and gazed at Elaine. "I woke up and heard him, but I couldn't get down before he went out and slammed the door. Will he make a nuisance of himself?"

"If he's allowed to," said Nicholas.

"Well, you won't be able to stop him," Julia pointed out sensibly. "You'll be in your office, and Elaine'll be with me at the Red House."

"You're all very good, and I'm very grateful," said Elaine, "but I'm quite capable of dealing with Kenneth by myself — and if I can, I'll see he doesn't come here any more. I seem," she added slowly,

"to have made a wonderful mess of everything."

"You seem to have been dealing, if I
may say so, with people who are not very
reasonable," said Miss Cornhill. "I think
we will do well to go to bed now, and talk
this over coolly in the morning."

"In the morning, early, I'd like to move
to the Red House," said Elaine. "Kenneth
can make his next scene there."

Miss Cornhill glanced at her white,
drawn face.

"Go upstairs and I'll bring you up a hot
drink," she said.

"I'll make it," offered Julia. "Don't you
wait up, Miss Cornhill."

Miss Cornhill, after a moment's hesitation, followed Elaine upstairs, and Julia
looked at Nicholas.

"Hot drink for you, too?" she asked.

"Not hot; just strong." He poured himself out a drink and carried it to the
kitchen. Pulling out a chair with his foot,
he sat down and, cupping the glass in his
hands, stared moodily at the table.

"Were you really kissing her?" Julia
asked.

He looked up at her.

"What were you doing — hanging over the banisters, listening?"

"There wasn't any need; Kenneth was really letting himself go. But were you really — "

"Yes, I was, if you want to know."

"Well, of course I want to know." She measured milk into a saucepan. "I wouldn't have said Elaine was the sort of girl who'd let you get away with it."

"Get away with what?"

"With kissing her so soon."

"Just for the record," said Nicholas slowly, "the initiative was all on my side. And now perhaps you'll mind your own business and — "

"What should I do — pretend I didn't hear Kenneth shouting?"

"That would be the delicate thing, yes."

"Do you have to be delicate with your brother?"

"You have to be delicate about delicate matters, whether they affect your brother or somebody else's brother. If I make a damned fool of myself and have the misfortune to be caught making a damned fool of myself, the least you can do is — "

"But all I wanted to know was whether

you kissed her with what Luke calls deadly intent, or whether — "

"With what Luke calls *what*?"

"Deadly intent. He says that even given the time and the place and the girl, a man needn't lose his head; he can still make a planned approach. That is, he can decide in his mind whether he wants to let the atmosphere engulf him or whether he'll keep it cool. If he really wants the girl, then he kisses her with deadly intent. Do you follow?"

"I can't say I do. Is this the kind of thing Luke always talks about?"

"How should I know? I only met him a week ago."

He stared up at her in amazement, striving to fit the words she had spoken so coolly and sensibly to the slender girl standing before him. This was Julia. He had to believe that she had just said all she had said. She had sounded completely and reassuringly adult — but before his eyes swam visions that accorded not at all with the words. Long, bare legs flashing from a high tree house. A face freckled, mud-streaked; a grimy little girl appearing at meals and being sent away to clean herself up. A thin, childish figure rolling on the drawing-room carpet, locked in combat with Simon or Dominic or — dear Lord! — Derek Arkwright. School reports that deplored her lack of attention, her disorderliness, her ability or determination to learn nothing but poetry.

"When and where did you grow up?" he asked her slowly.

The smile was the old Julia — warm, radiant, flashing out and irradiating her face.

"Do I look grown up?"

"You sound a bit too sophisticated for my liking."

She smiled gently.

"Two years in Rome," she reminded him, "surrounded by impressionable Italians. The first year, I didn't seem to have much to impress them with, but towards the end of my stay, things began to move. And when young Italian men move, they move awfully fast. Can you imagine an Englishman, for example, passing you in a car — when you're driving with somebody else — taking a look as he flashes past and then bringing his car to a stop, getting out and kneeling beside it in an attitude of supplication as you come up?"

"Frankly, I can't. I hope the one you were driving with ran him down."

"Why? The one I was driving with regarded it as a natural tribute to his good taste. Can you imagine an Englishman standing on the pavement under your bedroom window at three in the morning singing, while millions of scooters fly along the road behind him, making a fiendish row?"

"Drunk?"

"Only with emotion. Do you know that you sent me to Italy without once taking me into your study and giving me a brief talk on the facts of life?"

"That wasn't my job. You had two married sisters, one of whom was around all the time. It was your job to check up."

"It was, and I did. And that answers your question about my growing up, so you can answer mine. I asked you whether you were sorry you'd kissed Elaine — because if you are, I'm sorry, too."

"And why?"

Julia waited until the milk began to rise, and lifted the saucepan off the stove. Then:

"Because she's alone," she said, "and things are pretty difficult for her, and she's in an awkward enough position without having to feel that you think she's one of those. If she thought you really wanted to kiss her — moonlight apart — it would have been rather a comfort, I should think. After all, in a sense she's under your protection, and she'd like to feel that you're not sorry that — "

"If you want to know, and if she wants to know, I'm not in the least sorry about anything."

"Not even about Kenneth catching you at it ?"

"Not even about Kenneth, as you so delicately put it, catching me at it."

Julia put the milk saucepan on to the table, sat down and cupped her chin in her hands, staring thoughtfully at her brother.

"Does it happen ?" she asked.

"Does what happen ?"

"Love at practically first sight ?"

"Hadn't you better deal with that drink before the milk gets cold ?"

"I can heat it up again. Are you in love with her ?"

He spoke irritably.

"How the hell can anybody answer a question like that?"

"By a simple Yes or No. I'm only trying to find out, because if you are, it'll make her future so much clearer than it is at this moment."

"If she heard you talking like this, she'd get out of this house and out of this town so fast that nobody'll see her leave. The — "

"She can't hear. Do you love her?"

There was a long silence. They looked at one another; her gaze was intent, his absent and dreamy.

"Well?" she prompted after a time.

"You know, it's got nothing whatsoever to do with you. This is purely between Elaine and myself."

"I suppose," agreed Julia. "But this affair hasn't been running along the usual lines. Things have, so to speak, been snatched out of your hands. Normally, I'd say nothing to you, and just talk about it behind your back, but I like Elaine and I loathe Kenneth and when I hear that you were out there with her in a clinch, I just like to find out what was behind it; whether you were just carried away, or whether you sensibly, seriously, soberly kissed her."

"I was carried away and I kissed her, but there was nothing sensible or sober about it."

"But it was serious?"

"They say we all spring from fish. You must be the limpet family. Yes, it was serious."

Julia drew a deep breath.

"I'm glad. She'll be glad, too."

"What about?"

"She wondered whether you were living a bit in the past."

He regarded her frowningly.

"Don't you talk a bit too much?" he enquired coldly.

"Perhaps." She rose and poured the milk into the cup and held it out to him. "Here's her drink. Will you take it up to her?"

"Me? Go into her bedroom?"

"Where's the harm? You're fully dressed, and you can leave the door open, say good-night, tell her in two sentences what you think about her, and explain that you'll take care of her future — in whichever way she wants you to. Then she'll feel as though she's got somebody to lean on. It can't be much fun to be in her position, and the fact that most of it is her own fault doesn't make her feel any better. Here, take it."

He shook his head moodily.

"No. You take it."

"All right. Good-night."

"Good-night."

The door closed behind her, and he sat staring straight ahead, his mind in a daze. Elaine . . . Julia . . . Kenneth . . .

He looked down at his untouched drink, and lifted the glass — and then put it down again. His head, he decided, was going round too fast already. Life, which had been going on at a moderate and steady trot, had suddenly broken without warning into a swift gallop; had, in fact, bolted. All he could do was hang on and take vague note of things as they flashed by. A near-brawl at the airport, a threat of police; a girl materialising in the dusk. A large, aggressive man with a grievance . . .

He was hanging on — but he had already been swept out of the past. Left behind for ever was a woman called Estelle Dryden and a small, freckled girl called Julia

Wayne. They had been there last night — vague, indistinct, but identifiable. Tonight they had vanished and would never return. Tonight Estelle Dryden emerged as a housewife living in California, with three children who on Paul Moulin's colour slides looked typical young Americans. And Julia had become an intelligent young woman with a firm grasp on life.

And Elaine . . . Sitting here, with no moonlight, with nothing but a kitchen sink and kitchen cupboards to provide atmosphere, he could still feel her in his arms, still feel the warmth of her lips under his. His thoughts were with Julia, going into her room, sitting on her bed and watching her as she drank her milk. Elaine Morley, who — Julia said, and rightly said — was under his protection.

Elaine Morley. He said the name aloud. A week ago, she had been a girl standing a little apart at a crowded, confused airport. Tonight she was in his house and —

He paused. Deadly intent. He was alone, and the room was quiet, and he could think before he plunged. He was still on the edge; if he went in, he knew with absolute certainty that he would go down deep and stay down. He could still, on the brink, step back and consider matters coolly. He was free.

And then he knew that he was no longer free, and that he no longer wanted to be free. He was in love, and he was happy as he had scarcely imagined he could be happy: happy to know that he loved, happy to trust the Fate that had brought Elaine to him, happy to believe that Fate would not take her away again.

In love.

Perhaps, after all, he decided, he did need a drink.

CHAPTER VIII

"AND then?" asked Jeff.

Once more, he should have been working; once more, he was listening with deep absorption — this time, to Nicholas's account of Kenneth's arrival the night before.

"I've told you. Miss Cornhill took charge. And when we'd argued for a time in the drawing-room, he went off, promising to drop in next time he was in the district, and I said, 'Do, old chap; do, by all means.'"

Jeff looked across his desk intently.

"You're in a funny mood this morning, aren't you?" he asked.

"Relief," said Nicholas. "If Miss Cornhill hadn't come down just in time, I'd have been laid out on my back on the floor of the hall, with a swelling coming up rapidly on my . . . well, wherever he chanced to hit me. That wouldn't have sent up my stock with Elaine, would it?"

"How do I know? You've only told me half the story. What happens now?"

"It's happening. Lady Templeby's in action. She may have her faults, but you can't say she doesn't warm to friendly actions."

"She warms to unfriendly ones, too."

"Naturally. But Paul Moulin's right at the top of her list now. First thing this morning, she sent the Rolls, chauffeur-operated, to the Red House to take Paul and his luggage to the station. Then it went back to take his housekeeper and her luggage to catch the next train. Then Lady Templeby drove up in person — not in the Rolls, but in the station waggon, driven by Derek, and arrived at the Red House just as I was unloading Elaine and Julia and their gear. She brought bed-linen, towels, tinned food, frozen food, fresh food and so much fruit that Derek and I had to make six trips before we got it all into the house."

"What time do the wedding guests arrive?"

"Eleven thirty. But I haven't finished. Next at the Red House were Miriam and Leopold, with all his gear."

"He's moved out of Templeby?"

"Well, naturally. He had to get out

before the wedding. I've an idea Lady Templeby meant to put him and his brother at Wood Mount at the last moment — but she changed her mind when Paul came up with his offer. So he's at the Red House — and after him came Charlie's mother, and then Charlie."

"What's Charlie doing there? Oh — the tinned food and the frozen food and the — "

"He looked in to see if there were any odd jobs he could do before going to work. Then Luke Hayman dropped in to see what he could do. So we've got" — Nicholas counted on his fingers — "one, Lady Templeby; two, Derek; three, Luke; four, Mrs. Bush. The house will be pretty well manned when Kenneth next shows up. I'm not counting Leopold and his brother and the others — they'll all spend most of their time over at Templeby."

"Does Springer know where Elaine is?"

"Not yet. He took it for granted she was staying on at Wood Mount, so that's where he'll go first."

"Where's he staying?"

"No idea. But he must have had a long search before he found anything."

"If he found anything."

"If he found anything. His car's forty feet long — he could sleep comfortably in that." He turned as the door opened to admit Joey. "Come on in."

Joey came in, but for once he seemed unable to match Nicholas's mood of cheerfulness.

"Something on your mind?" Nicholas asked him.

"Yes. Your secretary. Miss B. Stocker," said Joey despondently.

Nicholas looked at him with a puzzled frown.

"It's funny," he said. "You have a peculiar effect on her. Before you turned up, she was a girl I would have said nobody could rattle. But you've managed it."

"Who rattled her?" Joey's voice held a note Nicholas had never heard in it before: injured innocence. "I didn't rattle her! I behaved to her just as I behave to most people I come across — but I rubbed her up the wrong way, and I finished it off by telling her that I was one of a family of twelve."

"What's wrong with that?" Jeff wanted to know.

"Ask her. We were a fine, happy family, but before I could say a word more, she'd got us all in a couple of dingy rooms in a slum — and what's more, she'd got my father lined up as a . . . Well, we won't go into that. A nicer fellow never lived."

"Well, I'll tell her — when we're not so busy with the wedding," said Nicholas.

"Wedding, wedding, wedding," complained Joey. "What's a wedding? A short ceremony followed by something to eat. How-come this town's turned itself into a — "

"You ought to alter the commentary of your film: show the world how a small town rises to its great occasions."

"You call this wedding a great occasion?"

To Joey's surprise, Nicholas's reply was made soberly.

"To some of us, it is," he said slowly. "Some of us — most of us, I think — have a rather special feeling about it."

"Because of Miriam Arkwright?"

"Yes. You've only dropped into Greenhurst now and then, so you haven't seen it all. Jeff and I have. We've seen her through most of her stages. And if you'd known her when she was younger and well under her mother's thumb, you'd never have guessed that she'd become the sensible, happy, co-ordinated woman she is today. Most weddings are nice affairs, but Miriam Arkwright's wedding to a nice fellow like Leopold is something special."

"I see. But she can be happy and get married, can't she, without all this turn-out-the-town? Go and take a look outside; when I came here ten days ago, that was a quiet, typical little High Street leading up to a nice little market square. That's how I filmed it. Now look at it — go on, take a look; the wedding guests are coming in already — two days before the event — and the place is so stiff with foreigners that it looks like Edinburgh during the Festival."

"The town's got a lot of interest in this wedding," Jeff pointed out. "Lady Temple-by's paying half its housewives good money to put up her guests. She's using a local caterer. She's using a local florist. She's using Brett's cars. So you see, everybody's got a finger in the wedding cake, and everybody's happy."

"I'm glad," said Joey. "I'm very, very

glad. But I didn't come in here to talk about the wedding. I came in to ask about this Springer fellow — Kenneth. I went along to the Red House just now, and Julia told me he'd turned up last night. Where's he got to now?"

"Nobody knows. But he'll be back," said Nicholas.

"Of course he'll be back. That's why I came in to see you. We've got to have a plan. We've got to think of some way of getting that girl Elaine behind some sort of protective screen. So this is what I thought: I'm free until the wedding and so's Luke. He and I will take turns at the Red House — you know, just dropping in and being there in case Kenneth shows up. Then when you close the office, you can take over."

"You think it's necessary?" asked Nicholas.

"Necessary?" Joey looked surprised. "Didn't I understand from Julia that she'd walked out on Kenneth and his mother?"

"Yes, but — "

"Well, I've tried to tell you this before, but I'll say it again: I've been around a lot more than you have, and I can spot the kind of fellow who doesn't stop short at the point which most people feel is far enough. That Kenneth's a muscle man; he'll talk for a spell, and if you don't appear to be impressed by what he's saying, he'll go into action."

"What sort of action can he go into here? All we've got to do is convince him that Elaine intends to stay away from him; once he sees that — "

" — he'll get dangerous." Joey rose. "Now, I've warned you. And while you chew it over, I'll do as I said: I'll stick around with the girls. If Kenneth comes in here, you can send him round with the knowledge that somebody'll be there to receive him. The only thing: if you get a chance, and you know he's on his way, pick up a phone and just give us a moment or two's warning."

"Well — thanks."

"Nothing. Well, I'll leave you."

"You're still looking worried," said Jeff.

"I'm not worried. But I keep thinking of something the Count said the other night — that I was like Miriam's mother. We both had the same technique, is what he said; we both used people, and the only difference was that I'd got the thing polished up to the point where people didn't notice what I was doing."

"You merely ask people to help you; what's wrong with that?" asked Nicholas.

"I use people. I used your secretary, just because she was there giving a good performance as an efficient typist; I handed over my bits of work and said: 'Here, do those.' And now I'm sorry."

"Well, tell her so."

"She won't speak to me. She — It's nothing to laugh at."

"I'm sorry. But I'm busy. I've got to go," said Nicholas.

Nicholas went away, and it was not long before Miss Stocker opened his door and ushered in a visitor.

"Miriam! Come on in." Nicholas rose and came round to shake up the chair cushions. "Sit down. Cigarette?"

"Thanks. I'm not staying," she said, when he had held a light for her. "When I came into town with Leopold this morning to take his things to the Red House, I heard a little more about Elaine Morley. Julia said she'd left her home. Is that really true?"

"Yes. It's what you might call an awkward situation all round. She arrived at or after ten o'clock at night at a stranger's house, to see a man she didn't know the first thing about — and she arrived without luggage. She didn't even bring back the green bag that caused all the trouble — the bag that had Julia's underwear in it."

"She came to warn you that the police — "

"She could have telephoned, written, wired — anything."

"How did she know who and where you were?"

"Her fiancé remembered my car number. She had a row, and after that, she walked out and . . . Good Lord, when you think what she might have landed herself into! She goes to a strange town, walks off a bus and up a drive into a stranger's house without knowing the first thing about — "

"She knew some things," said Miriam.

He looked at her.

"What, for instance?"

"She had plenty of time at the airport to study Julia. If you look at Julia, you see a lot of nice things and you're entitled to conclude that she belongs to a nice family.

Her brother comes to meet her, and she has time to study the brother. He's pretty reassuring, too. She sees Julia's affectionate greeting — and she hears it. I wasn't as near as Elaine Morley was, and I heard it. We all heard it. We heard about Pietro and Miss Cornhill and we could sketch in, if we wanted to, a very detailed picture of a home with friendly people in it. I saw you walk away with Julia to get the luggage — her hand in yours, both of you happy to meet again, anxious to get home. Perhaps Elaine Morley thought she was coming to Greenhurst to warn you about the police — but I think she was walking towards a gleam of light. I don't suppose she worked it out any more than I worked out my gradual realisation that I had to free myself from my mother — but when she set off for Wood Mount, she had a fairly clear idea of the sort of people who'd be living in it."

"That makes some sort of sense, but it isn't the kind of thing you could explain to Kenneth Springer. Leaving home the way she did — "

"How else could she ever have left?" Miriam seemed to put the question to the pale blue smoke swirling up from her cigarette. "How else? It sounds a bad way, but in the end, it's a clean way. It's easy for people like you to advocate reason, to point out how much better it would have been to think over the matter, come to a firm decision, notify your parents or guardians of your intention, pack your things, say good-bye and thank you — and go. That's the way it would work out if one of your brothers or sisters ever found the home weight too crushing. The door would be open, and there'd always be a welcome if they came back. Other people . . . some other people find it more difficult. And some people find it impossible. Parents or guardians who for any reason at all — selfish or unselfish — want to keep you, begin by laughing: 'Nonsense, dear; you mustn't be so silly.' If you persist, they go on to argument: 'Where will you go? What will you do? How will you support yourself?' From argument to anger, and from anger to the most wearing stage of all: pleading. 'Remember what we've done for you. Think how we need you. Don't throw all our love, our kindness, our devotion in our faces.' I don't know Elaine Morley's background, but I can tell you fairly accurately what she's been through, because I went through it. In the end, you go — but not with any dignity. You just go; you walk out — or rush out, like Elaine Morley. You gave me an excuse to go, and I took it — but up to the last, my mother held out against my going, because she knew that in one sense, I'd never come back. You gave Elaine Morley an excuse, and she took it, and I'm glad she did."

"Perhaps I'm glad, too. But leaving the way she did, she gave Springer good grounds for making trouble."

"He mustn't be allowed to make trouble. And that's what I came to talk to you about."

"Have you talked to Elaine?"

"Not yet. I wanted to talk to you first."

"If you've got any idea what we can do with her when this wedding of yours is over, I'd be grateful. All I can think of is sending Miss Cornhill back with her to wind things up with some kind of dignity. Nobody could look at Miss Cornhill without realising that — "

"Just a moment. Miss Cornhill's everything you say, but what's needed, Nicholas, is somebody with status. Miss Cornhill

has calmness and dignity and control —
but she's only, after all, your housekeeper,
and what you need, what Elaine needs is
somebody behind her — no, somebody in
front of her — who'll provide the kind of
authority and status that's essential."

"Well, who, for instance?"

"My mother," said Miriam.

Nicholas stared at her in astonishment.
"Your mother!"

"Yes." She leaned forward, crushed out
her cigarette and went on speaking calmly.
"My mother is the person you want. I
know a lot of things about her that I don't
care for, but when it comes to solid, basic,
rock-like family background, she's got it —
and to spare."

"But — "

"Wait a minute. If you'll let me talk to
her, I'll tell her the whole story. I gather
from Julia that she and my father already
have Kenneth Springer filed under I for
Impossible. I shall tell them that he
followed Elaine Morley here — and the
rest, I think, you can leave to my mother."

"But why should she — "

"Interest herself? Because she's interested in the Waynes. And because under

all that bossiness, she's got a good heart. And because when the wedding's over, she'll be left with a blank; not the usual blank left by a departing daughter, but the blank that follows a period of intense activity. She won't be able to do anything before the wedding — and in any case, until Saturday and for a day or two afterwards, Elaine and Julia will be at the Red House surrounded by their scouts. When the wedding's over, she'll adopt Elaine for a time. If I know her, she'll put her into the Rolls and go off to tell Kenneth Springer's mother that owing to the unfortunate behaviour of her son, Miss Morley will be spending some time at Templeby. May I talk to Mother? I've got to get her views before talking to Elaine."

Nicholas looked across at the plain, smiling, sensible face.

"If it could work out like that . . ."

Miriam rose.

"It will."

When she left the office, Nicholas glanced without interest at the pile of work on his desk, and then walked through Miss Stocker's room, through the hall and into the rooms occupied by Jeff.

"Busy?" he asked him.

"Yes. I thought you were too."

"I got side-tracked. Miriam came in. And she had a good idea — to talk to her mother and tell her all about Elaine and ask her to — "

" — take her under her wing?"

"Yes."

Jeff looked impressed.

"If the old lady'd do it," he said slowly, "it would be a wonderful way out of a very awkward situation."

"Miriam says she will do it. I think she will, too." He paused. "It's odd . . ."

"What's odd?"

"It's odd that at this moment, all I feel for Springer is sympathy."

"For why?"

"Because he's on the losing·end. I don't wonder he's acting belligerently. Fellows on the losing end can either retire gracefully, or they can relieve their feelings by violence. It's unfortunate that he's got the wrong idea about Elaine and myself."

"About you and Elaine?"

"Yes."

"You mean he's convinced there's more in the bag?"

269

"You trying to be funny?"

"Yes."

"Well, don't. Until Elaine Morley turned up at Wood Mount, I'd seen her for exactly five minutes. If you can make anything out of that, you're welcome to."

"It would be a neat finish," pointed out Jeff mildly.

"What would?"

"You and her. She's more than pretty, as Julia pointed out. She's a nice girl — my mother said so, and my mother always knows. She's homeless. And as for you, it's time you looked at a girl again — gave a girl more than a passing look, I mean. You're rising thirty-three, you've got a fair income and a nice home. The two cases seem to me to dovetail nicely. Not," added Jeff, who had discussed the point exhaustively with his mother, his wife, Joey Helyon and his confidential clerk, "not that I'd mention this to anybody but you."

"When I decide to marry," said Nicholas, slowly and with emphasis, "I won't come and ask you whether you think it's time I did or not. And I won't pick on a girl just because she happened to show up on my doorstep. Is that clear?"

"Absolutely. If I get a chance to talk to Springer before he gets a chance to talk to you, I'll point that out to him. And he might believe it, but I don't, because I've known you for thirty years longer than he has, and I know when you're lying. And these glasses I'm wearing help me to see quite a lot, and what I've seen of you this morning has been — for a fellow who knows you as well as I do — very, very revealing. And what I see, I'm glad to see, because if you don't grab a girl like that while you've got the chance — if you've got the chance — you'll be a bigger fool than most of us can be on occasions. If you take your eye off the essentials and start thinking about a lot of unimportant details such as how long you've known her or whether it's more sporting to wait till she gets on her feet again, you'll be crazy and you'll ruin your life and perhaps hers, too. And now get out of my office and let me ring up Roselle and tell her what's cooking. And after that I might ring up a bookmaker and lay my bets. See you later."

Nicholas went outside and stood hesitating. He wanted more than anything in the world to go to the Red House. He had said nothing to Elaine this morning except brief sentences relating to Kenneth's probable reappearance. They had breakfasted together; she had sat beside him and he had found himself relatively uninterested in his food and had realised that Miss Cornhill's eye, mild but all-seeing, was upon him. He longed to leave the office and drive over to the Red House and see Elaine and try to get her alone and talk to her.

But there was work to be done. Reluctantly, he went to his office. He walked past the busily-typing Miss Stocker, went into his room and stared with distaste at the pile of papers on his desk.

He did not know how much time elapsed before he heard Miss Stocker's discreet scratch on his door. It opened, and behind her, already brushing her aside and entering the room, was Kenneth Springer.

Nicholas got slowly to his feet and nodded to his secretary.

"All right, Miss Stocker; thank you."

She closed the door, and Nicholas indicated the deep leather chair.

"Sit down, won't you?"

"No I, won't." Kenneth stood, feet planted firmly, his expression set and brooding.

"I'm not staying. I came in to ask you a question or two."

Nicholas looked at him. Behind the aggressiveness, the now-familiar bullying manner, he saw something else, and recognised it as bewilderment, and understood its cause. Last night, Kenneth had left Wood Mount and had driven into Greenhurst in belligerent mood, resolved on getting a bed for the night at the local inn and resuming this morning the business which had brought him to Greenhurst. He was large, handsome, titled, and would normally have had no difficulty in finding a place for himself in the town and obtaining any services he was prepared to pay for. Moreover, at any other time Greenhurst would have been aware of him. He would have been studied, discussed, questioned, and then Greenhurst would have pronounced itself for or against him.

But he had arrived on the brink of the most exciting event that had taken place in the town since Lucille Wayne's wedding to Robert Debrett, a day still remembered for the dazzling crowd of celebrities that had glittered on Wood Mount's lawn. Miriam Arkwright was now to marry, and there was scarcely a man, woman, or child in the town without a keen and utterly personal interest in the event. Greenhurst was excited because Greenhurst was getting married; what had once been a pretty little village was now a flourishing little town, but the village spirit of unity remained. And Lady Templeby had brought custom, prosperity, and colour to Greenhurst. She had never been loved, but she had been respected, and her knowledge of and liking for the town had never shown itself more clearly than in the general invitation which she had issued to the wedding. Greenhurst would come, and she would provide food and drink for all, and Nicholas knew that the people of the town would show their appreciation of this lavish and kindly hospitality by keeping themselves strictly apart from the guests who had received more personal invitations. He knew that the town would be there, eating wedding cake; he knew also that there would be no misapprehension anywhere as to the demarcation line between those who would drink champagne, those who would prefer cider cup, and those to whom a nice cup of tea would be above all things preferable. Democracy took many forms, but in Greenhurst it operated in a way of its own. The words humble or servile had no place in the town; respect and delicacy were not words, but feelings, and by these Greenhurst allowed itself to be led.

But Kenneth Springer, Nicholas felt, would not have understood any of these things. He would only remain puzzled by the fact that he had been unable to make his presence in the least felt.

He sat down and looked across the desk at his visitor.

"What can I do for you?" he enquired.

Kenneth came a step nearer and halted, brought up by the desk, which Nicholas for the first time noted was broad and solid.

"You can tell me where my fiancée is, for a start," he said. "I went out to your house and I saw your housekeeper. She refused to let me in and she refused to say anything except that Elaine wasn't there — which is probably a lie."

"Miss Cornhill is very truthful," said Nicholas.

"And pretty damn unco-operative, too. What do you all think I am? I come here all the way from Wiltshire chasing a girl who appears to have lost her head in a big way. I get to your house, you try to give me this line about having had no hand in getting Elaine there, you send me out into the night to fix myself up in a town which you know quite well has only one pub, which happens to be full. I make enquiries and I find that the only place that can offer me a room is four or five miles out at a place called Stenby — a stinking little pub in a God-forsaken neck of the woods. The next morning, your housekeeper treats me to a frozen stare and behaves as though I were some fellow trying to pick Elaine up. So I came here. Now: where's Elaine?"

"Miss Morley and my sister are at the Red House, about a mile from here; they are staying there for four or five days, to help Lady Templeby by accommodating some wedding guests."

"Templeby? The textile Templeby?"

"Yes."

"And whose wedding? Don't tell me that Miriam Arkwright finally made it?"

"Miss Arkwright is being married on Saturday."

"Well, well, well." Kenneth's sneer

broadened. "So that's why the town's all at sixes and sevens? I know Miriam. We used to have jokes about her at my club."

"I'm sure," said Nicholas, "you must have enjoyed them. You look to me the kind of man who would."

Had he said that? he wondered hazily. The one thing he had warned himself when Kenneth had walked in was to lay off provocation. The one thing he had told himself was simply to tell him where Elaine was, safe in the knowledge that Joey, Luke, Derek, Julia, and probably Uncle Tom Cobley would be there, too, and after that, to shut his mouth. But he'd opened it — too far. The dark colour suffusing his visitor's face told him how much too far.

Watching the big, powerful man leaning over his desk — thank God for solid mahogany, thought Nicholas — he became aware with a sense of shock that for all his light talk of belligerence, for all Joey's warnings regarding men who used their fists, he had never really contemplated, never completely faced the possibility that a man, a stranger, a person against whom his only fault had been committed unknowingly, could subject him to actual physical violence. Until this moment, when he realised clearly that but for the desk between them and the narrow space round it, this man, his face suffused with rage, would have struck him, he had done no more than glance lightly at the possibility.

Violence. Here in his office; here between walls which had hitherto heard nothing more violent than the views of clients whose holidays had not come up to their expectations.

Violence. Blows, bruises. Blood. The kind of scene he had not witnessed since his brother Dominic had stopped fighting Derek Arkwright, ten or more years ago.

Violence — from a stranger; violence against which he could put up no more than a token resistance.

Men, reflected Nicholas in the next tense ten seconds, ought to keep on their toes. He had done two years in the Army — but after that? A round or two of golf at the weekends, some fairly strenuous tennis in summer, some quick walks to work off the effects of too much food at a party, cold baths with a sly splash out of the hot tap to ensure that the chill wasn't too chilly — and what else? Nothing. None of that kept a man in the sort of trim he'd have to be in to ward off attack from anybody whose biceps bulged, billowed as healthily as Kenneth's. One light tap from that ham-like fist, clenched now at the end of an arm that was waving across the desk like an elephant's trunk, one tap and the fight — could you call it a fight? — would be over. He'd be laid out as flat as the hearth rug and as cold as the grate; Kenneth would go away and Miss Stocker would come in and apply restoratives.

He found himself getting to his feet. It was silly, he told himself; it would be much safer to remain sitting down. On the other hand, it would be nice, before the end came, to try and make a mark — just a little tiny mark — on Kenneth.

His vision cleared. He saw Kenneth Springer taking a deep, difficult breath and realised, with a feeling between relief and inexplicable regret, that the moment for violence had passed.

"All right." Kenneth was speaking thickly. "I'll deal with you later. Where's this Red House?"

"Anybody will direct you. You cross the market square and turn right. You pass a group of cottages and then there's open land. Beyond, you'll see chimneys above the trees. That's the Red House."

Kenneth had opened the door and was already striding through the outer office. Miss Stocker, getting up and closing the door he left swinging, turned and walked to Nicholas's open door.

"Was that Miss Morley's fiancé? The one she gave the push to?"

"That's the fellow."

Miss Stocker hesitated and then spoke slowly.

"If he's going round to the Red House, hadn't you better — "

She paused, and Nicholas finished the sentence.

" — be there? No. He won't see her alone. That is, not unless he first disposes of Julia, Derek, Joey Helyon, Luke Hayman, and Mrs. Bush."

Miss Stocker stared at him for some time with her mouth open.

"I see what you mean," she said at last, and went back to her desk.

CHAPTER IX

HAVING located the Red House, Kenneth Springer made several attempts to see Elaine alone, and then appeared to realise that, for the present, he had very little chance of breaking through the cordon that surrounded her. Nicholas, walking round at lunch time to see how matters stood, learned from an unlikely source that Kenneth had fallen in with somebody who, like himself, was waiting impatiently for the wedding to be over. As he passed Brett's garage, Charlie came out and greeted him.

"Mornin', Mr. Wayne."

"Good-morning, Charlie. I can't stop, I'm afraid; I'm on my way round to the Red House."

"I'll go with you," said Charlie affably, falling into step. "Not all the way; I 'ave to keep on the 'igh Street, where people can see me. Mr. Brett's let me orf until Monday to look after all these foreigners. Look" — he displayed a large cardboard badge on the lapel of his jacket — "I made it. It says 'Guide' — see?"

"And do all the foreigners know what a guide is?"

"Most of 'em seem to. I'm getting a lotta tips."

"I hope you're saving them."

"I 'aven't decided. Talking of tips, you know that chap Miss Morley chucked?"

"Sir Kenneth Springer?"

"Yeah. 'E's staying at Stenby — did you know that?"

"Yes. He told me. I'm afraid he won't be very comfortable."

"No tips from '*im*. Mean with money, 'e is. I shouldn't like to 'ave many financial dealin's with 'im. 'E brought that car of 'is into the garage just now." He sighed with pleasure. "Beautiful job it is; beau-ti-ful. Well, I went up to it to do the usual — you know, open the front, give the windscreen a wipe, and that. What does 'e do? 'E gets out of the car and gives me a push and says: 'You keep your filthy 'ands orf.' Well, I don't say my hands was clean, but there's ways and ways of tellin' a person so. I said so to 'im, and he said a lot back to me, and we was just gettin' worked up when Mr.

282

Brett came up. You could see 'e wasn't taken with the bloke, either, cos when 'e'd gone, 'e didn't say one word to me about givin' the customer any back-chat. 'Ow a girl like Miss Morley could've — "

"Well, don't let me keep you, Charlie."

" 'Arf a minute; I was just tellin' you. In the car with 'im was this Delphi."

Nicholas looked down in astonishment. "Who?"

"That Delphi. The fellows in the garage told me he'd just picked 'er up at the George. Twin spirits, they are — the only two people in this town who don't give tuppence for the wedding. They're at the George now, in the bar. You could've seen 'em if you'd been looking. They're just sittin' there looking gloomy; not sayin' anythin'; just sort of brooding."

Nicholas, turning off the High Street and leaving his informant behind, walked on with greatly relieved feelings to the Red House, there to discover that Kenneth Springer was not the only one who found it impossible to get a private word with Elaine.

The house seemed, he thought, irritation mounting in him, to be swarming with people. The guests had arrived and had been allocated to their rooms: Leopold's godmother in the quiet room on the first floor overlooking the garden; next door to her, her French companion. In the big double room overlooking the drive were Leopold's aunt, an Austrian, and her six-year-old son, whose name sounded like Toto.

On the floor above were Leopold, his brother and best man, Rudi, and an extremely stout man of about forty who begged to be called Francisco, claimed to be Leopold's oldest friend, announced in a garbled sentence that he was fluent in English, and showed no disposition to leave the house and his charming new friends Julia and Elaine.

"I don't see," Nicholas said angrily to Julia when he caught her for a moment alone in the kitchen, "why Elaine can't come home to lunch with me. Kenneth's out of the way, and she can't be so busy that she hasn't time to."

"Well, you can ask her," said Julia, "but you can see how it is."

"I thought you agreed to do bed and breakfast only."

"We agreed to look after the guests. If they don't want to have lunch at the George, and prefer sandwiches and coffee in the house, it's not much trouble to provide it. Luke and Derek want to stay, too. Why don't you? Lady Templeby left us a huge cooked ham — delicious."

Delicious or not, Nicholas did not want it. All he wanted, he explained tersely to his sister, was to see Elaine by herself.

"What about tonight?" he asked. "You can't be providing dinner for all this lot as well as lunch?"

"No. Lady Templeby's giving a buffet supper for all the guests. Tonight and tomorrow night."

"Tomorrow night is Leopold's bachelor party, and I've got to go to it."

She piled sandwiches on to plates and looked at him sympathetically.

"I'm sorry. I know how you feel. Come in to a scratch supper tonight and we'll try and push most people off to the Templeby party."

There was no time for more; Francisco had appeared with an offer of help. Nicholas, not in the mood for sandwiches and coffee and company, walked angrily back to the office, picked up his car and drove to Wood Mount.

"How," asked Miss Cornhill, "are the girls getting on?"

"The house looks like Victoria Station with the Golden Arrow just in," Nicholas told her. "An Italian godmother and a French companion and an Austrian widow with a small boy with a name like a poodle. And a fat fellow called Francisco. To say nothing of Luke Hayman and Derek Arkwright and Joey."

Miss Cornhill looked at his moody expression and found her opinion of Elaine Morley — already high — rising even higher. A girl who wanted a private word with a man could usually arrange to have one. But a girl who had found things moving a little too fast for her was wise to withdraw and sort out her feelings. About the feelings of the man sulkily pouring himself out some beer in the drawing-room nobody could be in any doubt; he had, she thought, the look that Long John used to wear when, having buried a particularly juicy bone, he had forgotten to mark the spot and could not locate it: bewilderment, anger, a sense of injury were all evident.

Simon and Dominic and Julia, all digging furiously in likely places, had never been able to restore Long John to his bone — and nobody could do anything now to help Nicholas on with his affair. He had got off to a flying start, with music and moonlight; now he was checked, and would have, like Kenneth Springer, to exercise patience.

At a small table in the overcrowded dining-room of the George, another man was sitting moodily over a meal. Joey Helyon was thinking about Miss Stocker, and thinking brought no solution to his problem. Something had gone wrong and he did not know how to put it right.

He rose impatiently from the table and, on an impulse, made his way to the office. If he put the matter to Nicholas, if he laid the whole case before him, Nicholas would tell him what could be done. Nicholas would give him good advice.

But Miss Stocker, looking up from her work, told him that Nicholas would be back late from lunch.

"He went to the Red House first," she explained, "so he didn't get to Wood Mount until nearly two."

"I'll wait," said Joey. But he did not

move from the desk. Staring down into Miss Stocker's upraised brown eyes, he spoke slowly and regretfully. "I don't know how it is," he said, "but something went wrong somewhere. Between me and you, I mean."

Miss Stocker took her fingers off the typewriter keys. The office was very quiet. Outside in the High Street, there was little traffic; the guests that would throng the street later were lingering over their after-lunch coffee at the George. Inside, the man and the woman looked at one another in silence, and in Joey's puzzled gaze, Miss Stocker read the bewilderment of a man who had meant no harm and who for once had come up against somebody who did not understand his free-speaking ways. Something had gone wrong, but Miss Stocker, who had learned early in life that things could not always go right, would have left it at that. In the stillness of the room, she realised for the first time that she had never learned the art of making friends — or she had never had the confidence to reach out and grasp the hand of friendship. She had taught herself to do without a great many things: money, a home, luxuries, and even comforts. And friends. Friends, she had decided a long time ago, were tricky; they might stick to you or they might not. In any case, they cost time and money.

She heard Joey speaking.

"I've been thinking," he said. "You and I . . . Well, we got off on the wrong foot."

Miss Stocker, wanting very much to make a warm reply, found herself speaking impassively.

"You, not me."

"Me, then. From the first, I wanted to make a good impression, and from the first, I didn't."

"That's right," agreed Miss Stocker.

"And I'm sorry, because . . ." Joey stopped and then plunged on. "Well, the fact is that when I came back to Greenhurst, I tried . . . I wanted to make a good impression." He put his hands on the desk and leaned on them. "Why do you think I came in to the office so often?"

"You wanted your work typed out."

"That was just by the way. Or perhaps it was that at first, if you want me to be honest. But afterwards. There was something about you I . . . well, what's the use of trying to explain? The long and the short of it is that I was scheduled to leave this town as soon as the wedding's over, and . . . well, frankly, I don't want to go."

"Why not?" enquired Miss Stocker in the most impersonal manner possible.

"Because . . . Well, it all came back to you, whichever way I thought about it. And what I've been thinking about was this: If I stayed on for a bit, and you got to know the other side of me, perhaps we . . . well, it struck me that we could make a match of it," ended Joey with a rush.

There was a long silence. Miss Stocker's face slowly darkened with suspicion.

"You haven't been drinking?" she asked.

"Drinking? No. And if I had, it would have been moderate drinking and it wouldn't have affected my head. I know what I'm saying and I never thought I'd hear myself saying it, and if I did, I didn't think I'd say it to anybody like you. I — "

"Why not?" enquired Miss Stocker so quietly that Joey was lured into fatal frankness.

"I thought of somebody young and — and sort of cuddly, if you follow me."

"I follow you. Go on."

"Somebody people could look at and understand what it was that bowled me over, if you know what I mean."

"Yes, I know what you mean."

Her brown, unblinking regard held nothing that could explain the sweat that was breaking out on his brow.

"But there was something about you that seemed to get me," he struggled on. "I couldn't make out at first what it was."

"Oh no?"

"No. I told myself that I ought to have my head examined. I told — "

"What for?"

"What for? Well, for . . ." Joey, for the first time seeing the precipice yawning at his feet, strove wildly to maintain his balance. "Well, there was I, a man who never thought he'd find himself wanting to settle down, picking on somebody who — "

"Who?"

" — somebody who didn't, at first, look like . . . look like . . ."

"Like?"

"I admired you, of course; right from the start. I said to myself: 'There's a woman you shouldn't take at her face value; a woman . . .'" Joey paused, took out a handkerchief and wiped his brow. "Beauty," he explained desperately, "is only skin deep, and . . . Look," he pleaded, "do I have to take the thing step by step? I saw you and if anybody'd told me that you'd ever get me into this state, I'd . . ."

"You'd — ?"

"I've said I want to marry you," ended Joey doggedly. "At this moment, the idea might not appeal to you. But if you take time, if you think it over, maybe you'd see some things about it that would paint me in a — in a more rosy hue, if you follow me. I'm not young, and you're not young; I'm nothing much to look at and . . . and as I said, if you think it over . . . Well, what d'you say?"

"The answer," said Miss Stocker without hesitation, "is no. Thank you for your offer, and thank you for all the nice things you said about me. I'm sorry your passion for my beauty got the better of you, but if *you* go away and think about it, maybe you'd see some things that would paint you in a less rosy hue, if you follow me."

"Look. In the whole of my life, I never once said to a woman what I've just said to you."

"Then you're lucky. If you had, you might have got your face slapped more often."

"I never had the gift of tongues. I put you up an honest offer and — "

" — and I'm giving you an honest reply. What woman would take you on? In the first place, you're a flitter."

"I'm a what?"

"You flit from here to there, and you don't often flit back again. You've got itchy feet. You haven't got a settled job. You're a man who spends half his life and all his spare time among men, in bars. You've lived for about twenty years on your own, without responsibilities, putting up at hotels where they do for you and leave you with all your spare time for amusement. When you get tired of one spot, you move on. You don't like the idea of a steady job; you like to be free. So now you can add it up: itchy feet, roving job, man's man, rounds of drinks, and half a lifetime of doing what you like where you like. For marriage, you need a steady job and a liking for your own fireside, with no hankering after the boys in the bar. For marriage with a woman like me, you need to stay permanently in Greenhurst, because that's where I'm going to be for the rest of my life. I've found a place I like and I'm going to stay in it, and the difference between you and me is that after twenty years of being on my own, I've grown to like it — and you've grown sick of it. Thank you for all those compliments you paid me, that brought the blushes to my cheek. Thank you for all that po-try you read out about my charms. Thank you for screwing yourself up to the point of overlooking my deficiencies and persuading yourself that I'd do as well as anybody else to carry up your cupper tea in the morning and make you a hot meal at night. Thank you for nothing."

She had risen. Too dazed to speak, he saw through mists of shame and self-hatred that she had gone to the hat-stand and had taken down her hat and put it on. She jerked her coat from its hook and walked with firm steps to the door and opened it and went out. The door closed behind her and he stood listening to the sound of her footsteps across the hall, down the three steps, along the High Street, fainter and fainter . . .

He was still standing there when Nicholas came in — and Nicholas, absorbed as he was in his own troubles, saw that the other man was looking totally unlike the Joey he knew.

"What's up, Joey?" he asked. Then something strange about the office penetrated his wandering mind. "Where's Miss Stocker?"

"Eh? Oh, she went."

"*Went?* Went where?"

"Home, I suppose. She got up and she put on that pudding basin she calls a hat, and she took down that pepper-and-mustard coat, and she walked out." He turned to face Nicholas. "I've done it, Nicholas boy; I've torn it up. I've wrecked it. I've dished it once and for all."

"Dished what?"

"I asked her to marry me."

Nicholas drew a deep breath.

"You . . . you *what?*"

"I asked her to marry me. Not marry me at once, but marry me later, when she'd had time to think about it. But I waded in out of my depth, and I got into rough water. I forgot that honesty's only all right in places. I was laying bare my little heart, but some of its secrets should've stayed under cover. I was being honest, and in some circumstances, Nicholas boy, honesty is only another name for stinking bad tactics. I hurt her — I hurt her badly. I wanted to tell her that I liked her flat, funny face and her bulging brown eyes and her hair done in that baker's bun. I was going to explain, when I got round to it, that in all my career, gazing through the lens at the world's most glamorous women, all I'd ever done was think about poses and highlights. It took B. Stocker and her homeliness to reach down and touch something in me that went right back to my own homely, happy beginnings. I was going to tell her that — but she walked out. And perhaps it was the Lord's own mercy, she did, because the next thing I was going on to say was that I wanted an anchor, and that a woman of her weight and solidity would make a ruddy fine one. She walked out. She . . . What did you say?"

Nicholas was looking at his watch.

"Ten to three," he repeated.

"I'm boring you?" asked Joey bitterly. "I'm taking up your time?"

"I said it was ten to three — and she walked out."

"I've told you — I hurt her feelings. I —"

"That wouldn't have made Miss Stocker walk out. If I know anything, she's been hurt before, and stuck it. She's always put her work first, as well as second and third, and her feelings are something she thinks of as strictly personal, to be kept hidden away and taken out after five o'clock, if necessary, to be examined or soothed or repaired. If she got up off that chair, leaving work undone, and walked out of this office, she did it without knowing she was doing it. Does that hold out any encouragement?"

"Not to me it doesn't. If she didn't walk out to spare her own feelings, she could have walked out to spare mine."

"You really" — Nicholas looked at him — "you really know what you're saying? What you're doing?"

"Of course I know. Do you think I haven't thought about it? I'm not a boy; I don't have to float round in a pink cloud for months just enjoying the sensation. I'm ready to settle, and I'd like to settle here, and I'd like to settle on Miss Beryl Stocker. If I'd had any sense, I'd have asked Julia to scratch me up a nice bit of poetry, and I'd have recited it instead of charging into it feet first and blowing the whole thing to hell. How could I *do* it, Nicholas boy? How could I stand here and say all those things I did say? Honesty? Insults. But that wasn't why she turned me down. It was on account of my itchy feet. Hop from bough to bough, she said I did, and from bar to bar — with the boys. If I'd hopped with the girls, I could've understood her attitude. But that's one charge she couldn't level at me; my feet never itched after women."

"I wouldn't take it as final if I were you, Joey. Would you like me to talk to her?"

Talk to her . . . What did one say? wondered Nicholas. If he did it well enough, he would lose the most efficient secretary he could ever hope to have. The office . . . without Miss Stocker . . .

Joey was speaking.

"No; leave it, Nicholas boy. I'll have to do it on my own." He opened the door and stood swinging it morosely. "I'll go and buy one of those Teach Yourself books:

Teach Yourself Courting. Lesson One: Don't be too honest." He looked at Nicholas. "What's wrong with honesty?"

"It's all right in business, Joey. In business, it's an asset, but — "

"Truth's truth, isn't it?"

"Of course. But when you're dealing with women — "

" — I should stick to embroidery. I get it."

He went out, but for the rest of the afternoon Miss Stocker did not come in. She did not telephone and she did not reappear; her absence and her silence added up to something so uncharacteristic of her normal changeless, calculable behaviour that he could only conclude that Joey's proposal had affected her more deeply than Joey could have hoped.

For the rest of the afternoon he ploughed doggedly through his own and Miss Stocker's work, irritation mounting steadily. When at last he had piled the letters up for the post and tidied the two desks, he was in a state in which he would have welcomed a visit from Kenneth Springer.

He decided to go home to Wood Mount;

going to the Red House would mean only a repetition of the morning's frustration. He would be able to see Elaine only over a sea of heads. There would be no hope of talking to her alone, no hope of even a word in private. All he could hope for — like Kenneth — was the departure of the wedding guests, the emptying of the town, the restoration of peace and normality — and the chance to talk to a girl alone.

He would go home.

But his car seemed of its own volition to deposit him at the door of the Red House — and once inside, his worst fears were realised. Joey, Luke, Derek, Jeff, and Roselle, Miriam and Leopold and Rudi were all comfortably established in the drawing-room, and with them was the adhesive Francisco.

"Has it," asked Nicholas moodily, following Julia into the kitchen, "has it been like this all the afternoon?"

"Has what been like what?"

"This house — like an annexe of the George."

"It's been fun. The George is terribly crowded, and so Luke has been coming over here. Derek's driving his mother around, but he's coming along here for dinner. We're going to have a sort of picnic meal; I hope you won't mind."

"Don't worry about me. Is all that lot staying?"

"No. Why are you cross?"

"Who's cross?"

"You are. You're as mad as mad, and if it's because you can't talk quietly to Elaine, you oughtn't to be worrying. This job has been a godsend; she's enjoying it, she feels she's being useful, she's getting to know people and she doesn't feel in the way any more. She's happy, and you ought to be happy that she's happy. And here she is. Elaine," she continued, "I've just been telling Nicholas that you're happy. You are, aren't you?"

Elaine, with a glance at Nicholas's far from happy face, said tranquilly that she was.

"I came out for some water and some more glasses," she added.

Nicholas got them for her.

"There's news of Kenneth," he said. "He's filling in his time with Delphi, so he'll probably be out of the way until the wedding's over. He's bored and she's bored, so they've, so to speak, gravitated towards one another."

And you'd think, he told himself angrily, that Kenneth was some stranger in whom she hadn't the faintest interest. She couldn't even stop to ask for more details. She'd smiled — and gone back to the drawing-room.

He followed her, to find everybody but Luke and Francisco on the point of leaving. When the others had gone, he walked over to Francisco and tried a little prising.

"Aren't you," he asked him, when delicate hints had fallen, unheeded or unnoticed, round the fat, genial form, "aren't you expected at Lady Templeby's?"

"It is a choice, she told me: go, don't go," said Francisco. "I don't go."

"That's a pity, in a way," said Nicholas. "It's a beautiful house, and the grounds are magnificent."

"At the wedding I see them."

"You're not interested, by any chance," asked Nicholas, "in English inns?"

Francisco pondered.

"No," he said. "Not."

"The George is very old, and some of

the beams are the original ones dating from — "

"Beans ?"

"Beams."

"No, I am not interested in beams. You are very kind."

"If you want a lift anywhere, I'll be only too glad to take you."

"A lift ? Oh, in a car ? Thank you. Not."

Nicholas, walking into the dining-room to watch Elaine laying out food on the table, announced total failure.

"If you want him out, you'll have to blow him out," he said. "Want me to carve ?"

"Yes, please. Don't be too liberal. Who's left in the drawing-room ?"

"Julia and Luke and that Francisco."

"Well, Derek's coming back. Will you put an extra plate out for him ?"

Nicholas, putting out an extra plate, doled out thin slices of cold tongue and cold beef, and took the precaution of making himself a thick sandwich and eating it as he worked.

"Don't go hungry," said Elaine, watching him. "We'll all make do on what you don't want."

He stared at her across the table, sandwich in hand and an irritated frown on his face.

"Do you realise," he said, "that I've been trying to talk to you — talk to you alone — for the whole day?"

"Yes," she said tranquilly. "I've been rather wanting to talk to you alone, too. But it'll have to wait."

"I'm glad you can take it so calmly. Myself, I would have said that we left one or two matters outstanding last night."

"That's what I would have said, too. Would you put some ham out on all the plates?"

He took the ham from her and began to lift the thin pink slices on to a fork and drop them beside the slices of beef.

"Don't you," he asked, "want to talk about anything? About you? About me?"

She turned to face him and spoke quietly.

"There's quite a lot to say," she said, "but at the moment, there are quite a lot of things to do. I've got problems, and I'm thinking about them — but for the next two or three days, they'll have to take second place because I've undertaken to do a small job in this house, and I'm doing it. And it's fun, and I'm grateful."

He said nothing. A fusillade on the front door had announced the re-arrival of Derek, and with his entrance, those in the drawing-room began to make a move towards the dining-room.

Julia seated them and counted heads and plates.

"Luke hasn't come in," she told Nicholas. "Go and tell him to hurry."

Nicholas went out of the dining-room, closing the door angrily on the buzz of talk. In the drawing-room he saw Luke standing staring out of one of the long windows, and spoke to him briefly.

"Ham and beef next door. Unless you'd rather have another drink first. I'm going to."

Luke did not turn.

"No, thanks. I think I'll just get on," he said.

"Well, there's no need. There's enough to eat. At least, almost enough."

"If you ask me," came over Luke's shoulder, "the place is too overcrowded as it is."

This remark, which Nicholas took to be

a friendly comment on his own difficulties, warmed him a little.

"You're right," he said. "You try to get a girl alone and — "

" — and you can't." Luke swung round and broke into rapid and impassioned speech. "You said it. You just can't. Nearly two weeks. For nearly two whole weeks I've been trying it, and as you said — it's impossible. It's like . . . like chasing rainbows. You can quote it, even if it sounds corny. Rainbows — or wild geese. But I've hung on. If I'd been a guy with any pride, I'd have read the signs and moved on — but you go on hoping, don't you ? Don't you ? My job with Joey's done; for the present, he doesn't want me any more. I can go — but I don't. I thought you didn't know why — but I'm glad you do. Until you said that just now, I was afraid you were just waiting to tell me it was no good and I'd better get out. But I'm still here, because I still don't know what's in that Arkwright's mind, if he's got a mind. Back home, I guess I'd know how to make him come out into the open — or get right out and stay out. But how do you ever know what the English are thinking? Does he love Julia the way I do? If he doesn't, why does he keep on hanging round her? If he doesn't, why is it that every single time I've tried to get her alone, he's materialised out of the air and hung on just the way this Francisco hangs on — freezes on? If I knew for certain whether he was after Julia, too, I'd be able to figure out a plan of action — but what does he do? He just does this known-the-girl-all-my-life stuff, and hobbles round on his good foot, and sticks. Sticks and sticks. He — "

Only one word came out of the confusion in Nicholas's mind.

"Derek?"

"*You* know him. Do *you* know what he's thinking? *Do* you?"

"I . . . Me?" Nicholas pulled himself together. "I don't know what anybody's thinking. And I don't quite follow you — "

"*He* does," said Luke bitterly. "Oh, he sure does! If I've ever got Julia with me, you can bet he's around too. If I hear breathing, I know for sure, without looking round, who's showed up."

"You mean you . . ."

"I mean I'd like to go after your sister,

if it's all the same to you. I mean I'm in love with your sister Julia. I mean that I've been trying to tell her so, just to get her reactions, ever since I saw her. And ever since I saw her, I've had to have this Arkwright in the picture, too."

"But . . . but Derek's been one of the family for — "

"Oh, sure, sure. The guy next door. Well, if you want to know, I'm sick of him. I asked Julia if he'd staked a claim or anything, and she said no, he hadn't. Well, if he hasn't, he ought to get the hell out of it and give other guys a chance."

"Then why don't you tell him so?"

"Because you said it just now: one of the family. Say one word against him, and she goes up right through the chimney. So I keep quiet, hoping he'll break the other leg and have to stay home for awhile — and time's going, and soon I'm going, and how do I know what chance I'd ever have? How do I find out? How . . ." He paused. "I suppose you think I'm crazy? I suppose you think that before I make up my mind I'm in love, I have to go away and think about it? Well, I don't have to. I saw her at the airport and I watched her.

I said to myself: 'That's the kind of girl your mother prays you'll bring home one day' — but you never do because some lucky guy's got there first and taken her home to *his* mother. I'm twenty-three; money, lots of it; a job. Steady and mostly sober. And I'd like to stay right here in Greenhurst and try to get Julia to marry me — and this minute, I don't think it's one damn bit of good." He paused once more, his eyes meeting Nicholas's in sudden, desperate young appeal. "Do you know any way . . ."

Nicholas said nothing. His eyes had dropped from Luke's unhappy face to the framed photograph that stood on the desk before him. Twenty-three, and in love.

Thirty-two . . . and in love?

The room, the framed likeness, the young man standing at the other end of the room faded from his mind. He seemed to himself to be floating on something that might be a sea of time, upheld, suspended, pictures coming and going with sharpness and clarity before him. E for Elaine. E for Estelle and e for emotion and e for ephemeral episode; for ember, for end. For exit. For error? No. Dimly he saw the man across the room, and remembered that he was called Luke and remembered that he was in love — with Julia. He could feel, somewhere deep down within him, some of the old agony of doubt, of fear; he could feel the scar, but now he could probe without pain. E for ecstasy — or for echo. E for Elaine — and for exchange. And, of course, for experience. Luke, twenty-three and in love. Himself, thirty-two and in love — once more. Between himself and the other man, ten years and the knowledge that if there was pain, it would pass; if there was loss, it would one day be unremembered.

He came back to the present and felt Luke's eyes on him.

"I can't help you," he said. "I don't know what's in Julia's mind. Up to this moment, I've never given a thought to — to anything of this kind in connection with her."

"You're her brother; I forgot." Luke's voice held hopelessness. "But is this Derek guy after her?"

"I can't even answer that." And then, as Luke seemed to lose himself in an unhappy dream, he recalled him. "I think it would be as well if we went along and had this so-called dinner."

He sat at table almost as silent as Luke and Derek; if he had had thought to spare for Francisco, he would have been grateful to him for his blissful unawareness, his anxiety to talk and to keep on talking. But he himself was thinking of Julia; a glance or two showed him that she seemed oblivious to the silence of Luke and Derek. She was listening to Francisco, her eyes amused, her tongue giving assistance when Francisco's sentences became too involved.

Did she know what she was doing? Nicholas wondered. Did girls know what they put men through? Some girls did, of course — but what about the Julias? Did she know that Luke was in a state of misery and frustration? And Derek: why hadn't he looked at Derek before? Well, he had — but seeing something or somebody constantly made one blind to the fact that they might be changing, developing. But then again, the blindness didn't seem general; if Derek hadn't observed changes in Julia, he wouldn't be sitting here now looking determined to outstay, to outlast Luke Hayman.

And how much had Julia changed? He ought to be able to see her, since Luke's outburst, at least from a more detached point of view. A nice girl — a girl with something about her that had made her, in Greenhurst, beloved beyond all the other Waynes. But that was a general liking; there had been nothing so far, it seemed to him, to cause anybody to think that she could make two attractive and eligible men sit glowering at one another across a table. Had she really changed so much? Take a look; a long clear, steady look. Slender figure; some people would say no figure at all. Small nose, large mouth, and eyes you didn't notice until you talked to her, when you couldn't help being struck by the way they seemed to express everything she was saying. Red hair done in the silly way girls did their hair today; it suited her — but apart from all this, one had to face the fact that beside Elaine Morley, Julia looked . . . he searched for a word, and settled on homespun. Not homely; certainly not homely in the American sense — but in his opinion, a girl he wouldn't have said possessed any quality that could drive a sane young man like Luke Hayman into the state he had been in in the drawing-room.

He was glad when the meal ended. When they all rose from the table, Francisco, who came from a country in which the servant problem was not pressing, ignored the litter and proposed a drive. It was a good night, he pointed out; there was a moon; they would drive. Who would drive?

Who would wash up? countered Julia. He and Elaine would see to it, promised Nicholas, and he and Elaine watched the others going out to Derek's car. Francisco's politeness did not permit a lady to sit beside the chauffeur; he handed Julia in beside Luke, and shut himself in firmly beside Derek.

"Nice drive they'll have," Elaine commented, as the car went out of sight, and there was a dry note in her voice that brought Nicholas's eyes round to study her.

"You didn't have any brothers, did you?" he asked.

"If you don't count Kenneth . . . no. But if I'd had brothers, they wouldn't have been able to see me in the right light any more than you're able to see Julia."

"Are you going to tell me that you knew what was going on?"

"Of course. Come in off the front doorstep. I don't trust you on front doorsteps. I'll wash and you can dry."

"I'd rather wash."

"Too bad; some other time." Her tone was abrupt, and he stared at her in surprise.

"You wouldn't," he asked, "be pushing me around?"

"All through dinner," she said, beginning to clear the sideboard with swift, angry movements, "you've been peering through your eyelashes at Julia and deciding that Luke and Derek must be suffering from some kind of sex-starvation. Haven't you?"

"No, I haven't. All I — "

"You have. I saw your conclusions on your face. You peered and you peered, and then you got a sort of hopeless look, because you'd decided that Julia really had nothing that anybody could see that would account for any man's falling for her."

"Well, if I did, it's merely because I'm her brother."

"No, it isn't," said Elaine. "It's simply because you're you."

There was a note of exasperation in her voice. He paused in his absent-minded clearing of the table and stared at her.

"Why the tone?" he enquired. "Are you angry about something?"

"No, I'm not angry. Why should I be angry just because a man I don't know has an outlook that won't stretch? Are you going to finish clearing the things, or shall I do it?"

He caught her arm as she made a move towards the kitchen, and holding it, spoke slowly.

"The table can wait," he said. "So can the washing up. So can the drying up. You said — "

She drew her arm away, walked into the kitchen and began to wash the dishes and plates. After a moment, Nicholas finished clearing the table and followed with a laden tray.

"Tell me," said Elaine, after a strained silence, in the tone of one determined to make polite conversation, "about Julia's music. She isn't going to take it up?"

"No. You feel" — his tone was as distant as hers — "you feel she should?"

"If she's decided and Monsieur Moulin

has decided, that's enough, isn't it? You'll find another cloth in that drawer."

He took it out in silence. Two shocks in one evening, he decided morosely, were two shocks too much. Julia emerging as a man-killer, and this girl, who before her unheralded arrival had never so much as set eyes on the Wayne family — you couldn't count the airport — beginning to air her views about them all. To accuse him, without the slightest justification, of having a narrow outlook . . . .

"Where do the clean plates go?" he enquired coldly.

"Big ones there, small ones on the shelves behind you. Any more things in the dining-room?"

"Nothing to be washed."

The work was finished in silence. She dried her hands, hung up the cloths and then led the way out of the kitchen and into the hall.

"Well, thanks for the help," she said. "I think I'll go up to bed now; I'm rather tired."

"Then I'll say good-night." He was walking towards the drawing-room, his feelings chaotic, but anger beginning to predominate. He had wanted, above all else, to talk to her. Well, he was talking. He had longed, with a longing that had shaken him, to see her alone. Well, here they were — alone. Just he and she. They were alone, and they were talking. And she had said plenty. Narrow outlook . . . Well, if she thought that she could turn him out of a house whose owners he had known since he was born, she could think again. "I'll just have a drink and a cigarette before I go. Don't bother about me; I know where the drinks are kept."

He walked into the drawing-room and stood staring unseeingly at the carpet, misery beginning to oust anger from his mind. Coldness and anger — was it for these that he had worked throughout the long day? What had gone wrong?

His eyes went to the photograph of Estelle Dryden, and he walked up to the desk and picked up the photograph and stared at it thoughtfully. And then he heard a sound, and turned to find Elaine at the door.

"I came to tell you," she said quietly, "that one of my many failings is to open my mouth too wide. While it's open, things come out of it that I don't always mean. I'm sorry."

"There's nothing to be sorry about." He paused to replace the photograph on the desk. "If you find me as blind as a bat to my sister's charms, and with a small-town outlook, there's no reason — "

" — why I shouldn't say so? Some reasons," she corrected. "Politeness, gratitude for what you've done for me, and the fact that I don't know any of you well enough yet to say what I said. I'm not usually outspoken to the point of rudeness. I think perhaps I've been sitting on things too long. Remember that I've only just finished clearing out an assortment of things that have been building up in my mind for years and years. Having seen the light in one direction, I suppose it annoys me to watch you writing off an attractive girl like Julia just because . . ." She pulled herself up. "Don't start me off again," she warned him.

"Drink?" he asked.

"Yes, please. Something long and cool. I need it. Something lemony, with a lot of water and some ice. I'll get the ice."

"No; stay here. I'll get it."

"Why don't you sit down?" he asked, when he returned.

"No; it's getting late."

"You can't go to bed until you've told me why I've got such a narrow outlook."

"Can't you forget that?"

"No. Nobody's ever said it before. I told you why I didn't get out of this town. I — "

"It's got nothing to do with getting out or staying in any town. It's just a matter of . . . of development."

"I see. I'm an arrested type?"

She stared at him across the desk that was between them.

"You're trying to make me angry," she said.

"That's right." His voice was cool. "Then you'll have another outburst and I shall hear more about the Waynes. How did you size up Roselle and Jeff? You saw them — didn't you — for a few minutes?"

"Look" — she put down her unfinished drink and turned to the door. "I think I'll — "

"Don't go. You have such interesting views on everything. And everybody."

She turned, and he wondered whether

he would have taken back the words if he could — and decided not. A girl couldn't throw an accusation at a man and stroll away. She had to . . . well, she ought to explain it or retract it. There was no need for her to stand there looking as though he'd been the one to start all this off.

"I find you," she said levelly — too levelly — "rather boring."

"You don't look bored."

"The reason I said you had a narrow outlook was because you've got a narrow outlook."

"That's as good an explanation as any," he said.

"I feel grateful to you because you've been kind, but you must know as well as everybody else that people from the outside see a different picture and perhaps a truer picture."

"Onlookers and the game? Quite so. I'm only sorry we weren't all here — Lucille and Simon and Dominic; you could have seen us as a whole, and made a report."

"I didn't mean that you were narrow in outlook. What I said, or meant to say, was that in the short time I've been here, two facts have been sticking out so far, so high, so clearly that nobody could have helped seeing them."

"One was?"

"One was the fact that your sister Julia is devastatingly attractive."

"Julia?"

"You see? You don't even *know*! Every time anybody mentions her — anybody new like me — you tell them the old, old story: red stringy hair, freckles and all the rest of it. That's *gone*! That's the past, and it's dead. That was one of the stages of development, and what you don't see, and what you should see if your opinions or your advice is to have any value for her, is that she has turned into a girl who can . . . who can lay men out in rows. She isn't pretty; perhaps she isn't even good-looking in the conventional sense. I saw you looking from her to me tonight, and you said, as clearly as though you'd said it aloud, that it was a pity she didn't have my hair or my eyes or my skin. Or my figure. All you saw was what she didn't have. What you don't seem able to see — and why should I let it worry me? What do *I* care? — is what she *has* got: a sort of slender, supple figure and a way of moving that makes you think of shy young animals in woods. A small face, ridiculous nose, a lovely, lovely mouth and hair that's a delicate kind of auburn I've never seen before. And eyes . . . if she had nothing else to draw people, can't you see what beautiful eyes she's got? When she talks, they're like . . . like mirrors; you can see reflected in them everything she's saying. The first time I saw Luke Hayman look at her, I knew how he felt about her. Derek Arkwright feels that way, too. But you don't know. You think Derek's filling in time with Julia until her brother Dominic comes home, and making things difficult for Luke Hayman. Of course he's making things difficult for Luke Hayman! He hates Luke Hayman, and Luke Hayman hates him, and what worries me is to watch you watching them — and seeing nothing. Until tonight, when I suppose Luke said something to you in this room, you hadn't the faintest idea that anything was going on."

"And everybody else in Greenhurst had, I suppose?"

"Almost everybody. Joey Helyon. The people at the George; they've been laying bets. Jeff and your sister Roselle know. And I'm pretty certain that your Miss Cornhill has a pretty shrewd idea."

"It's odd — isn't it? — that not one of them has — "

" — said anything to you? No, it isn't odd. Jeff's probably holding Roselle back because he wants to see how long it'll take you to realise that the Julia you see doesn't exist any more — except perhaps underneath. Miss Cornhill feels she isn't in a position to point out something you ought to be seeing for yourself. If you were a parent, one wouldn't be surprised; parents are older, and some sort of instinct — an instinct, perhaps, to put off counting the years — makes them fundamentally unable to realise that their children have changed or developed or grown up. They're usually shocked into seeing it. But you're not a parent; you're young enough to be able to notice that two young men have been sticking close to your sister ever since she came back from Italy; you ought to be alive enough to be asking yourself why. And so . . ." She stopped abruptly. "And that's all, and I'm sorry, and I shouldn't have said any of it, but you brought it on yourself by making me angry, and now if you don't mind, I'll go upstairs to bed."

"One moment."

There was a calm, authoritative note in his voice that made her pause and turn on her way out of the room.

"I'm tired," she said.

"You must be." His tone was dry. "But you mentioned two points; you've only dealt with one. They were both sticking out — you remember? — far and high and clear."

"You won't goad me into talking too much again, if that's what you're trying to do. The second point is . . . none of my business. Julia was different; I've spent some time with her and I've got some grounds for saying what I did. And don't run away with the idea that I go round giving out unwanted opinions about the people I run across. If I hadn't happened to like you and your sister, if I hadn't happened to get interested in your family, I wouldn't have spent two minutes thinking about any of you. Liking you all and being interested in you all didn't give me the right to say what I did just now — but you insisted."

"And point two? Perhaps you'll let me tell you what point two was? It wouldn't be — would it? — the fact that you feel I've clung too long to an old love?"

Her gaze was cold.

"If you've clung, didn't I say it was your own affair?"

"You feel that ten years is a . . . shall we say a long time?"

"Too long for clinging."

"Perhaps the fact that I lost my head the other night made you feel that I was suffering from — what was the term you used — sex-starvation? It might interest you to know that it wasn't the first time in ten years that I held a girl in my arms and kissed her."

"It doesn't interest me to know."

"When you fall in love," said Nicholas, "you perhaps choose — at twenty-two — a woman who represents some kind of ideal. If you lose her, perhaps you go on looking for something in other women that she had, or that you thought she had. If you don't find it, perhaps you're entitled to tell yourself that you might find it one day — if you wait. If that's a narrow outlook, it must be a pretty general one among men.

To fall into the arms of the next woman who comes along . . . that might be a solution, but I never felt it was a permanent one. Not to want to spend too much time in this house, in this room, because it happened to bring up certain memories I wasn't too keen to revive . . . that might be narrow, too, but perhaps it's also natural. And it's also natural, when you come to think of it, which of course you haven't time to do, that if a man conducts a love affair under the eyes of a town in which every inhabitant knows him and his family well, he can't exactly put the whole thing behind him and cover it with a decent veil. People don't like it. People prefer the popular idea of loving for ever. They — "

" — put you in the part and you had to go on playing it ?"

"By no means. But to this day, if a stranger's in a shop I happen to go into, I know what he's told about me — or what she's told about me. I see kindly glances; sympathetic glances. The old tale — and the veil lifted again and again and again. That's something that wouldn't have occurred to you in your snap-summary of us all."

"And so when you took these women in your arms and kissed them during the last ten years — what was that? Trying them for size? Testing your reactions to see if they were as potent as the ones Estelle Dryden aroused in you? Or was it just keeping your hormones active so's they wouldn't get rusty with disuse? Or was it a sort of test of this dedication: a watch-me-and-see-if-I'm-disloyal-to-my-ideal love?" She came a step nearer. "Ten years," she said slowly. "Ten years in the life of a young man . . . just remembering. Perhaps I'm wrong; perhaps I've got no finer feelings; perhaps I haven't got a proper spirit of . . . of dedication. But in my opinion, you've lost ten good years of good, clean, full, progressive living. Look at you! You're tall and strong and so good-looking that when I think of those girls — those other girls — who had the brief pleasure of being pressed to your faithful heart, I wonder how you managed to detach their clinging arms. You lost a girl you loved; too bad. It must have been hell, and I'm sorry. I'm not so insensitive that I can't imagine a little of how it felt. But you loved and you lost and you had to go on living. You had to realise that things didn't stop just because the girl you wanted, the girl you could have married and lived happily with, married somebody else. You should have seen, years and years ago, the danger you were in: a small town you'd lived in all your life, where people would do their best to spare your feelings by never mentioning Estelle Dryden's name out loud, but where every street, every shop held some memory, however slight, of her presence; where people began to point you out, after a time, as a man immune from the usual allure of women because you were keeping a flame alight in your heart. Well, keep it. Don't, whatever you do, let it go out. Don't give any other woman a chance of marrying you and having nice, tall, strong, handsome children by you."

She came to a breathless halt. They faced one another, flushed, their eyes full of anger and outrage, the silence lengthening between them.

"Anything else?" enquired Nicholas coldly at last.

"Nothing whatsoever." She went to the door. "It was a good friendship while it lasted, wasn't it? So interestingly begun — and so brief. You can draw a line under it now; it's over."

The door crashed behind her, rattling the ornaments in the room. The sound stilled and silence fell, and he stood unmoving and heard the crash of her bedroom door, and then there was nothing to listen to but the echo of her words in the room. It was over.

He went quietly out of the house and drove himself home. He stopped the car outside Wood Mount, but he made no move to get out. His elbows on the wheel, his eyes fixed unseeingly ahead, he sat — he could not have told how long.

And then he switched on the engine, turned the car and drove back to the Red House.

He walked up the steps, opened the front door, walked unhesitatingly up two flights of stairs and knocked on Elaine's door.

It opened and she stood before him. She had not begun to undress, and he saw that she had been crying.

"I came back to say just one thing," he said. "You're as blind as I've ever been. I love you. I've loved you since I held you in my arms — "

"Please!" She broke into his firmly-delivered speech, her low tone enjoining silence. "Julia isn't back, but . . . but the others are. They're in their rooms and . . ."

They were not, Nicholas saw, in their rooms. The godmother, the French companion, Toto and his mother were on the staircase, their necks craned upward. Francisco's door was open and his head was showing round it. Leopold and Rudi appeared and stood rooted. There was a dead, expectant hush.

"As I was saying, I love you," said Nicholas. "If you'd stay on in Greenhurst and try to get over your first unfavourable impressions of me, I'd like you to marry me. I love you with all my heart, and the only reason I was holding that photograph tonight was to thank Estelle Dryden — and to say good-bye. I love you. I — "

"Hush. Oh, please . . . hush," implored Elaine.

"I love you." He took a step forward and drew her firmly into his firms. "I love you, Elaine. I love you very much. I — "

Tears were pouring down her face, but her arms, he noted, with a tremor that shook his whole body, were creeping round his neck. She was close to him, clinging to him.

"I love you," he said.

"Hush, oh hush . . ."

He brought his lips down gently, firmly on her mouth, and kept them there. From around, there came the sound of long, satisfied sighs, following by the sound of gently closing doors. When Nicholas at last raised his head, he saw that they were alone.

He was never afterwards able to recall how he got back to Wood Mount. He found himself in the hall; in a daze, he shut and bolted the front door. As he did so, the door of Miss Cornhill's sitting-room opened and she came out, switching off the light behind her, a book under her arm to take up to her room. For a moment she stood still, looking at him, and he wondered whether his state of mind showed on his face. If it did, he mused, she would soon be reaching for the sedatives.

He addressed her almost absently, his hand still on the heavy chain of the door.

"Would you say," he asked quietly and evenly, "that Julia was . . . devastating?"

Miss Cornhill's face kept its habitual look of calm.

"She changed a lot in Rome," she said after a brief, thoughtful pause. "She has grown very attractive."

"And have you noticed a couple of young men who've noticed that?"

"Most people," said Miss Cornhill calmly, "have noticed it."

"I see. And would you say that for ten years, I've been moving around draped in sackcloth?"

"You have given," said Miss Cornhill judicially, "less attention to young women than most men of your age." She frowned. "You haven't been . . . drinking?"

"Yes. Yes, I have, as a matter of fact. One small whisky. Come to think of it," he added thoughtfully, "I didn't finish it. I . . . I put it down and . . . and forgot it."

"Well, I'll say good-night." Miss Cornhill turned and had gone up three stairs when he stopped her, standing and looking up at her.

"Would you say," he asked, "that I was exceptionally obtuse?"

Miss Cornhill studied him for a few moments.

"Do you remember what Alice said to the Queen?" she asked.

"Frankly, I don't. What did Alice say to the Queen?"

"She said that she couldn't believe impossible things."

"Then I sympathise with Alice. I'm finding it hard — very, very hard — to believe impossible things. What did the Queen say to Alice?"

"The Queen said that Alice hadn't had much practice; then she went on to say that she herself always practised for half an hour a day, and sometimes she had believed as many as six impossible things before breakfast. Is that all?"

"Not quite all," said Nicholas. "Since you've got on to Alice, you can tell me that other bit — about the Cheshire Cat. Didn't the Cheshire Cat disappear?"

"It did. It vanished quite slowly," Miss Cornhill reminded him. "Beginning with the end of the tail, and ending with the grin."

"That's it." Nicholas's gaze went absently to a point past her head and seemed to be riveted there. "That's all. It vanished quite slowly. It took about ten years to vanish."

Miss Cornhill had gone on up the stairs; she turned at the top and looked back.

"And if you remember," she said, "the grin remained some time after the rest of it had gone."

Nicholas was left in the empty hall, but he did not move.

"That's right," he said aloud at last. "The grin remained."

CHAPTER X

NICHOLAS left the house early the next morning, but he did not go straight to the office. His first call was to the florist, his second to the Red House; it was not a prolonged call, but it was a satisfactory one. Everything that there was to be said had been said last night, and he had no doubt that a number of foreign ears had been glued to bedroom doors, listening to every word. If he had to talk to Elaine while she and Julia prepared breakfasts, laid them on trays, and handed them to him to carry upstairs, he did not much mind.

It was not until he at last announced, reluctantly, that he had to go to the office, that Elaine gave him a piece of news.

"About Luke," she said, wiping her hands on her apron and looking at him from her place beside the stove. "He's gone."

There was a short silence.

"When?" he asked.

"Last night. At Templeby. Julia took him outside because he wanted to see the lake, and he plunged — into a proposal."

She paused.

"And she doesn't want to marry him?" asked Nicholas.

"No. She likes him, and that's all."

"Was she upset?"

"A bit. I told her that the time to worry was when they went away without proposing."

Nicholas went thoughtfully away. He knew what Luke must be feeling — but for Julia, there would be little time for regrets; this afternoon, Lucille and Robert were to arrive from London, and driving down with them was Dominic. Without Simon, it would not be a complete family reunion, but Dominic would claim a good share of Julia's attention.

There was one more call to be paid before he went to the office. He stopped his car outside the George and went in to find Joey.

Joey was in the dining-room, a sparse breakfast before him. He greeted Nicholas soberly.

"Glad you came in," he said. "I was wanting to talk to you."

"Well, I want to talk to you," said

Nicholas. "About Miss Stocker. Having cleared up my own affairs, I'm now at liberty to clear up yours."

"Clear up? I was just sitting here," said Joey, "thinking that the best thing I could do was clear out — like Luke'"

"I'm sorry about Luke."

"So'm I. He wasn't a chap who got bowled over easily."

"Where has he gone?"

"London. If Delphi'd known in time, she'd have gone with him — but he didn't stop to ask her." He raised worried eyes to Nicholas's. "If I went along to the office — " he began.

"Not this morning. This afternoon. I won't be there, because I want to be at Wood Mount when Lucille and Robert and Dominic arrive. They're lunching on the way down and they ought to be here about three. So I probably won't hurry back to the office after lunch. If I were you, I'd look in."

"That's what I did before — look in. And look what happened."

"Go in behind a screen of expensive flowers, and say what you've got to say from behind it."

"Flowers!" Joey's face brightened. "Now, why didn't I think of flowers?"

Nicholas thought, sadly, that the answer was that people did not often think of flowers in connection with Miss Stocker. They thought of less flowery matters: efficiency, loyalty, good hard work and an untiring attention to detail. But not flowers.

"What'll I say to her?" asked Joey.

"The only thing you can say is that you're a heavy-footed idiot, but you love her and want to marry her. Leave it at that. You talked too much before; this time, let her do the talking."

"Can you," asked Joey solemnly, "see me as a married man?"

"Why not? I hope she'll have you."

Joey signalled to the waiter for an extra cup and poured Nicholas some coffee.

"I never," he said slowly, handing it to him, "wanted to be single all my life. I've got an idea that after a certain age — about forty, to be exact — a bachelor stops being a confirmed bachelor and becomes a confirmed spinster. I wanted to settle down, but I'm not a man who'd suit everybody. There was something about Miss Stocker

— Beryl — that made me think she'd do. She was plain and down-to-earth and — "

"There you go again."

"There I go again."

Nicholas drained his cup and rose.

"I've got to go. Remember — a thousand bunches of the most expensive flowers they've got in the shop. And good luck."

He went to the office and found Miss Stocker looking — except for a certain pallor — exactly as she had looked for the last six years.

"I'm sorry about leaving early yesterday," she said, as he entered the room. "I had a headache."

And the headache, thought Nicholas, as he uttered his sympathy aloud, was coming back this afternoon — with flowers.

He could not bring anything like concentration to his work, and after ringing up Elaine several times and ascertaining that her feeling for him was unchanged, he decided to go home to lunch. He telephoned to Elaine once more, to ask her to accompany him.

"You ought to be there when they arrive," he urged. "This is my family — you've got to meet them."

"Later," she said. "In the first place, Julia isn't here and I'd like to stay. In the second place, I'd like to meet your family after you've had time to give them a few explanations."

"Well, I'll see you in a few minutes, when I call round to take Julia home."

"You won't have to call. Derek came in an hour ago and drove her to your house. He's having lunch there, to be on hand when Dominic arrives. Now will you go home and stop wrecking my morning with phone calls?"

He went home and ate lunch with, for once, no interest in food. Afterwards, Miss Cornhill found his restless pacing too much even for her calm nerves, and as a telephone call from Joey reporting a moderate success did little to distract him, she suggested that he should go out into the garden and do some weeding.

From the drawing-room window, Julia watched him, smiling.

"It's nice to see him happy," she said to Derek. "Gosh! we've got a lot to tell Dominic?"

Derek made no reply. He was staring up at the curtain hooks, one of which had detached itself from its ring and was hanging loose.

"Can you fix it?" Julia said.

"Yes. If you hold this chair on this table I think I can get up high enough."

She held it and he clambered up and then stood upright, groping and finding the hook and pushing it back into its ring. But Julia, his feet just above her head, was regarding the bandaged one compassionately and failed to note the exact moment of Derek's descent. There was an ominous swaying of the chair, a warning cry from Julia, and then he had leapt down, just in time to avoid the fall of the table, and had landed lightly on his feet and was coming towards her to take the table down again, laughing at her look of alarm.

And then he halted, and the look on Julia's face changed and the alarm gave way to something else.

There were some moments of dead silence. The clock gave its loud, relentless, steady beat and Julia remembered nights on which she had opened her bedroom door in order to be able to hear it, and had lain awake with a difficult passage going again and again through her mind to the metronome background of the clock. She was waiting now for a sound that did not come. Derek's lips were closed and looked as though nothing would ever part them again.

She was staring at him, and then her eyes travelled downwards until they rested on the thick bandages round his ankle.

"Your . . . your foot," she said

He said nothing. She glanced up at his face, trying to read its expression, but Derek, like Dominic, could present a blank face when he wished to.

"Your foot," she said again, and this time the dazed note had left her voice. Realisation was coming, and found expression. "There's . . . nothing the matter with it. It's . . . it's all right. Isn't it?"

"Yes," said Derek. "It's all right."

Her eyes narrowed as she stared into his, seeking for an explanation, seeking for reasons.

"But . . . but *why*? *Why*?" she brought out at last. "You mean to say you've . . . you've just pretended about it all this time?"

"All this time," he said.

She sat slowly down on the sofa and stared up at him.

"I thought I knew you," she said slowly, "but this is . . . Why did you do it?"

"To get home."

"To get home? Home from where?"

"Home from Norway."

"But . . . but good Heavens, if you wanted to come home, what was to stop you?"

"Nothing."

"Then —"

"But if I left Dominic a couple of weeks before our climbing programme ended, he'd naturally want to know why."

"Well, I naturally want to know why, too."

"I wanted to come back to Greenhurst. And I wanted to come back without having to answer a lot of questions from Dominic. I wanted a good excuse — and the only good excuse I could think of was to fake an injured ankle. So I did."

"You mean you didn't know Dominic well enough, after all these years — after all your life — to say to him: 'Look, I'm tired of climbing and I'm going.' Is that what you mean?"

"I wasn't tired of climbing. I just wanted to come home, that's all."

"But . . . but why?"

"To see you," he said.

He saw, as he watched, the surge of amazement that passed over her, leaving her limp. He followed her changes of expression from complete blankness to bewilderment, from bewilderment to incredulity.

"Me ?"

"You."

"You mean you . . . you came back to Greenhurst because . . ."

"Because you were coming back from Rome. I wanted to see you — without Dominic around. Simon wasn't here; there was a chance that for once in my life I could have you — without the others. Have you to . . . to myself."

There was a long pause.

"You . . . you haven't lost your mind or anything, have you ?" she asked slowly at last.

"I don't think so." He smiled. "It rather breaks your theory down, doesn't it ?"

"My theory ?"

"About the advantages of growing up together. Miriam and Leopold, you said, couldn't share their . . . what was your word ? It doesn't matter. We grew up together, but your memories and mine aren't at all the same. This proves it, doesn't it?"

"Go on talking," said Julia. "I don't feel awfully well."

He gave a short laugh and sat beside her, his eyes on her, his hand going out to take one of hers and hold it loosely, almost absently.

"What you remember, and what I remember," he said slowly, "can't be the same, because for years you haven't known what's been in my mind. Sometimes I've hardly known myself. When I first got into this house, I tried, for nearly two years, to model myself on Dominic. I wanted to be cool and unmoved, like him; unruffled, like him; I wanted to be as like him in every way as possible, to consolidate my position here. After that, I relaxed because I realised I was in for good — as myself. And everything was all right until you told me you were going to Rome. You told me quite casually. I'd got back from Oxford and I'd seen you once or twice and you hadn't even mentioned it — and as I was going home one evening, you looked up and said good-night and added that it had been decided you'd go to Rome to study for two years under that Italian teacher."

"And you said: 'Take a scooter with you; everybody rides scooters in Rome.' "

"Yes. That was the body twitching after the head had been lopped off. I felt myself walking out of the house and across the lawn and climbing over the wall, and I knew quite well — at least, one part of me knew quite well what had happened to me, but the rest of me couldn't, wouldn't believe it."

"Careful," put in Julia.

"It wasn't what you're thinking. It was just that things had been so natural, so brother-and-sisterish, that I couldn't believe that some part of me, all the time, must have been sizing you up in an entirely different way; looking at you from an entirely different angle."

"Why didn't you say anything then?"

"Say anything? I sweated all night wondering whether Dominic had had any idea . . . whether he'd suspected anything. If he'd come to me then and asked me to tell him, on oath, whether I thought I was in love with you, I'd have lied."

"Why?"

"To protect my tiny, tender, delicate little shoot. It needed warmth — the warmth of my heart — and darkness; the darkness of secrecy. It had to grow, slowly, surely, in safety, protected and sheltered."

"How could one word from Dominic have blasted it?"

"One word from anybody would have forced it out into the open — and you would have seen it in all its poor, shivering little bald, unfeathered state. Nobody would have been unkind, but I couldn't have borne anybody to know — just then."

"So I went to Rome without knowing."

"Yes. I went twice to Rome to see you. Each time, I was surer of my own feelings, more certain that I could never be happy without you. I would have got out of going to Norway if I could, but it was difficult. I went — and when I thought of you coming back here, I wanted more than anything in the world to come home and be here, too."

"You mean . . . nobody suspected?"

"No. I went to a chemist and bought bandages and tied up my ankle and met the others and told them it was all right, and didn't hurt, and they thought I was taking it pretty well. My mother was a bit of a danger when I came back — she insisted on my going to the doctor, and in the normal way, she'd have been after him to find out how long I had left to live, but Miriam kept her mind busy with wedding chores and I didn't have to make a report on what the doctor'd said. Which was just as well, because I didn't go to the doctor."

"Miriam knew?"

"Yes. She didn't know much about sprains, but she once did a course of First Aid, and apparently it included bandaging. She had a long look at mine one evening and made two and two into four. And she said I ought to say something to you — but there was this Luke fellow hanging round you, and I knew he was in love with you, and I didn't know what to do. I didn't know whether I ought to ask you whether you liked him . . . or not. I decided to wait until after the wedding. And now I've told you. All I haven't put in is all the agony I went through when I'd been to see you in Rome the second time. I'd never seen you with men before. I'd never imagined you'd have men round you — "

"Careful, I said."

"I'm being careful. Julia — "

"Yes?"

"Did they ever . . . kiss you?"

She looked at him in mild astonishment.

"You ought to look up Italian in the dictionary," she said. "The Latin *Italia*; the Greek *Italos*, which means a bull. They were — "

"All right; I get you."

"Every girl should go to Italy for a time. Most Italian men have a rooted idea that foreign girls go there for the express purpose of sleeping with them. I tried to explain, as I was running round and round the largest piece of furniture in the room, that a number of us were as pure as lilies and were going to stay that way until we joined the other lilies up at the altar, but it was like talking to air. Very warm air. I learned every evasive tactic in the book." She paused, frowning a little. "I wish I'd known, when I was saving my virtue, that you were interested in it all the time. I wish you'd said something before. I wish I could have known what you felt."

"Why?"

"Because I could have thought about it; thought about you. I could have taken you out of the Simon–Dominic bracket and put you apart and really looked at you."

"You're looking now."

"Yes."

He held one of her hands against his cheek.

"Julia . . . Could you ever ?"

"Love you? In one way," she said, "I love you now."

"Would you marry me ?"

She waited, and for a time he did not urge her. Then:

"Well ?" he asked.

"Can you — honestly, Derek, can you imagine me marrying anybody else ? Can you ?"

He could not. So much at least he could hold on to. He did not know what he had hoped; less, perhaps, or more — he did not know. But he was aware that one part of her at least was his, and he was aware that he was part of all that she loved, all that she prized in life.

He had told her. He had told her briefly, baldly, rather badly, in an attempt to approach her gently and by degrees. She knew — and she was Julia, honest and open and guileless, and one part of her loved him.

"Julia — "

"Well ?"

"If I kissed you passionately, what would you feel like ?"

She came a little nearer, warm and soft and sweet.

"Try it and see," she suggested.

"That's right," came in Dominic's even, amused voice from the doorway. "Try it and see."

CHAPTER XI

THE wedding morning was misty, but there was a promise of sunshine to come. Every office in Greenhurst was closed; every shop was staffed with what might with truth be called a skeleton staff: aged crones, grandfathers or great-grandfathers assisted from their beds and propped up behind counters to keep off sneak-thieves, while every able-bodied citizen dressed in his best and hurried off to find a good place from which to see the bride and bridegroom and the guests go into and out of church.

Nicholas, dressed for the wedding except for his morning coat, wandered up to the top floor to inspect his sister, Lucille, in her finery; told her that she was even more beautiful than he remembered her, and strolled into Robert Debrett's dressing-room to talk to him as he dressed and to share the coffee Lucille brought in. He was at peace with the world, happy as he had never been before, impatient only to get Kenneth Springer out of Greenhurst, out of his life and Elaine's.

He went downstairs to his own bedroom, stopping to lean against the open door of Dominic's room and study the tall, incredibly handsome figure in his hired morning suit.

"I look something, hm?" Dominic turned to demonstrate the swing of his tails.

"Why did you bother to go to Moss Bros.?" asked Nicholas. "The new tailor in the High Street would have arranged it for you; he got this outfit down for me, and he'll pack it up and save me the trouble of sending it back to London."

"He had time to measure you and get you a decent fit. What do you make the time?"

"Just on two. We're early. In one hour and three — no, two minutes, Miriam'll be a Countess." He peered at his brother critically. "Aren't those trousers too long?"

"I can hitch them up a bit."

Nicholas left him hitching them, and went into his room to complete his own dressing. He was reaching for his coat when he heard rapid footsteps on the stairs — Julia's footsteps — and waited for a knock. Even Julia, nowadays, knocked before entering.

But there was no knock. The door was flung open, and to his amazement he saw Julia, white and breathless, in the doorway. There was panic in her eyes, and in three strides, he was across the room and had taken her arm in a steadying hold.

"What is it?" he asked.

"Miriam. Have you . . . have you seen her?"

He frowned in bewilderment.

"Miriam? No, of course I haven't seen her. What's the matter? What's happened?"

"Leopold."

He released her slowly.

"An . . . an accident?"

"I don't know. Nobody knows."

"What the hell do you mean by 'nobody knows'?"

"Just what I say. He isn't at Templeby. He isn't in town. He isn't . . . he isn't anywhere."

There was silence. They stared at one another, and some of her panic communicated itself to him and he made an effort to fight it.

"Start at the beginning," he ordered.

"Rudi went over to Templeby at about

354

ten o'clock this morning — he left Leopold at the Red House, having breakfast with the others. Then Rudi came back and he thought Leopold was in his room, dressing for the wedding. All the others — the other guests — got ready and went off for an early lunch at the George. They were to go straight on to the church, but Leopold and Rudi were going to have lunch with Elaine and myself at the Red House. Well, when all the others had gone, Rudi went along to Leopold's room to say something to him — and found he wasn't there. He wasn't anywhere in the house."

"What time was this?"

"About half past twelve."

"Had he changed?"

"Rudi had, but not Leopold. His clothes were all laid out on the bed."

"If he went out, didn't he tell anybody where he was going?"

"No. At least, he didn't tell me or Rudi or Elaine."

"Hadn't you, hadn't Elaine, hadn't anybody heard him go out?"

"No."

"And had he said nothing about going out?"

"No. That's what made Rudi worry. There was nothing for Leopold to go out *for*."

"Didn't you — "

"Rudi rang up Miriam, and — "

"The damn fool. The damn, damn fool," groaned Nicholas. "Go on."

"Miriam said he'd probably turn up soon; she had no idea where he could be, but she said she'd ring back in a quarter of an hour. She did. She sounded worried, Nicholas. She sounded . . . But there was no news of him."

"Didn't you *do* anything?"

"Yes. After that, we did, because we were getting frightened. I rang the George and talked to Joey — no news. Leopold hadn't been there. Then Derek arrived from Templeby — Miriam had sent him. He said they hadn't told anybody — "

"Thank God. How did you get here?"

"Derek brought me. He's downstairs, phoning. Joey's doing a round of the shops, just looking — not asking. We don't want to — "

" — spread the alarm. Where's Rudi?"

"He drove along the road to Templeby; he thought Leopold might have gone to meet him or something. But he's back at the Red House now, waiting. He said he'd ring you up if Leopold turned up. Nicholas . . ."

"It'll be all right," said Nicholas calmly, and found himself praying. It couldn't happen to Miriam. Other brides might wait at the altar; other brides; not Miriam. Not in Greenhurst. Not with every man, woman, and child in the place crowding into the church on the heels of the guests to see her married. Not with every citizen of Greenhurst remembering, as they waited for the missing bridegroom, that once she had been a very different Miriam Arkwright, who ran after men and failed to catch them.

Not Miriam; dear God, not Miriam, just as she's found happiness, he prayed desperately. Not a hold-up of the wedding, with people beginning to wonder, to question — to speculate. Wherever Leopold was, safe or harmed, he must be found. Any news — any, any news, even news of the worst kind, was better than an agonising time of suspense, suspense peculiarly agonising for this bride.

He heard footsteps on the stairs, and put

Julia aside to confront Derek. Dominic had come out of his room and stood silent, anxious and expectant.

"Nothing," said Derek, and his face was chalk white. "Nothing whatsoever. He's just . . . he's just disappeared. But we've found out one thing — why he went out. Rudi said there'd been a mistake — the carnations for Leopold's and Rudi's buttonholes had been sent by mistake to Templeby with the ushers'; Joey asked at the flower shop whether they'd managed to provide Leopold with two more, and they said they had — he'd come in for them himself and he'd waited for a moment while they got them ready, and he'd taken them away."

Taken them away. Nicholas stood still, his mind racing over the possibilities. Leopold had gone to fetch the buttonholes — and then? The flower shop was in the busiest part of the High Street; to walk back to the Red House would have taken, at the most, ten minutes. But he hadn't gone back to the Red House. He had vanished.

He turned and caught up his morning coat from the bed and went downstairs, followed by Julia and Dominic and Derek. The front door was open, and through the open doorway Nicholas saw Miriam's small grey car come racing up the drive. He was down the steps before she had brought the car to a stop — and then he had opened the car door and was bending to talk to her in rapid but calm tones.

"Listen, Miriam — "

She put out a hand and laid it on his sleeve.

"Nicholas . . . I'm frightened."

"Don't be. Something's happened — something small, something probably absurd. We'll find him."

"But if you . . . if you don't ?"

He looked at her, and something in her eyes made the blood recede from his cheeks. For a moment, helplessness gripped him, and then he heard himself speaking, to his own surprise, in a voice in which the calmness and confidence were no longer feigned. He seemed to see, as he spoke, his life here in Greenhurst, bound loosely with hers but bound by a thousand common memories. They had grown up here, neighbours and, of late, friends. He had seen her grow almost lovely in the warmth of her happiness — and if he could do anything to serve her now, he would not spare himself.

"Listen, Miriam. Go back to Templeby They must be wondering where the hell you are. Go back and get dressed — quietly and calmly. Say nothing to anybody. Think of nothing — nothing but the wedding. Keep yourself from remembering anything but the fact that in an hour you'll be going up the aisle to meet Leopold."

"If he's there. Oh, Nicholas . . ."

"He will be there. People don't disappear in a law-abiding town like this one. He lost his way, he forgot the name of the Red House — there are hundreds of reasons why he might be lost for a time."

Hundreds, he thought desperately — and nobody can think of one.

"If he's hurt — "

"I don't think he's hurt. If he were hurt, somebody'd know; somebody would have told us. I think he's lost — somewhere. Go back and don't worry; do you hear? Don't worry. This is your wedding day and things have got to go well. One hint of this to your mother — or to anybody at Templeby

— and the whole set-up will crumble and there'll be confusion — and worse. Go back — will you promise to go straight back and think of nothing but getting ready and getting to the church?"

She said nothing, and he knew that she was trying to keep from weeping.

"If you cry," he warned, "it'll show."

"What are you going to do?"

"Get into my car and comb the streets. I'm going to find him. I swear it. Now go."

He watched the car out of sight, and then went back to the house.

"I've sent her back to Templeby," he told Derek and Julia. "I'm going into town to find Joey. Derek, look after the girls and see they get to the church — and see that nobody gets wind of anything. Dominic, take Robert's car and see if he's anywhere between here and Templeby."

He was in his car, speeding towards Greenhurst. He had no hope, he saw on his arrival, of getting the car near the George, for the pavement was lined with cars of every size and make. In the George itself, when he had left his car and walked up to it, the buzz and chatter of hundreds of lunchers filled the air. As he pushed open the wide glass entrance door, he saw Joey coming towards him.

"Anything?" Joey asked.

"Nothing. Will you come with me and see what a tour of the streets will do?"

"How can he be wandering about?"

"Everybody's making for the church; if he lost his way and wandered a bit off the beaten track, he mightn't find anybody who could put him right. Come on, Joey, let's go."

"Half a minute." Joey held his arm. "Here's Elaine."

She was half running, half walking to the George, but at Joey's hail, she turned and came towards them. She looked at the two men, and spoke without preamble.

"I think Kenneth's in this," she said.

Nicholas stared at her in bewilderment.

"What in the world could he — "

"I *know* he's got something to do with it," she broke in, her voice trembling. "He was in town this morning — he came to the Red House. He said he'd had a letter from his mother and wanted to discuss it with me — and I told him it was impossible and he went away."

"What time was this?" asked Joey.

"Early — about eleven. I can't explain what I feel, but I know he's mixed up in this somehow. I need a car. I want to drive over to this place Kenneth's staying at."

"Stenby?" Nicholas hesitated for a moment and then took her arm and turned her towards the car. "Come on, Joey," he said. "We may as well go. It might lead somewhere."

They walked swiftly, three abreast, halting for a moment to give way to one of the Brett fleet of cars, beribboned for the wedding, the gay effect somewhat spoilt by Charlie, a boiler suit under his shabby jacket, seated beside the driver. He hailed them as he passed, and leaned out to speak, but Nicholas did no more than raise a hand in return; then he was leading Elaine across the road and going round to settle her in the car.

"Hey — Mr. Wayne!" came Charlie's voice.

Nicholas turned; the thin, undersized figure was running towards him. He shook his head to indicate that he had no time for conversation, and got into his car.

"Hey — Mr. Wayne! Wait a minute — I want you!"

363

Charlie, breathless, had come up to the car and was addressing Nicholas through the window.

"Look, Charlie, we're in a hurry. Some other time," said Nicholas.

"I jes' wanted to ask you somethin', that's all."

"It'll keep," said Nicholas, and switched on the engine.

Charlie stepped back, his expression irresolute. Nicholas had backed to ease the car out of the parking line before he spoke again.

"It was jes' this Leopold — " he began.

Nicholas brought the car to a neck-jerking halt and turned to stare at him.

"What did you say?" he asked incredulously.

"Well, the bridegroom." Charlie stepped up to the car. "We passed that other chap's car on our way into town, and 'e was in it."

"Which car? Whose car?"

"That . . . the Springer fellow's car. 'E and that Delphi, and the Springer fellow was driving. Three of 'em."

"I told you. I knew he was in this," said Elaine.

"Driving towards Greenhurst?" Nicholas asked Charlie.

"Naw!" Charlie's scorn was abysmal. "Could we 'ave passed it if we'd been going the same way? Not bloomin' likely! They were going towards Stenby, and I said to m'self, 'Well, that's funny; if 'e's going to be married in a matter of an hour or so, 'e — ' "

"Get in," ordered Nicholas.

Joey had opened the door and was pulling the boy in. Then they were on their way to Stenby, Nicholas silent and absorbed, one half of his mind attending to the driving and the other half racing with futile speculation. Leopold in Kenneth's car, driving towards Stenby . . .

Joey was the first to break the silence.

"What the devil," he asked wonderingly, "could he hope to get out of it? Springer, I mean."

"You can't take a fellow anywhere against his will — or can you?" asked Nicholas. "Charlie" — his tone brought Charlie in as a full partner in the investigations, and brought a flush of pleasure to Charlie's cheeks — "Charlie, you couldn't have got much of a look at the car as it passed; how can you be sure you saw the Count?"

"The hood was down. The three of 'em were sittin' together. Two of 'em I didn't 'ave to look at. That fellow Springer and Delphi's been in that car goin' up and down and back and forwards to Stenby for the last day or so, and all of us in the garridge 'as got used to seein' 'em. I took a look at the third one, and it was the Count."

"You're absolutely certain?"

" 'Course I am."

"Did the driver of your car see him, too?"

"I didn' ask. If you see a bridegroom leavin' town in a 'urry just before 'is wedding," said Charlie shrewdly, "you take a minute or two to wonder wot 'e's up to. Then I thought that if 'e was up to wot I thought 'e was up to, I'd better find you and ask you wot you thought about it, seein's you was brought up with the bride an' all."

"Charlie, you're a man after my own heart," said Joey. "Nicholas boy, how much longer before we get to Stenby? My watch tells me it's two twenty."

Two twenty . . . Forty minutes; less

than forty minutes to go. Forty minutes in which to find the bridegroom, dress the bridegroom and get him to his place up at the altar, awaiting the bride. Forty minutes. Nicholas, without comment, applied himself to getting the maximum speed from the car, and longed for more power to eat up the mile and a half that still divided them from their destination.

He took a long, low hill and brought the car to a stop at the top. Below them they could see the winding little river, the wooded hill beyond, the quiet country road widening after the bridge and then joining the main road that led back to Greenhurst. The air seemed strangely still; the car engine ran quietly, but above it there was no other sound. The branches of the trees were motionless; a quivering reproduction of the bridge lay along the river. It was a scene of peace and beauty, natural, unspoiled save for three incongruous features; the AA telephone box at the junction of the two roads, the ill-kept and unpicturesque inn — and before it, the long, gleaming expensive car owned by Kenneth Springer.

"Let's go," said Nicholas. "He's there."

He brought his car to a halt behind the other man's; in a few moments they had all got out and were hurrying through the inn's crookedly-hanging door. Inside, the sole occupants of the shabby and comfortless lounge, sat Kenneth and Delphi Dunn.

Nicholas wasted no time and no words. He walked up to the table at which the two sat, and greeted them briefly.

"Good-morning. You brought the Count out here a short while ago. Will you please tell me where he is ?"

"The Count ?" Kenneth had not risen; after a glance beyond Nicholas, he got to his feet in a manner that made it clear that it was to Elaine and not to Nicholas that he extended the courtesy. "Well, Elaine," he asked her, "what brings you here ? I thought you told me you were busy with preparations for the wedding — somebody else's wedding."

"Where is he, Kenneth ?" she asked. We've got thirty-five minutes in which to get him to the church. Where is he ?"

"The Count ?"

"Come on — don't stall," broke in Joey angrily. "You brought him here. Where is he ?"

"You're wrong, my dear fellow; quite wrong. I didn't — I did not bring the bridegroom here."

"You're lying," said Joey bluntly. "You were seen. He was in your car."

"Oh!" Kenneth's tone was one of enlightenment. "Oh, now I follow you! You misled me; you said that I brought him here!"

He spoke slowly, drawlingly, a smile on his lips, his eyes going now and then to the clock behind the bar.

Elaine stepped up to Delphi and looked down at her.

"Can you tell me where the Count is?" she asked.

Delphi yawned; it was a natural yawn of complete and utter boredom, and hope began to die in Nicholas. What had looked like an unlikely, melodramatic incident now seemed to be nothing but a stupid mistake. Kenneth might be playing for time; Kenneth might be lying — but Delphi's manner was without any sort of pretence — and it was the manner of a woman totally uninterested in everything that was going on. If she had known anything, she could not, Nicholas felt, have remained so entirely uninterested and aloof.

"The Count *was* in the car?" asked Elaine.

"Please?"

"You had somebody in the car with you just now."

"In the car? Oh, yes; yes. The Count. He wanted to have a . . . a lift, you call it."

"Where did you take him?"

She shrugged.

"He got out."

"Got out where?"

Delphi pointed vaguely towards Greenhurst.

"On the hill. To walk. To walk back," she said.

Nicholas hesitated. They had brought him as far as the hill; he had got out and was now . . . where? Walking back to Greenhurst by the long way? It seemed the only possibility; their only hope, now, was to speed back along the main road and pick him up — if he had not tried to find a short cut across the fields.

He looked at Joey, in whose eyes he read nothing but frustration. But Joey had two suggestions to make.

"I'm going upstairs to look through the

rooms," he said. "You find the landlord and see if he knows anything."

Joey sped up the stairs, Charlie at his heels; Nicholas and Elaine found the landlord and his wife in the dingy room overlooking the wild, wooded garden. Neither of them, it was clear, knew anything about Leopold, and Nicholas knew them well enough to be certain that they would not act against his interests. Kenneth might have offered to bribe them, but a bribe from a passing stranger would have to be substantial to operate against a lifetime of benefits from the Waynes.

"He didn't come here?"

"Nobody." The landlord's voice was firm.

"Nobody," corroborated his wife. "We heard the car come up. I went out to see, and those two were just coming in. I asked if they wanted anything, and when I found they didn't, I shut the door and left them to it."

Joey and Charlie came down with nothing to report; every room was empty.

"We tried the cupboards, too," said Joey. "I wouldn't put anything past that ... that ..."

" 'Arf past two," said Charlie, his face puckered with worry. "Wot do we do, Mr. Wayne?"

"We drive like hell along the other road back to Greenhurst, and hope to pick him up," said Nicholas, but his voice was lifeless. Half an hour. It couldn't be done. He had told Miriam to have courage; to have faith; to go to the church. He had tried to save her from humiliation — and he had done nothing. Whispers would soon start in the crowded church; agitation would grow and the news of the missing bridegroom would reach Lady Templeby — and Nicholas knew that her dignity, her pride, her grand manners were not proof against a situation of this kind. Her husband would do nothing that could curb her panic — and Miriam...

There was nothing left to do but drive; drive as fast as the car would go, which wasn't fast enough. Drive — and hope to pick up Leopold — Leopold, who had inexplicably asked Kenneth Springer for a lift — and who had got out at the top of the hill and gone... nobody knew where. He had asked for a lift out of Greenhurst an hour before his wedding. Nobody could do more than hold on to the fact that, as far as anybody could judge, he was a decent, straightforward, honest and uncomplicated man sincerely in love with Miriam Arkwright.

There was dead silence as Nicholas started the car. Only Charlie's anguished murmur sounded as he leaned forward on his seat at the back, his head close behind Nicholas's, as though by adding his efforts to the driver's, he could make the car move faster.

"Nearly twenty-five to, Mr. Wayne."

Twenty-five minutes. It was all over. Leopold would reappear — perhaps — and the wedding would take place at some other time; there was no reason to suppose otherwise. He had not been abducted — his momentary belief in so melodramatic a development filled Nicholas with shame. If Leopold wanted to get out of the car, Kenneth wouldn't feel that it was his business to point out that time was getting short. There was mystery somewhere; the thing didn't tie up — but there was nothing to be gained by trying to see what lay behind Kenneth's faintly triumphant grin.

He drove towards the junction of the

two roads. Before them stretched the main road, empty of traffic, empty also of any trudging figure. Empty. But they could only drive, fast and faster. They could only —

"*Hey!*"

Charlie's piercing scream, uttered no more than an inch away from Nicholas's ear, tore through him and set every nerve in his body quivering. But before he could do more than open his lips to utter a violent protest, Charlie was thumping crazily on his back.

"Stop, Mr. Wayne! Stop, stop, *stop*, I tell you!"

Nicholas, the car at a standstill, turned to face the yelling boy and saw to his amazement that he was trembling violently.

"What's the matter, Charlie?" His voice was eager. "Have you seen him?"

"Seen 'im? No! Turn 'er, Mr. Wayne; turn 'er round and go back!"

His tone was too urgent, and Nicholas's opinion of his quick wits too high to make him anxious to waste precious moments in argument. If Charlie wanted to go back to the inn, if he had thought of something that had not previously occurred to any of them, he was only too willing to go. He swung the car in a wide circle and headed once more for the Stenby Inn. His foot went down on the accelerator — and then a shout, almost as nerve-jangling as Charlie's scream, sounded in his ear.

"Stop! Stop, I said, Mr. Wayne!"

Nicholas stopped and sat looking right and left. They were back at the junction of the roads; there was nothing but the inn, the bridge, the river —

"Come on!" shouted Charlie. "Come on!"

He was scrambling out of the car, the patched pocket of his jacket catching on the door handle and giving way with a rending sound. Joey was scrambling out behind him, and Elaine, tears of hopelessness streaming down her face, was fumbling at the door handle on her side. Nicholas leaned over and pushed the door open, and then turned and was out of the car and staring incredulously at Charlie, who was standing beside the AA telephone box, desperately turning out his pockets, diving again and again into one and then the other, his shaking hands groping and coming out again empty.

"I 'ad one. I 'ad one, Mr. Wayne! I 'ad a key; I always carry a key cos Mr. Brett says we 'ave to. I had it on me! I did, I did!"

Nicholas, for a few moments, was unable to move. Behind, beyond the despairing wails of Charlie were other sounds — a beating, a hammering on the door of the telephone box, cries and shouts . . . cries and shouts in Leopold's voice.

"Let me out! Let . . . me . . . out!"

Charlie was still searching his pockets — but Nicholas's eyes had left him and had met Joey's. In them he read the bewilderment that was in his own mind.

"Wait a minute, Charlie." Joey took his arm. "There's no need to look for a key."

"But 'e's locked in there,"cried Charlie, "an' — I 'eard 'im as we drove by. I 'eard *something*, and then I knew . . ."

"But nobody can get locked inside an AA box. If the door shuts, it can only be opened from the outside by a key — but the guy inside only has to walk out; that's the kind of lock it is. You can't get stuck in. Ah — I thought so!"

He had followed Nicholas, who had run

round to the front of the telephone box and had dropped on his knees and was pulling, wrenching with all his might at the enormous, flat, heavy stone that was wedged against the door, ensuring that Leopold could not get out until he was let out. Nothing could have testified more clearly to Kenneth Springer's great strength than the fact that the removal of the obstruction necessitated the combined efforts of Nicholas, Joey, and the panting Charlie.

"He must," gasped Joey, as they fought desperately to free the door, "he must have been able to h-hold the d-door shut with Leopold in there pushing his whole weight against it — and then bent down to fix this so's the door c-couldn't move. He must have . . . Now then: One, two, three — heave!"

The door moved. From within, Leopold's desperate pushing gave it the final impetus. He was out, his hair disarranged, his hands scraped and bleeding from his onslaughts on the door. He was out of the telephone box and in the car, and the car was moving — but it was moving not towards Greenhurst, but towards the inn.

"Later," groaned Leopold. "After the

wedding, you can attend to him! I beg you . . . take me back . . ."

Nicholas had stopped the car behind Kenneth's. In a flash he was out, opening Elaine's door, Charlie's door — but Joey, guessing his intention, was already out and running towards the other car.

"It's here!" he shouted. "The key's in it!"

"Thank God," said Nicholas, and leapt into the driving seat. He set the car in motion before the other three were more than half in, before Kenneth could do more than reach the door of the inn and begin running towards them.

They were away. They were moving at a speed at which Nicholas had never driven before. His eyes were on the road, but his mind was caught up in a delirious realisation of the power, almost unlimited, at his call. Seventy . . . eighty; the road stretched empty and inviting. Ninety . . . thank God for Kenneth's money, that could buy this salvation for them all. Thank God . . .

Behind him, Leopold's gasping explanation told them what had happened.

"I was at the flower shop, for the — the

buttonholes, you understand? I came out; he was in the car, with the girl. He leaned out, very kindly, very helpfully, and said 'You wouldn't by any chance like a lift?' I said but of course I should like one, because I knew that I must hurry — and so I got in. When I saw that we were going away from Greenhurst, I asked him what he was doing, and he was still very friendly and said that he was sorry, but he had remembered something he must pick up from his room. He was driving very fast, and I hoped that I was only imagining that he was deliberately taking me away from Greenhurst. We got near the inn, and he slowed down, and I looked at him across the girl — and he smiled. And the way he smiled, I knew that in some way he did not wish me to be at the wedding . . . in time. I asked to be put down; I was afraid — a little afraid that if I went to the inn he would be able to prevent me from leaving. I began to walk back — you may imagine what I was feeling. . . . And then I saw his car; he had left the girl at the inn and he had come back, and I was glad, because I thought that I had been foolish, and let my imagination run away with me. He would take me back to Greenhurst, he said. I got into the car. He stopped at the telephone box; he said please would I get his purse, which he had left there when making a call. I got out quickly — and when I went in, I knew only that the door was shut behind me, and he was making sure that it did not open. It was of no use to push, to call, to shout. If you had not come . . ."

Nobody else spoke. As Leopold's account came to an end, they reached the Red House, and saw Rudi, white-faced, sick-looking, standing in the drive. There was no time for speech. Rudi had got his brother out of the car and, an arm about his shoulders, his lips murmuring fervent prayers of thankfulness, was rushing him up the stairs and into his bedroom. From the hall, Charlie chanted the passing minutes. Elaine, with shaking hands, poured drinks and Joey rushed them upstairs. And upstairs, Leopold had become a puppet, a dummy on to which Rudi and Nicholas put clothing, swiftly, deftly, silently.

Ten to three. Charlie's chant floated up the stairs, but they were already hurrying Leopold down. From the pocket of his discarded suit Joey had snatched two carnations, white, limp, and dishevelled, and had restored them to a semblance of their morning freshness and given them to the bridegroom and the best man. Then they were all in Kenneth Springer's car, Charlie clinging to the side, his face bright with joy, his hair floating in the breeze like a banner, his voice uttering a shrill cry of triumph.

" 'E couldn't catch this car, could 'e, Mr. Wayne? 'E couldn't catch us!"

"Three minutes to," said Joey. "We've made it."

Three minutes, and the church before them, with the eager crowds outside and the whispers already, Nicholas saw as he came to a halt at the bottom of the wide, shallow steps, the whispers already beginning to stir. And here was the bridegroom — late, by local standards, but not too late; here was the bridegroom, accompanied by his brother, entering the church. Here was the bridegroom . . . a well-set-up man, a good-looking man; every inch, thought Greenhurst, a Count. Three minutes at the altar; not long, but long enough. And another stir, and — yes; here came the bride. Here came Miriam Arkwright, who'd turned out better than anybody would ever have thought; here she came on the arm of her father, who was so seldom seen and who was almost never remembered.

Here came the bride . . .

Nicholas fought his way to a precarious foothold just inside the church, and over the heads of the tightly-packed spectators, met Miriam Arkwright's glance for a moment, as she entered on her father's arm. He was dimly aware that what passed between them during that brief look was a summing-up, a crowning of their lifelong association. She was taking with her into the church thirty years of both their lives; they had never been close, they had never been more than friends — during their early years they had been less than friends. But there had been, nevertheless, a link so strong that his happiness today had depended upon hers. Her humiliation would have been his. The years had forged ties that neither of them had fully understood — until now.

And at the exact moment that she reached Leopold's side, Nicholas felt a touch on his arm, and turned to see Kenneth Springer, dark with fury, behind him.

"Step outside," he invited in a low, deadly tone.

The age-old, the time-honoured invitation ...

Nicholas hesitated. This was sanctuary, wasn't it? This was a church, and better men than he had sought its safety in the past. Even a man in the state Kenneth Springer was in must be aware that a church offered a man a refuge from his pursuers.

To stay — or to go.

Staying meant safety. Staying meant being surrounded by a tightly-packed, reassuringly friendly press of friends, old friends. Even if Kenneth tried to hit him, he could scarcely reach with any effect across the entire Wheeler family and their ex-Greenhurst cousins who had come over from the other end of Hampshire simply because one of them had been Miriam Arkwright's nurse and had been invited to see her married.

Staying meant safety. Going meant a very unpleasant interview with a man whose fists were already clenched in readiness to by-pass argument.

He turned and shouldered his way out of the church, and Kenneth led the way. And Nicholas remembered that it was more than ten years since he had used his fists; during his period of compulsory service in the Army, a fellow-recruit had called him — in no complimentary spirit — a gentleman, and he had felt compelled to do something about it. He had come off worst then, and he was shortly going to come off worst again.

Kenneth walked steadily down the steps of the church, and Nicholas followed him, and both men were too absorbed to see that, after a brief agony of indecision — wedding or fight — half the occupants of the back pews of the church had followed Nicholas.

Round the back of the church and into the graveyard — ominous, Nicholas thought fleetingly . . .

It was just beside the grave of Mr. Brett's first wife that Kenneth came to a halt, swung round and invited Nicholas to put them up. It was across the grave, after the shortest fight in the history of Greenhurst

—one second by Mr. Wheeler's watch, and one crashing blow from Kenneth — that Nicholas went down and stayed down.

CHAPTER XII

HE awoke some time later to a confused feeling of regret that the wedding had turned out so rainy. A pity, he muttered, exasperation in his tone. Happy the bride the sun . . . the sun . . .

The rest of the saying eluded him. It would come back some time — some other day, when whatever it was that was making his jaw feel unfamiliar would stop.

Jaw. Chin. There was something . . . One would have to work backwards, very, very carefully. Chin. Swipe. Graveyard. Kenneth.

He opened his eyes. The first thing that became clear was that the rain was coming not from Heaven, but from Earth. And it wasn't rain. It was tears.

Elaine was crying.

Nicholas put up a hand and with a careful forefinger caught a tear as it coursed down her cheeks, and balanced it for a moment.

"Nothing to cry about," he said.

"The brute," sobbed Elaine; "the beast . . . the brute."

Nicholas, in silent agreement with these sentiments, was examining his surroundings, and discovered that he was in a totally unfamiliar bedroom. There seemed to be a large number of people round the bed: besides Elaine, he saw Lucille, Jeff, Dominic, Robert Debrett, Derek, and Julia.

It was Robert who spoke first.

"As an actor," he said, "I have to tell you that I don't like what you did."

"What did I do?" Nicholas, debating whether he should sit up, decided against it; it was madness to detach himself, remove himself from a pair of warm, loving arms. "What did I do?"

"You stole the show," said Robert. "Only half the local population stayed in church; the other half were engaged in chasing your unsuccessful rival out of town."

"Unsuccessful? Feel my chin," invited Nicholas.

"You must have b-been out of your m-mind," sobbed Elaine. "You needn't have have f-followed him out of the ch-church."

"He used a magnet. Whose bedroom is this?" enquired Nicholas.

"Miriam's." Jeff answered the question. "She's down there now, trying to keep her mind on the reception, but she's refused to leave until you come round. Leopold, too."

"You're not a hero," Julia said. "Everybody thinks you were crazy to follow him and just stand there and let him bash you."

"Where is he now?" enquired Nicholas.

"On his way," said Jeff, "wherever his way is. Half the onlookers stopped to pick you up, and the other half — led by Joey — legged it after Kenneth."

"You mean Kenneth ran?"

"Of course he ran. He may be an ox, but he's not an ass; he can size up the mood of a crowd and assess his own danger. He really ran. He got to his car eight seconds before the crowd reached it — and after that, of course, he was safe. He must have been doing ninety at the Greenhurst bend. By that time, the wedding was over and the two halves of the congregation met, and Lady Templeby heard that Kenneth had chased you into the church."

"I hope that's all she heard," said Nicholas.

"That's all. The full story'll leak out, of

course," said Jeff. "Charlie Bush will see to it personally. But for the moment — "

He paused. The door had opened and Lady Templeby, breath-taking in wild silk and ostrich-feathered hat, appeared in the doorway.

"How is he?" she enquired, in hushed tones.

Nicholas struggled to a sitting position.

"I'm fine, thanks," he said. "Thank you for — "

"Now, now, now," she broke in, "not a word. I'm going to send everybody away and — "

"Not everybody," said Nicholas.

"Everybody except Elaine, and then you must decide whether you feel well enough to come down and see the last of Miriam as a bride." Lady Templeby was shepherding everybody to the door as she spoke, and soon only she and Nicholas and Elaine were left in the room. "If you don't come down," she said, "I shall have something to eat and drink sent up to you."

Nicholas got slowly to his feet and looked at Elaine.

"I'll be down," he said. "We'll be down . . . presently."

And Lady Templeby, not normally noted for tact, withdrew quietly and closed the door behind her.

THE END

This book is published under the
auspices of the
ULVERSCROFT FOUNDATION,
a registered charity, whose primary
object is to assist those who experience
difficulty in reading print of normal
size.

In response to approaches from the
medical world, the Foundation is also
helping to purchase the latest, most
sophisticated medical equipment desperately needed by major eye hospitals
for the diagnosis and treatment of eye
diseases.

If you would like to know more about the
ULVERSCROFT FOUNDATION,
and how you can help to further its work,
please write for details to:

THE ULVERSCROFT FOUNDATION
The Green, Bradgate Road
Anstey
Leicestershire
England

We hope this Large Print edition gives you the pleasure and enjoyment we ourselves experienced in its publication.

There are now 1,000 titles available in this ULVERSCROFT Large Print Series. Ask to see a Selection at your nearest library.

The Publisher will be delighted to send you, free of charge, upon request a complete and up-to-date list of all titles available.

Ulverscroft Large Print Books Ltd.
The Green, Bradgate Road
Anstey, Leicester
England

B.U.

85 33352

DATE DE RETOUR
Veuillez rapporter ce volume avant ou
à la dernière date ci-dessous indiquée.

1 1 JUIN 1992			
0 1 JUIL. 1992			
1 0 JUIL. 1992			
0 3 JAN. 1993			
0 2 JUIL. 1993			
6 JAN. 1994			
8 AVR. 1994			
2 3 MARS 1996			

No 16 – "Bibliofiches"

BIBLIO. PIERREFONDS/D.D.O.

009097 8